FRANKENSTEIN;

or,
The Modern Prometheus

Mary Shelley

Adapted by H.B. Ambler

Modern Classics Publishing
Providence, Rhode Island

Published in 2020 by Modern Classics Publishing,
Copyright © 2020 by H.B. Ambler

For more information,
visit modernclassicspublishing.com
Modern Classics Publishing,
Providence, Rhode Island

ISBN 978-1-7357640-0-9

Note on the Adaptation

Sometimes the most influential book written in a given language hides in plain sight, and so it is with *Frankenstein*. References to Shelley's novel, published when she was a twenty-year-old with a turbulent past and an infant child, appear everywhere in the English-speaking world.

Whether it is used to characterize a strain of science, a political movement producing panic, or the family dog just back from the animal hospital with a prominent scar, it is not uncommon to encounter the phrase "Frankenstein's monster" as a means of describing things that have a thin, or nonexistent, connection to the "real" monster in Shelley's book. We find such references strewn throughout the speech and work of novelists, modern journalists, and everyday folk in equal measure. It little matters whether the person using the phrase has read the novel. "Frankenstein's monster," both as a phrase and as a singular literary creation, will be with us until the end of time.

This creature, known for his violence and hateful appearance, also happens to be one of the most articulate and impassioned characters to plead for a parent's love in English literature. He is heartbreaking, earnest, and human. It was almost as though Shelley, in a bid not to further alienate a father with whom she would reconcile shortly, had to hide her own deep sorrow in a monster's heart, the better to cloak and ultimately reveal it.

While several themes in Shelley's most read book are wildly fascinating, that of science without forethought and conscience is the one that is the most thoroughly understood. But among the other reasons the novel continues to resonate was its author's deep-seated sense of place. Her own travels facilitated some of this pleasure for her readers, but when it comes to the semifrozen Arctic Ocean and remote regions within northern Russia, Shelley would have had only her research and imagination to guide her. It is to her credit that alongside the "serious" themes of her masterpiece, the book also serves as a feast of changing locales and cloak-and-dagger stalking that readers will intuitively recognize as a precursor to the modern spy novel and, perhaps most of all, the modern spy movie.

I undertook to write this adaptation to help high-school students understand what for them was, well motivated and bright though they were, an impenetrable book. As I began to rewrite key passages to get them through various difficult parts of the narrative, I realized that at least some students who had the book assigned a generation earlier would have had a similar experience. And so it was that I came to recast Shelley's story in somewhat easier language. If the new version manages to gain for Shelley an even wider audience, that will be a suitably modest accomplishment for a middle-aged English major who still loves his old books.

—H.B. Ambler

Frankenstein

Did I request thee, Maker, from my clay
To mould me man? Did I solicit thee
From darkness to promote me?——

PARADISE LOST.

To William Godwin,
Author of *Political Justice*, *Caleb Williams*, etc.
These Volumes
Are Respectfully Inscribed by the Author

Preface

The event on which this fiction is based has been found by Dr. Darwin and some scientific writers in Germany to be at least theoretically possible. I ask that no one associate my own thoughts on science, and what it may one day achieve, with this work of the imagination. Nonetheless, I believe I have done more than weave together a sequence of supernatural terrors, and most will allow that the central event of the narrative makes this something other than a mere ghost story. Indeed, the scenes described include situations never before put in print, and reveal experience in a way that no other set of circumstances could.

I have made every effort to maintain the truth of basic human nature, while allowing myself the luxury of combining humanity's traits in ways that fit my tale. *The Iliad*, the tragic poetry of Greece, Shakespeare—in the *Tempest* and *Midsummer Night's Dream*—and especially Milton—in *Paradise Lost*—all play by the same rules. Certainly, a humble novelist such as myself may be allowed equivalent freedom to describe the truth that the great poets of the ages have always taken.

The idea for the tale arose in conversation. The actual account set forth here was begun partly as a way to pass the time and amuse a few friends and partly to see what kind of intellectual powers I might develop. Various sources of inspiration popped up along the way. I fully understand that the moral situations detailed in the story will produce reactions, some of them strong, on the part of my readers. However it may appear, let it be known I wished to avoid the dull nature of the novels being published in our time, and to highlight the kind and noble nature of human kind. The particular stance on science, as well as that on the nature of morality, stated by the hero of this book, should under no circumstances be seen as representing my own thoughts. Nor should anything else in these pages be taken as proof of the author's own opinion on the scientific method, the state of science, or scientists at large.

Many have found interesting the fact of where I happened to be when I began creating the book. I was in the beautiful terrain of and around Geneva, Switzerland, when the ideas came to me, and it is there the story is mostly set. The majestic sights and the wonderful company I shared in that summer of 1816 tug upon my heart still. Despite the calendar, which indicated the finest season of the year, the weather that summer was cold and rainy. After taking our supper at night, we crowded around a blazing fire, and sometimes retold German ghost stories that had found their way to us. Some were so good we could not help ourselves from wanting to create our own similar tales. Two friends who were present—one's writing is vastly superior to anything I will ever produce—and I made a pact: each of us would write a tale based on a supernatural event of some kind.

Ironically, the weather suddenly turned pleasant, and my two friends left for a journey in the Alps, leaving me at the inn where we were staying. As they ventured among high peaks in the glory of summer, the strength of the ghostly visions they so recently had experienced dissipated like so much morning mist. The following tale is the only one to be completed.

Volume I

Letter I

To Mrs. Saville, England
St. Petersburg, Dec. 11th, 17—.

You will be happy to learn that my undertaking so far has not produced any of the disastrous results you have so feared. I arrived yesterday, and wanted to let you know I am safe and well, and feel more optimistic about my plans by the day.

I am already far north of London; and as I walk the streets of Petersburg, I feel a cold northern breeze touch my cheeks, and I am renewed by it. Do you understand this feeling? This breeze, which has travelled from the regions I have begun to approach, gives me a foretaste of those icy climes that I will be visiting soon. With my daydreams given life by each gust, the pictures in my mind are more vivid than ever. I try in vain to hold a respectful fear of the frozen wilderness awaiting me at the pole, but instead it presents itself to my imagination as a scene of shimmering beauty and peace. There, Margaret, the sun is always visible; its broad disk moves in a circle just above the horizon—never dipping below it—and bathing everything in its soft light. As far as danger, you should know that earlier navigators tell us that snow and ice are banished from the atmosphere here in summer, and the surface of the sea wonderfully smooth. With our sails pushed by the gentlest of winds, we will be delivered to a land more exquisite than all others, overhung by a sky of pure wonder. Indeed, the secrets of the heavens may be revealed to us—for what may not be expected in a land of eternal light? I may discover the power drawing the compass needle northward, and find the explanations for other celestial observations that have long confounded mariners. I will satisfy my intense curiosity by seeing a part of the world never before visited, and may tread pieces of earth never before imprinted by the foot of man. These are the things enticing me, and they are sufficient to win out against all fears of danger and death, and to allow me to start a forbidding trip with the joy a child feels when he embarks in a little boat, with his holiday mates, on an expedition up his native river. But even if I learn far less than I hope, you must admit that discovering a passage near the pole to the Pacific and determining what pulls the needle northward will represent significant gifts to mankind.

These reflections have dispelled the agitation with which I began my letter, and I feel my heart glow with such hope that heaven seems within reach; nothing is better for one's spirits than having a steady purpose. The heart and mind align when such a goal is chosen, and when it comes to my own situation I have been thinking of this trip since I was a boy. For, pulse racing, I have read the descriptions of attempts to find a northern passage to the Pacific. We both remember accounts of these voyages filling whole walls in our Uncle Thomas's study. They were all the books he owned! What an effect each had on me, and what an impression they made on me collectively! On the one hand, my burning interest in the subject led to my ignoring other disciplines; on the other, it made me the most passionate reader I could have ever been, poring over the stories day after day and night after night. All that passion and all those hours only made it more devastating when, as a child, I learned my father's dying command to my uncle was that he never allow me to embark upon a seafaring life.

These visions of exploration faded when I read, for the first time, our great poets' work, which healed my soul and lifted it to heaven. For a year, I lived in a paradise of my own making, thinking I might become immortal, like Homer and Shakespeare; alas, my eagerness exceeded my talent, and my ambition was soon dashed. You of course remember how hard failure was on my spirits. But just at that time I inherited my cousin's estate, and my thoughts returned to their earlier bent.

Six years have passed since I committed to my present undertaking. I can, even now, remember the hour I committed to this great endeavour. First, I had to strengthen my body and numb it to the pain the trip would bring. I volunteered on several whaling expeditions to the North Sea, and during them all I sought out cold, hunger, thirst, and lack of sleep. I worked harder than the crew during the day, and spent nights becoming an expert in math, medicine, and all physical sciences that would most benefit a naval adventurer. Twice I actually got myself hired as an under-mate on a Greenland whaler, and earned the admiration of my fellows. I must say it made me a little proud when the captain pleaded with me to stay on as his second in command; so valuable did he find my services.

And now, Margaret, do I not deserve to accomplish some great purpose? My life might have been spent on an estate in ease and luxury; but I preferred glory to every temptation wealth placed in my path. Oh, that I might receive word from the heavens confirming the wisdom of my plan! My courage and resolution is firm; but my hopes fluctuate, and my spirits are often depressed. I am about to set out on a long and difficult voyage, one whose emergencies will require all the strength I have gathered; at the lowest points, I will be forced to raise the morale of others, but also sometimes of myself, even when there is scant hope to be found.

This is the most favourable time of year for travelling in Russia. They fly quickly over the snow in their sleds, far more smoothly than the coaches traverse the roads in our country. The cold is not excessive, if you are wrapped in furs, a custom I have already adopted; for there is a difference between walking the deck and remaining seated motionless for hours, when no exercise prevents the blood from actually freezing in your veins. It is not an ambition of mine to die on the post-road between St. Petersburg and Archangel.

I will depart for the latter city in two or three weeks; and once there I will hire a ship, which can be done by paying the insurance for the owner, then hire sailors accustomed to the whale-fishing for my crew. I will be taking only men who have whaled extensively in the northern seas, where I have manned the oars and harpoons myself. I do not intend to sail until the month of June—and when will I return? Ah, dear sister, how can I answer this question? If I succeed, many, many months, perhaps years, will pass before you and I may meet. If I fail, you will see me again soon, or never.

Farewell, my dear Margaret. May heaven shower blessings on you and save me, that I may again proclaim the gratitude I feel for the love and kindness you have always shown me.

Your affectionate brother,
R. Walton.

Letter II

To Mrs. Saville, England.
Archangel, 28th March , 17—.

How slowly time passes here, buried as we are under ice and snow; still, a second step has been taken towards my enterprise. I have hired a vessel, and am at work collecting my sailors; those I have already engaged appear to be men on whom I can depend, and they are all clearly in possession of real courage.

There is one absence I feel as a severe evil. I have no friend, Margaret: When in the course of this trip I am glowing with the enthusiasm of success, there will be no one with whom to share my joy; and if I am brought low by disappointment, there will be none to lift my spirits when they need it the most. Yes, I will write down my thoughts in letters, but ink on paper is a poor medium for the communication of feeling. You may think me childish, but I bitterly feel the absence of a friend. I have no one by my side, gentle and yet courageous, with a learned and strong mind, whose tastes are like my own, to approve or improve my plans. How much might this kind of friend repair the faults of your poor brother! I am too passionate in completing tasks, and too impatient when difficulties come. Worse, I am self-educated; for the first fourteen years of my life I ran wild on a town common, reading nothing but our uncle's books on sea voyages. While I did find poets whom I wished to emulate for a time, achieving even minor success in this regard would have required learning languages, and by the time I fully understood that fact it was too late. A boy of twelve can learn ten times the number of words and rules of grammar that a man twice his age can. It matters not why this happens to be the case; but it is so. As of this year, I am twenty-eight, old enough to realize that schoolboys of fifteen already have learning and sophistication that I will never have. It is true that I have reflected more, and that among my thoughts are ones possessing a certain magnificence, but at the same time they lack proportion; to gain that rare quality, I need a friend fond enough of me to help regulate my mind.

Well, these are useless complaints; I shall not find a friend on the wide ocean, nor in a port such as this, among merchants and seamen. And yet I see evidence of human nobility even here. My lieutenant, for instance, is a man of substantial courage and energy who is mad with desire to achieve glory. An Englishman, his fine character somehow survives amidst the tangle of nationalities and prejudices that one sees daily here. I originally became acquainted with him on board a whaling vessel; upon learning that he was unemployed in this city, I easily engaged him to join the expedition.

He is a man of dignity and goodwill who stands out among the crew for his gentleness, and the mildness of his discipline. His is, indeed, so kindhearted that, despite being an effective whaler at sea, he will not hunt on land, because he cannot stand to spill blood. He is, moreover, almost heroically generous. At some point in the past he was in love with a young Russian lady from a modest home. He saved money enough to marry the object of his affection and was engaged to her, after her father eagerly consented. He was able to spend a moment with her once before their wedding day, and saw she was crying. Before he knew what was happening, she had thrown herself at his feet, where she pleaded with him to spare her, informing him that she loved another. The one she loved was a pauper, she told him, and her father would never allow the union. When my generous friend learned the name of his rival, he consented to the young woman's desire to be released. And he did more: Having before bought a farm where he had intended to spend the rest of life, he transferred ownership of the farm to the shocked man and gave him the last of the money he had saved, urging him to purchase stock to secure his future. Lastly, he asked the father to provide his blessing to the marriage. The father said no, feeling bound in honour to my friend; but when he saw his request refused my friend left the region, and only returned after hearing that the young woman had finally married according to her heart. "What an astonishing person!" you will say. He is, indeed, but he has spent his whole life on board a vessel, and has scarcely an idea beyond spars and rigging.

Please do not assume, hearing all my complaints, and all my dreams of having a true friend, that I am any less devoted to success. I am as firm in my resolve as ever, and when the weather permits we will depart. The winter has been unusually harsh, but spring has gotten a fast start; and we may sail sooner than expected. But you understand my character well enough to know I would never leave on such a voyage without completing every preparation, particularly when the safety of others falls to me.

I am unable to convey the range of my thoughts as the trip draws near; the mix of hope and fear is like nothing I have experienced, being both a pleasure and a torture. We are going to unexplored regions, to "the land of mist and snow"; but I will kill no albatross, so you need not fear for my safety.

Will I meet you again, after crossing immense seas, and returning by the southern cape of Africa or America? I dare not expect such success, yet I cannot bear to contemplate what failure would mean. Keep writing; I may get your letters when I most need the hope they contain. I love you tenderly. Remember me with affection, all the more so should you never hear from me again.

Your affectionate brother,
Robert Walton.

Letter III

To Mrs. Saville, England.
July 7th, 17—.

My dear Sister,

I write these few lines in haste to tell you that I am safe, and well advanced on my voyage. If all goes well, my letter will get to England by a merchant marine ship now on its homeward voyage from Archangel. That vessel's crew are luckier than your brother, for I may not see my beloved country again for many years. I am, however, in good spirits: my men are bold, and appear to be firm of purpose; the floating sheets of ice that perpetually pass us, harbingers of the dangerous region we are beginning to approach, seem not to worry them in the least. We have quickly reached a very high latitude; summer is at its peak, and although it is less comfortable than the same season in England, the southern winds bring us a renovating warmth that I had not expected.

Nothing has happened so far worthy of even mentioning in a letter. One or two gales and the breaking of a mast are occurrences that experienced navigators scarcely remember to record; and I will be happy if nothing worse happens to us during our voyage.

Adieu, my dear Margaret. Be assured that, for my own sake

as well as yours, I will not needlessly seek out danger. I will be cool, persevering, and careful.

Please give my regards to all my English friends.

Most affectionately yours,
R. W.

Letter IV

To Mrs. Saville, England.
August 5th, 17—.

Something astonishing has happened; I cannot wait to write it down, even though you are likely to see me before these papers can make their way into your hands.

Last Monday (July 31st), we were almost completely surrounded by ice, which closed in on all sides and barely left the ship the sea room in which she floated. There was danger in the situation, especially as we were enveloped by a thick fog, and we decided to lay to, hoping that some change would take place in the atmosphere and weather.

About two o'clock, the mist cleared away, and we saw, extending in all directions, vast and irregular plains of ice, which appeared to have no end. At this point, some of the crew groaned, and my mind began to grow watchful with anxious thoughts, when a strange sight attracted our attention and distracted us from the risks we faced. What we saw was a large sled drawn by dogs travelling towards the north, half a mile away. On top of the sled there was some kind of low carriage and sitting on top of this and guiding the dogs was a being with the shape of a man but of gigantic stature. With our telescopes, we watched him make rapid progress, until he was lost amid the distant irregularities of the ice.

What we had witnessed generated our unqualified wonder. We were, to the best of our knowledge, hundreds of miles from land, but the appearance of the mysterious traveller forced us to consider the possibility that it was not as distant as we had believed. Shut in as we were by the ice, though, it was impossible to follow his track, which we had watched him make with supreme interest.

About two hours after this happened, we heard the ground sea; and before it was time to retire for the night the ice broke, freeing the ship. We remained anchored until the morning, however, fearing to strike in the dark those large loose masses that float about after the breaking up of the ice. I used the time to rest for a few hours.

In the morning, though, the moment it was light I went on deck and found the men gathered on one side of the ship, apparently talking to some one in the sea. It was, in fact, a sled, like the one we had seen before, which had drifted towards us in the night, on a large fragment of ice. Only one dog remained alive; but there was a human being on the sled, whom the sailors were in the midst of persuading to board our vessel. He was not, as the other sled driver had appeared, a strange giant from some undiscovered island, but a European. When my men saw me, the master said, "Here is our captain, and he will not allow you to die on the open sea."

Turning his head towards me, the stranger addressed me in refined English, although with a foreign accent. "Before I come on board your vessel," he said, "will you be so kind as to tell me the direction in which you are bound?"

You can imagine the shock I felt hearing this question from a man on the brink of death, and who should have seen our ship as a resource more precious than all the wealth in the world.

I replied, notwithstanding my surprise, that we were on a voyage of discovery towards the northern pole.

Upon hearing this he appeared satisfied, and agreed to come on board. Dear God! Margaret, if you could have seen this man who had been ready to refuse our offer of safety, you would have been astonished. His limbs were nearly frozen, and his body had been left perilously thin by fatigue and suffering. I had never witnessed anyone in such condition. We began to carry him to the cabin, but as soon as we had gotten him below deck away from the fresh air he fainted. Fearing we were accidentally harming him, or possibly putting his life at risk, we returned him to the deck and brought him back to consciousness by rubbing his icy hands, neck, and face with brandy; we dribbled a tiny amount over his lips and forced him to swallow a few drops. As soon as he showed signs of life, we wrapped him in blankets and put him near the chimney of the kitchen stove. By slow degrees he recovered, eventually eating a little soup, which put colour in his cheeks and restored him wonderfully.

Two days went by in this manner before he could speak; and I often feared his sufferings had deprived him of his wits. When he had recovered a little more, I moved him to my own cabin and took care of him myself, as much as my duties would allow. I never saw a more interesting creature: His eyes frequently resemble those of a wild animal, and when he seems more human, he looks at best mentally unwell. None of this is too remarkable, I suppose; much more so is the fact that whenever one of us does the smallest service for him, his face lights up with a look of warm appreciation and kindness that I never saw equalled. But he is generally quite melancholy; and sometimes wears a terrible grimace, as if he can barely stand the weight of the woes oppressing him.

When my guest was a little recovered, it was all I could do to keep off the men, who wished to ask him a thousand questions; but I would not allow him to be tormented by their idle curiosity, in a state of body and mind whose restoration evidently depended on full and complete rest. Once, however, the lieutenant asked, Why had he come so far onto the ice, headed away from civilization and safety?

The man's face again took on its most forlorn look, and he replied, "To find the one whom I am pursuing."

"And is the man you are looking for travelling in the same way?"

"Yes."

"Then you would probably like to know that we have seen him. The day before we found you, we saw dogs pulling a sled, with a man in it, across the ice."

Our guest's eyes widened, and he began asking his own questions, one after the next. What direction was the "demon," as the man called the one he pursued, travelling in? Was he making good time? And so forth. A short while later, when he was alone with me, he said, "I have, no doubt, aroused your curiosity, as well as that of your men. But you do not ask me anything yourself, out of consideration for my well-being."

"It would be rude, not to mention inhuman, to trouble you with any questions."

"Perhaps, but you have nonetheless rescued me from a strange and dangerous situation, and you have graciously restored me to health."

A short while later he asked if I thought the breaking up of the ice would have destroyed the other sled? I said I had no way of knowing. The ice had not broken apart until nearly midnight, several hours after we saw the first traveller, who might have arrived in a place of safety by then; there was no way of knowing.

From that point forward the stranger was keen to be on deck, to watch for the sled that we had seen first; but I have managed to talk him into staying below, for he remains far too weak to withstand the rawness of the atmosphere. I have promised that one of the men will serve as a lookout and that we will bring word straight away if any new object should appear in sight.

That apprises you of all that has happened in this regard up to the present day. The stranger has gradually improved in health, but is very silent, and appears uneasy when anyone except myself enters his cabin. Still, he maintains an exceptional level of grace and gentleness, and the sailors all remain interested in him, although they have had very little communication with him. As for me, I acknowledge that I am beginning to love him as a brother, and his constant and deep grief fills me with sympathy and compassion. He must have been a noble creature in his better days, being even in his broken-down state so charming and amiable.

I said in one of my letters, my dear Margaret, that I would find no friend on the wide ocean, but I have found a man who, before his spirit had been broken by misery, would have made a fine friend, whom I could have loved like a brother.

I will continue my journal concerning the stranger, whenever anything new takes place.

August 13th, 17—.

My affection for my guest increases every day. And yet two other feelings compete for prominence as I look upon him: admiration and pity. Seeing such a noble creature brought low by sorrow and misery makes my heart clench. He is so gentle, yet so wise; and his mind is so cultivated; and when he speaks, his words are chosen with the truest art, and yet they flow with effortless speed and great eloquence.

He is now much recovered from his illness, and is continually on the deck, apparently watching for the sled we first saw. Although he is unhappy, his misery does not distract him from an innate interest he has in what the people around him are doing. He has asked about my purpose in bringing a ship here, and I have explained the expedition to him; my trusting him seemed to please him, and he was kind enough to offer several slight changes to my plan, each well conceived, which, together, will prove exceedingly helpful to me. He is far from condescending; everything he does springs solely from the interest he instinctively takes in the welfare of those who surround him. Nonetheless, he is frequently overcome by gloom. When it happens, he retreats, sitting where he will not be disturbed and struggling by force of will to overcome the mood afflicting him. Eventually, the darkness passes like a cloud from before the sun, but the underlying sorrow remains. I have made efforts to win his confidence; and I trust that I have succeeded. I admitted to him that I have for a long time been looking for a friend, some one who would show me kindness as well as improve me. I said that I was not one of those who find advice poisonous.

"I am self-educated and sometimes forget what strengths I possess," I told him. "I would want a friend both wiser and more experienced than myself, who would counsel me in everything I do. I would want him to confirm and support the better parts of me, and to let me know when my thoughts and actions have gone astray. However difficult it might be to find such a person, I have held onto the idea that this could happen for me."

"I agree with you," said the stranger, "in believing friendship to be both a good thing and one possible for you. I once had a friend, the most noble of human creatures, and the memory of him allows me to judge such matters fairly. You have your hope, and the wide world before you, and you have no reason to quit your search for such a friend. As for me, I have lost everything, and cannot begin life anew." As he said this, his face took on an expression of calm settled grief, which moved me deeply. But he was silent, and after a few moments retired to his cabin.

Even in his broken state, no one can feel more deeply than he does the beauties of nature. The star-filled sky, the reflecting sea, and every sight provided by these wonderful regions, seems to still elevate his soul from earth. A man such as he has a double existence: he may be miserable, overwhelmed by disappointment; but at the same time there is within him a sublime fortitude, a realm where pain and sorrow may not go.

You could be forgiven for thinking that my impressions of this wanderer are full of contradictions. It is not possible to describe him in any other way. But as you consider what I have said, remember your own girlish innocence, and the simple, straightforward way you once considered the world. It is that very spirit one needs to begin to understand him. Know that my affection for him is merited, and that I will continue to write every day to show why this is so.

August 19th, 17—.

Yesterday, the stranger said to me, "You can easily see, Captain Walton, that I have suffered a series of terrible misfortunes. I had decided, not long ago, that the memory of my hardships would die with me, but your welcome and interest have inspired a change of heart. You hunger for knowledge and wisdom, as I once did, and I sincerely hope that being satisfied in your quest does not prove to be as painful for you as it was for me. There is no way for me to know if hearing my story will prove useful to you, but, if you are so inclined, listen to my tale. I believe that the strange events associated with it will give you a better appreciation of nature and her workings and widen your understanding generally. You will learn of occurrences and powers widely considered to be impossible, but you will recognize as you hear all the different parts of the tale that the whole of it is true."

You can easily understand why I was flattered that he wanted to tell me his story. At the same time, I feared his saying it aloud would greatly renew his grief. Two forces urged me to hear him out: one was simple curiosity; the other arose from a strong desire I had to improve his situation, if it were possible to do so. I expressed these feelings in my answer.

"Thank you for your sympathy," he said, "but it is useless; my fate is nearly fulfilled. I await only one event, and after it comes to pass I will embrace the eternal rest my soul requires." I made to interrupt him, but he dissuaded me with a gentle look. "My destiny is fixed," he said. "Listen to what I have to tell you, and you will understand why this is so."

He then added that he would begin telling me his story the following day, during my leisure time. I thanked him. I will write down each night what he tells me during the day, as nearly as possible in his own words. On those nights when the ship and the crew require my attention, I will at least make notes. I am confident that the manuscript will bring you great pleasure; but to me, who know him, and who hear it from his own lips, it will be with limitless interest and sympathy that I read it some future day!

Chapter I

I am a son of Geneva, and my family is among the most distinguished of that republic. My ancestors had long been lawyers and judges, and my father continued the tradition, serving in a series of public roles with honour and distinction. He was respected by all for his integrity as well as his enthusiasm for serving the public good. In his younger days, he was constantly striving to improve the workings of our government. It was not until late middle age that he thought to marry and confer to the state sons who could carry his virtues and his name down to posterity.

As the circumstances of my father's marriage shine light on his character, I cannot refrain from describing them. One of his closest friends was a wealthy merchant, who, after decades of living in elegant circumstances in Geneva's best district, experienced a lengthy period of ill fortune and eventually sank into poverty. His name was Beaufort, and, possessing a proud temperament, he could not face living so humbly in the same city where he had flourished. After paying his debts in an honourable fashion, he moved with his only child, a daughter, to Lucerne, where the two lived unknown and in wretched conditions. My father was exceedingly fond of his friend, and he agonized over his downturn. He committed himself to finding Beaufort and begging him to start his life anew with help from an old friend.

But Beaufort had been skillful in the matter of his disappearance. Even knowing what city his friend was in, it took my father ten months to learn his precise whereabouts. After eventually getting an address, my father had made his way towards it straight away and found it to be a small, dark apartment house in a rough neighbourhood near the Reuss River. When he came through the door, only misery and despair welcomed him. Beaufort had emerged from bankruptcy with only a tiny amount of money, enough for meager food and this grim shelter for a few months. He initially hoped to get a job helping the sort of prosperous merchant that he used to be himself, but in the absence of such opportunities, and with time on his hands for reflection, his grief became worse, his depression darker. In the end he became bedridden, able to do little more than eat and breathe.

His daughter looked after him with tenderness, but she saw with alarm that their meager funds were dwindling. No additional source of income could be found, and their bad situation grew truly desperate. But Caroline Beaufort had an uncommonly strong character; and her courage blossomed in her hour of adversity. She fought to keep the two of them going in whatever way she could, weaving straw into hats and place mats, and through this and other piecework earning enough to keep them from starving.

Months passed. Caroline's father grew weaker still, and she was forced to spend more and more time tending to him. As a result, both funds and sustenance inevitably diminished, and ten months into their stay in Lucerne her father died in her arms, leaving her an orphan and a beggar. Her father's death devastated her. She was kneeling by his coffin and weeping when my father entered. He came like a protective spirit to the poor girl, who consented to his care. After Beaufort's burial, my father conducted her to Geneva and there placed her under the protection of a relative. Two years after this event Caroline became his wife.

When my father became a husband and a parent, he found his time so occupied by the duties of his new situation that he gave up much of his public role, and devoted himself to the education of his children. I, as his firstborn, was the one destined to inherit what his hard work and reputation had earned over the years. No one could have had more tender parents than mine, both of whom gave me everything that a child could hope for, all the more as I remained for several years an only child.

But before relating more of my story, I must give an account of something that took place when I was four years old.

My father had a sister, whom he loved very much, and who early in life had married an Italian gentleman. Shortly after their wedding, she and her husband left for Italy, and for several years my father heard little from her. When I was four, this aunt died, and a few months later my father received a letter from the husband. The man explained that he intended to marry an Italian woman, and asked whether my father would adopt his infant niece, Elizabeth, the only child of his departed sister.

"It is my hope," the man wrote, "that you will consider her your own daughter and educate her accordingly. Her mother's fortune is now hers, and I will send the documentation to you with the hope that you will consent to the idea. Please consider whether you think it preferable for her to be raised in your own household or in that of a stepmother."

My father did not hesitate. He left straight away for Italy so that he could bring little Elizabeth to our home in Geneva personally. I have often heard my mother say that Elizabeth was from the time of her first arrival the most beautiful child she had ever seen, and that the girl showed signs in infancy of the gentle ways for which we would all come to know her. Seeing such a beautiful child blessed with an outstanding temperament, my mother forged an early plan for Elizabeth and me to marry, a hope she never abandoned. It was, she said, the only way for the harmony of the family to be preserved and raised to its highest level.

From this time Elizabeth Lavenza became my playfellow, and, as we grew older, my friend. She was gentle and good-natured, and as happy and playful as a firefly over a summer meadow. Although she moved easily from one happy pursuit to another, her inner life had great depth, and she was wonderfully affectionate. No one made better use of freedom than she, and yet she was unfailingly gracious when it came to accommodating the ideas of others. Her imagination was intense, and yet her ability to apply herself was extraordinary. In so many ways, she was her own most perfect creation. Her hazel eyes, though as lively as a bird's, possessed a beautiful softness. Her figure was slender and graceful, and while she could withstand deep fatigue better than anyone else, she appeared the most fragile creature in the world. While I admired her wisdom and spontaneity, I could not refrain from doting on her, as I would on a favourite animal; I never saw so much grace of body and mind brought together in a single person without at least a little pretension being the result. But there was none in my cousin.

Everyone in our household loved her. When the servants needed to communicate something to my father or mother, they turned to Elizabeth, and she delivered their message with tact. As for my cousin and myself, we were quite different, but that somehow served to make the harmony between us stronger. Of the two of us, I was more prone to silent reflection and philosophical thinking, and never as serene as Elizabeth, nor as comfortable to have around. I would study a subject for a longer period of time, but with less passion. I loved to learn about the physical universe, she to take in the truths left behind by the poets. To me the world was a puzzle that needed to be solved; to her it was a blank canvas ready to be painted with her imagination.

My brothers were much younger than myself; but I had one friend from school who compensated for this faint sorrow. Henry Clerval was the son of a merchant of Geneva, a close friend of my father. He was a boy of great talent and imagination. I remember, when he was nine years old, he wrote a fairy tale, which delighted and truly amazed all his young friends. He was always reading books about chivalry and romance; and when very young it was common for us to act in plays that he authored based on his favourite of these books, with their principal characters being Orlando, Robin Hood, Amadis, and St. George, the dragon-slayer.

No one's younger years could have been passed more happily than mine. My parents were generous, my young companions fond. Our studies were never forced; instead, we were always provided with the purpose for our work, which spurred us to apply ourselves with something akin to joy. In this way, in lieu of being fed dull facts to commit to memory, we were provided with the fuel for an intellectual curiosity beyond our years. Elizabeth was encouraged to devote herself to drawing, not to win any contest, implied or otherwise, with her companions, but to delight her aunt, through the representation of a favourite scene done in her own hand. We learned Latin and English in order to be able to read the writings in those languages; and as opposed to study being made hateful by having it handed down to us as a punishment, we loved our learning, and what we experienced as exhilarating fun was what other children perceived to be dreary toil. Perhaps we did not read as many books, or learn languages quite as quickly, as those who are disciplined according to the ordinary methods; but what we learned was impressed the more deeply on our memories.

As I describe our home life, I must include Henry Clerval, who in many ways was an extra member of the family. In the morning, he was at school with me, and in the afternoons he was at our house. He was an only child, with no playmate at home, and his father was pleased that he had companions at our house; we were never completely happy when Clerval was not with us.

It is a pleasure to think back on these days, before misfortune changed the appearance of the world from a hopeful to a dismal place and my own value within it from that of a truly useful person to a forlorn waste. Still, as I recount this period of my life, I must not fail to describe the events that led to the misery you see upon me today, all of which was unimaginable then. The passion that one day would claim me started as humbly as a high-country stream: a tiny trickle, coursing among a few rocks, increasing by the addition of a few other streams, and eventually becoming a raging mountain river carrying away everything in its path—hopes, aspirations, and joys.

What passion unlocked this power? It was the innocent pursuit of scientific knowledge. That is why it is important for me to share the circumstances that led to my initial interest in this subject. When I was thirteen, my family and I made a pleasure trip to Thonon; but bad weather forced us to spend a day indoors at the inn. In this house I chanced to find a volume of the writings of Cornelius Agrippa. I opened it in the grip of boredom. However, the theory Agrippa strives to prove in his writings, and the facts that he includes, soon changed my mood to wonder. My mind suddenly possessed a new light, and I went looking for my father to share with him this remarkable turn of events. I have to say that many a teacher fails the student in situations such as this, and that was what happened on this day.

Whereas all a teacher needs to do is direct a student towards more current, useful knowledge, too often the instructor will issue a blanket statement of disapproval about a subject with which he is less than exceedingly familiar. My father looked carelessly at the title page of my book, and said, "Ah! Cornelius Agrippa! My dear Victor, do not waste your time on this; it is sad trash."

If instead of this remark my father had taken the trouble to explain that Agrippa's principles had been entirely exploded, and a modern system of science had been introduced, one that held far more power than the ancient, how better for all of us it would have been! I surely would never have read another page of the man's work and would have taken the excitement that had been generated within me and studied the more rational theory of chemistry that has resulted from modern discoveries. It is even possible that with this one alteration in the course of my life, the chain of events that eventually destroyed so much of what was good around me, as well as all the happiness I knew myself, would never have begun. But my father had really only glanced at the writings of Agrippa when I held the volume out for him to inspect, leaving me unconvinced that he even knew what was inside it, and I continued reading with the greatest fascination.

When I returned home, my highest priority was to acquire Agrippa's complete works, and afterwards those of Paracelsus and Albertus Magnus. I read and studied the unrestrained conjectures of these writers with great delight. I perceived them to be treasures known to few other than myself; and although I badly wanted to communicate what I was learning to my father, his blanket rejection of Agrippa, my favourite, persuaded me against the risk of further rebuke. In Elizabeth I had a safer audience, but my discoveries proved of little interest to her, and I was left to pursue my studies alone.

It probably seems strange that some one living in our modern era would be so taken by the works of Albertus Magnus, but my family was not scientifically disposed, and I had never gone to any of the lectures given in the various schools of Geneva. My dreams were therefore undisturbed by reality; and I joined with great seriousness the search for the philosopher's stone and the elixir of life. And it was the latter that received my nearly undivided attention; wealth was no worthy goal, but what glory would be mine if I could banish disease from the human body and keep man safe from any but a violent death?

But my ambition went beyond even this. I went about summoning ghosts as well as devils, feats promised by my favourite authors. When I failed to achieve the desired results, I blamed my own inexperience and errors, rather than an absence of skill or good faith in my instructors.

I was fascinated by the natural phenomena that take place around us every day. Distillation, and the astonishing effects of steam, of which my beloved authors were ignorant, filled me with wonder. But my greatest astonishment was reserved for experiments on an air pump, which I saw used by a gentleman we regularly visited.

The ignorance of my favourite scientists on these and several other points diminished their value to me, but I could not entirely throw them aside until some other system could take up their place in my mind.

When I was around fifteen, we had moved for the summer to our house near Belrive, when we witnessed an unusually violent and terrible thunderstorm. It came from over the Jura mountains, with deafening thunder clapping from multiple directions. I stood in the doorway throughout the storm, watching it unfold with wonder and delight. Suddenly, I saw a stream of fire rise from a tall oak about twenty yards from the house. After the dazzling light vanished, only a blasted stump remained where the tree had been. When we visited it the next morning, we found the tree shattered in an interesting way. It was not splintered by the shock, but entirely reduced to thin ribbons of wood. I never saw anything so utterly destroyed.

I found the blasting of this tree completely astonishing, and I asked my father to tell me what he knew regarding the nature and origin of thunder and lightning. He answered, "Electricity"; and subsequently described some of the effects of that power. He constructed a small electrical machine, and performed a few experiments; he also made a kite, with a wire and string, which, astonishingly, drew down that majestic fluid from the clouds.

This impressive feat led to the overthrow of Cornelius Agrippa, Albertus Magnus, and Paracelsus, who had so long served as the masters of my imagination. But by some fatal flaw of character I did not yet hunger to begin studying any modern system; and my lack of interest was worsened by the following minor event.

My father expressed a desire that I attend a course of lectures on natural philosophy, to which I readily and happily agreed. Something I can no longer recall occurred to prevent my attending the lectures until the course was nearly finished. The lecture, being therefore one of the last, was entirely incomprehensible to me. The professor held forth with great fluency about potassium and boron, sulphates and oxides, terms about which I had absolutely no idea; and I became disgusted with the science of natural philosophy. Still, I continued reading Pliny and Buffon with delight, as they were authors, in my estimation, of vast interest and usefulness.

The bulk of my time at this age was spent upon mathematics, and most of the branches of study connected with that science.

I was hard at work learning languages. I knew Latin already, and was reading some of the easier Greek authors without a dictionary. I also perfectly understood English and German. And that is the list of my accomplishments at seventeen; you can put together on your own how industrious I had to be to acquire and maintain my knowledge in these realms at so young an age.

Another claim on my time arrived, when I was appointed my brothers' tutor. Ernest was six years younger than I, and was my principal student. He had been in poor health from the time of his infancy, when Elizabeth and I had been his constant nurses; he had a gentle way about him, but he was not able to work very hard or long. William, the youngest of our brood, was still an infant, and quite beautiful. His lively blue eyes, dimpled cheeks, and considerable charm inspired tender affection among all who knew him.

Such was our domestic circle, an island within Geneva that never knew care or woe, even for a day. My father held the responsibility for our education, and my mother was in charge of our enjoyments. None of us was more important than anyone else in the family; no voice of discipline was ever heard; our love for one another was sufficient to produce the harmony that all families require, and so few families know.

Chapter II

When I turned seventeen, my parents informed me that I would be attending university at Ingolstadt. Until then, I had gone to school in Geneva, but my father, especially, thought it best for me to become familiar with the customs of more than one place. My departure date was chosen with great purpose and hope, but before it arrived the first misfortune of my life took place—an omen, as it were, of my future misery.

Elizabeth had caught the scarlet fever; but her illness was not severe, and she quickly recovered. During the period that my cousin was confined to her bed chamber, my mother was often told, emphatically, to let others in the household comfort the patient. For a time, she accepted this wisdom, but when she heard that her favourite was recovering, she could not help herself from looking in on her. Unfortunately, the danger of infection was still present, and this wish to comfort her niece proved fatal. On the third day of Elizabeth's illness, my mother herself became sick. Her fever was extremely serious, and the servants' faces told me that the worst of all things was about to happen. On what proved to be my mother's deathbed, her strength of character and goodness were as present as ever. With so little time remaining for her, she joined my hands with Elizabeth's, and began to speak.

"My children," she said, "more than anything else I have

looked forward to seeing the two of you joined in marriage. Looking forward to this will now help your father as he grieves for his wife. Elizabeth, my love, you must take my place in the family when I am gone. I despise being taken from you, and, after all the tenderness we have known, it is hard to say goodbye. But I prefer not to be pessimistic; I hold onto the hope of seeing you again in the afterlife."

My mother died calmly, and her face showed affection, even in death. I need not describe the feelings of those who find themselves torn apart by the great evil of death, whether it is the emptiness created in the soul or the despair visible on the faces of those left behind. It takes time, a long time, before the mind can understand that some one whom we loved the most, whose very existence was part of our own, has departed forever. It is, at first, incomprehensible that the brightness of beloved eyes is permanently extinguished, that the sound of this one voice, so soothing and so familiar, will never be heard again. Thoughts like these come to the surface during the first days of grief, during which each hour brings anew the truth of the loss. After this preliminary phase, the bitterness of grief begins to take hold. Who has not been hurt by death in this way? It is a pitiful thing that everyone has felt, and must feel. But, as time passes, grief becomes an indulgence one allows oneself rather than a necessity. Eventually, one even permits oneself to smile without judging the moment of happiness, or forcing it to go away. My mother had died, yes. But we had to continue our lives as individuals and as a family and to focus upon the blessing that there were still people around us to love.

Preparations for my journey to Ingolstadt, delayed due to these events, began anew. My father gave me a few weeks to gather myself. Although my mother's death, and my forthcoming departure, depressed our spirits, Elizabeth worked to reestablish the spirit of cheerfulness within our little society. Since her aunt's death, her mind had taken on new firmness and energy; she intended to fulfill the duties entrusted to her with precision; she knew that the greatest of the responsibilities that had fallen to her was ensuring the happiness of her uncle and cousins. She consoled me, amused her uncle, and instructed my brothers; I never saw her more enchanting than during this time, when she was constantly striving to add to the happiness of others, and entirely forgetful of herself.

The day of my departure eventually arrived. I had already said goodbye to all my friends, with the exception of Henry Clerval, who spent the last evening with us. He said many times that he was upset not to be able to go with me. It tormented him to be unable to accompany me, but his father had decided Henry would become his partner in business and had expressed an unwillingness to be separated from his son and skepticism about higher learning. He believed that studying at university achieved nothing when it came to the business of everyday life. The truth was that Henry's mind was excellent, and he would never allow himself to pursue idle knowledge. Even though he was grateful for his father's trust and support in matters of business, he believed that a man could be a very good trader and yet have a refined understanding of civilization.

Elizabeth and I stayed up late, listening to his complaints, and making a variety of little arrangements for the future. Early the next morning I departed. Tears gushed from the eyes of Elizabeth, some from sorrow at my departure and some for another reason: She could not help remembering that, if the departure had taken place just three months earlier, a mother's blessing would have accompanied me.

I climbed in the carriage that was to carry me away, and indulged in a series of sad reflections. I had always been surrounded by friendly companions, with all of us concentrating on making one another happy, but now, for the first time, I was alone. At university, I would have to form new friendships and be my own defender. My life to this point had been unusually sheltered, to such an extent that even the thought of new faces made me uncomfortable. I loved my brothers, Elizabeth, and Clerval; theirs were "old familiar faces"; but I believed myself ill fitted for the company of strangers. Such were my reflections as I started my journey; but as I continued, my spirits and hopes rose. I was keen to gain knowledge, and I would have the opportunity to do so in my new environment. I had often, when at home, found it suffocating to remain cooped up in one place, and had longed to enter the world and take my station among other human beings. Now that my wishes were being granted, it would have been foolish to change my mind.

I had time for these and many other reflections during my journey to Ingolstadt, which was long and tiring. At length the high white steeple of the town came into view. A few minutes later I exited the carriage and was chaperoned to my solitary apartment to spend the evening as I pleased.

The next morning I delivered my letters of introduction, and paid a visit to some of the principal professors, and among others to Professor Krempe, one of the university's noted men of science. He asked me a series of questions concerning my progress in the different branches of science. I mentioned, it is true, with fear and trembling the only authors I had ever read upon those subjects. The professor stared: "Have you," he said, "really spent your time studying such nonsense?"

I replied that I had. "Every minute," continued Professor

Krempe with warmth, "every instant you have spent on those books has been utterly and entirely lost. You have burdened your memory with outdated thinking and useless names. Good God! in what wild land have you lived, where not a single person was good enough to tell you that these daydreams, which you have taken in with such hunger, are a thousand years old, as well as musty and useless? I admit I never expected in our enlightened and scientific age to find a disciple of Albertus Magnus and Paracelsus. My dear sir, you must begin your studies anew."

So saying, he stepped aside and wrote down a list of books on the natural sciences he wished me to obtain, and dismissed me, after mentioning that he would be starting a series of lectures the following week and that Professor Waldman, his colleague, would give lectures on chemistry the alternate days that he missed.

I returned home, not disappointed, for I had long known that the authors the professor scorned were useless. Still, I did not feel myself drawn to read the books I had collected at his recommendation. Professor Krempe was a squat little man with a gruff voice and a repulsive face; the teacher, therefore, did not predispose me in favour of his philosophy. Besides, the scientists on his list seemed bent on destroying the visions on which my own interest in their subject was based. Where in the past scientists had sought to fabricate gold and eternal youth, now they were content to accomplish things far more mundane. Their resulting science failed to capture my imagination, let alone to lift it to its former heights.

Such were my reflections during the first two or three days, which I spent almost in solitude. But as the next week got going, I thought of the information Professor Krempe had given me concerning the lectures. And while I could never stand to go and hear such a self-important little man deliver his thoughts from a pulpit, I remembered what he had told me about Professor Waldman, whom I had never seen, as he had until then had been out of town.

Partly driven by curiosity, and partly driven by having nothing better to do, I took a seat in the lecture hall, which Professor Waldman entered shortly after. This professor was very unlike his colleague. He appeared to be about fifty years of age, but with a look on his face of tremendous kindness; a few gray hairs covered his temples, but those at the back of his head were nearly black. He was not tall, but carried himself with pride; and his voice was the sweetest I had ever heard. He started his lecture with a retelling of the history of chemistry and the various improvements made by different men of learning, pronouncing the names of the most accomplished discoverers among them with reverence. He described the current state of the field and explained many of its elementary terms. After having made a few preparatory experiments, he ended with a tribute to modern chemistry, in words I will never forget.

"The ancient teachers of this science," he said, "promised impossibilities, and performed nothing. The modern masters promise very little; they know that metals cannot be changed into other materials, and have no illusions about creating an elixir of youth. But these men, whose hands perform crude tasks and whose eyes stare into the microscope and crucible from morning to night, have performed miracles. They have seen into the innermost workings of nature and have climbed with their understanding into the heavens. They have discovered how the blood circulates, and the nature of the air we breathe; they have acquired new and almost unlimited powers, allowing them to command the thunder in the sky, to mimic earthquakes, and to mock the invisible world with its own shadows."

I left highly pleased with the professor and his lecture, and paid him a visit the same evening. His manners were even more charming in private; there had been a formality to him at his lecture, whereas in his own home he was all kindness and warmth. He listened attentively as I told him about my own studies and smiled at the names of Cornelius Agrippa and Paracelsus.

"These are men to whom contemporary scientists owe a great debt," he said. "Without their passionate and patient work, nothing the modern scientist does would be possible. They made our task far easier than it would have been, arranging classifications and determining facts that we use every day; the work of men of genius, even when it is misdirected, is ultimately turned to the solid advantage of mankind."

I listened to this assessment, offered without airs or conceit, and told him his lecture had opened my mind to the work of modern chemists, before asking him what books I should be buying and reading.

"I am happy," said Professor Waldman, "to have found a new disciple. If your diligence is as great as your curiosity, your success is certain. Chemistry is the natural science that has made the most impressive advances until now, and it will likely see the greatest breakthroughs in the years to come. That is why I have made it my field of expertise. However, I have not neglected the other branches of science, and neither should you. A man would make a poor chemist if he mastered his own area of inquiry solely. If you wish to become a real man of science, and not merely some one who performs routine experiments, I suggest you study the other sciences seriously, including mathematics."

He then took me into his lab and explained the uses of the different machines, explaining what I needed to buy and offering to lend me his equipment after I had learned enough not to damage it. Then he wrote down the list of books that I had requested; I thanked him, told him goodnight, and returned to my apartment.

And so ended a day that would change the course of my life.

Chapter III

From this day forward the natural sciences, and particularly chemistry, in the widest sense of the term, became nearly my sole occupation. I read, pulse pounding, those works, so full of genius and clear thinking, that our modern researchers have written on these subjects. I went to the lectures, and became a friendly disciple, of the men of science of the university, and I came to see that even Professor Krempe had a deep understanding and real information on which I could draw, no less so for his repulsive face and manners. In Professor Waldman, meanwhile, I found a true friend. His gentleness was never tainted by pride or dogma, and his instructions were amiably given, without a whiff of self-importance. It may have been the kind personality of this man that pushed me towards chemistry, rather than any instinctive love for the subject. But that was true only at the beginning; the more I studied chemistry, the more I wanted to learn about it for its own sake. My work, at first intermittent and laboured, became so absorbing that the stars would disappear with the sun's first light while I was still performing my experiments.

Applying myself in such a way, it is easy to understand why I improved rapidly. My never-ending eagerness to study was shocking to my fellow students, but my professors praised me for my widening skill. Professor Krempe, with a smile both ironic and kindly, asked how Cornelius Agrippa was coming along, and Professor Waldman expressed deep delight in my progress. Two years passed in this manner, during which I never managed to visit Geneva, being too absorbed with the work of making scientific discoveries. Perhaps no one except those who have direct experience can appreciate the pull of science. In other realms of knowledge, you can travel as far as others have gone before you, but there is, typically, little remaining to uncover; but in science there is limitless food for discovery and wonder. A mind of moderate capacity, allowed to pursue an area of study without interruption, will become highly proficient in it; and I, as I performed my research, was supremely focussed on a single goal, and I saw my skills improve at a nearly unimaginable pace. By the end of the two years, I had made discoveries improving certain vital chemical instruments, and this work earned me wide admiration at the university. At this point, I had become as familiar with the natural sciences as I could under my professors, and thus living in Ingolstadt was no longer necessary, or even helpful, to my further progress. Indeed I was thinking to return to my friends and native town when a breakthrough occurred that lengthened my stay.

One area of inquiry that fascinated me especially was the structure of the human frame, and, indeed, any animal pulsing with life. From where, I wondered, did life itself spring? It was a bold question, one that had long been a mystery; yet how often are we just about to learn the truth about something when fear or a lack of vision holds us back? I overcame these in myself, and decided I would focus on physiology, and the other parts of science relevant to it. If I had not been motivated to an almost supernatural degree, my study of the subject would have been difficult and slow, like the worst drudgery. But I was driven by something more than curiosity. If I were to learn the causes of life,

I would need to come to a good understanding of death. I had by now become acquainted with the principles of anatomy and physiology, which were helpful, but I saw that I would have to observe the decay and corruption of a dead human body. My work would be made easier by the fact that my father had taken great pains during my education to make sure I was never exposed to any tales of supernatural horrors; I do not ever remember trembling at the telling of a ghost story, or fearing the appearance of a spirit, nor was I ever even the slightest bit afraid of the dark. A church burial ground on a moonless night, terrifying to many, to me was merely the receptacle of bodies deprived of life. That these forms, which had once been the seat of beauty and strength, were now food for the worm had little effect on my imagination. Thus it actually seemed routine to me when I found myself examining the causes of decomposition and spending days and nights in morgues and crypts. I fixed my eyes on objects that would horrify the sensibilities of most human beings. I saw the attractive lines of a face after they were degraded and shriveled; I saw death's darkening and withering quickly destroy the blooming rose of life; I watched worms make their way through the wonders of the eye and brain. I took my time about it, looking hard at the tiniest details of causality, as exemplified in the change from life to death, and death to life, until from the midst of this darkness a sudden light broke in upon me—a light so bright and wondrous, yet so simple, that although I became dizzy with the scale of what it was showing me, I was surprised that among so many men of genius, who had directed their inquiries towards the same science, that I alone should be the one destined to discover so astonishing a secret.

Remember, I am not recording the vision of a madman; rather, what I am affirming to be true has the same objective value as the sun itself shining in the heavens. Some miracle may have produced it, but the stages of the discovery were distinct and logical. After days and nights of incredible labour and fatigue, I managed to discover the cause of generation and life; no, more, I myself became capable of creating animation within lifeless matter.

The shock I at first felt about this discovery soon turned to delight and rapture. After so much time spent in painful labour, to arrive without warning at the summit of my desires was a more exhilarating realization of my efforts than I could have imagined. But this discovery was so great and overwhelming, that all the steps by which I had been progressively led to it were obliterated, and I could only see the result. What had been the study and desire of the wisest men since the creation of the world, was now within my grasp. Not that the great prize would be revealed to me all at once, by some magic; no, the information I had obtained was sufficient to point my efforts now to the real object of my search, rather than to bring that object into view for all the world to see. I was like the Arabian who had been buried with the dead, and found a passage back among the living, assisted only by one weakly glimmering light.

I can see by the wonder and hope in your eyes that you think I may be on the verge of revealing the secret I have learned, but that cannot be; listen patiently until the end of my story, and you will easily perceive why I am honour-bound to remain silent on that subject. I will not be the shepherd who leads you, unguarded and thirsting for knowledge as I was then, to your physical and moral destruction. Learn from me how much happier a man is who allows his native town to be the whole world, compared to the man who wants to be more significant than his natural gifts will allow.

When I found so astonishing a power placed within my hands,

I hesitated a long time concerning the way I should use it. Although I possessed the ability to give life, preparing a frame to receive the vital spark—with all its intricacies of fibres, muscles, and veins—remained a work of unfathomable difficulty and labour. I was unclear, at first, whether I would try to create a being like myself or one of simpler organization, but after my first success my imagination was too energized for me to doubt my ability to give life to an animal as complex and wonderful as man. Although the materials I had acquired were not yet adequate to such an undertaking, I did not doubt that I would eventually succeed. It was important, nonetheless, to prepare mentally for the inevitable series of failures that the endeavour would involve; my operations might leave me incessantly baffled, and my final product be highly imperfect; yet, when I remembered the improvements taking place daily in science and mathematics, I felt hopeful that my present efforts would at least lay a foundation for future success. I was unwilling, meanwhile, to consider the scope and complexity of my plan as proof of its impossibility. It was with these feelings that I began the creation of a human being. As the small size of many parts represented a hindrance to my speed, I decided, against my first inclination, to make the being of gigantic stature. He would be eight feet in height and proportionately large. After arriving at this determination, and having spent months collecting and arranging my materials, I began.

No one can imagine the variety of feelings that carried me forward, like a hurricane, in the first enthusiasm of success. Life and death appeared to me like walls hemming me in, which I would soon break through, before pouring a great stream of light into our dark world. A new species would smile upon me as its creator and source; many happy and good souls would owe their lives to me. No children in history had ever owed more gratitude to their father than these beings would feel towards me. Continuing these reflections, it seemed to me that if I could animate lifeless matter, I might eventually be able to renew life where death had seemingly set in motion the process of corruption within the body.

These thoughts kept my spirits hopeful, while I laboured on my project with unceasing passion. My cheeks had become sunken and pale from toil, and my body was becoming emaciated. Sometimes, on the very brink of success, I failed. Still, I held onto the hope that the next day or the next hour would bring me that much closer to my goal. No one knew about any of this work or about the scope of my ambition; with the moon gazing upon my midnight labours, I chased nature to her hiding places with breathless eagerness. Who can imagine the horrors of my secret toil, as I dabbled among the unholy damps of the grave, and tortured living animals to create life in others where there was none? My body trembles and my eyes swim with the remembrance. But during this long period of exhausting, furious effort, an overwhelming impulse urged me forward; I seemed to have lost all connexion with my soul and even my body, apart from the work before me. After this unparalleled fever of labour and estrangement from myself, I felt my normal range of sensations as I had before, if more deeply, as I resumed my previous work habits. I collected bones from the morgues; and disturbed with unrepentant fingers the tremendous secrets of the human frame. In a solitary apartment, or rather cell, at the top of the house, and separated from the other tenants' quarters by a long hallway and a stairway, I kept my workshop of filthy creation; my eyes were starting from their sockets as I tended to the details of my project. The university's dissecting rooms and the slaughter-house provided many of my materials; and often my human nature turned away in disgust from the work, and yet all the while I felt myself pushed forward by an ever-growing eagerness, as I brought my work close to conclusion.

The summer months passed while I was thus engaged, heart and soul, in one pursuit. It was a most beautiful season; never had the fields yielded a more plentiful harvest, or the vines produced a more refined vintage; but my eyes were by then blind to the charms of nature. And the same feelings which made me ignore the scenes around me caused me also to forget my friends so many miles away, whom I had not seen for so long. I knew my silence worried them; and I was haunted by the words of my father: "I know that when you are content, you will think of us with affection, and we will hear regularly from you. You must forgive me if I interpret any interruption in your correspondence to mean you are neglecting your other duties as well."

I knew well therefore the effect my continued silence would have on my father, but I could not tear myself from my task, which though hateful in itself had taken complete hold of my imagination. It was my preference to procrastinate everything related to my feelings of affection until the great object, now consuming my very life, could be completed.

At the time I thought my father would be unjust if he attributed my neglect to poor behaviour, or a lack of character on my behalf; but I now understand why he was justified in believing me not to be altogether free of blame. A human being doing as he ought should always maintain a calm and peaceful mind, and not allow passions or passing desires to upset his tranquil state. I do not think that the pursuit of knowledge is an exception to the rule. If something you would study will weaken your ties to those you love, and destroy the joy you take in life's simple pleasures, then it is destructive and in some way evil. The human mind should not be fed with such unconventional nourishment, if the unthinking pursuit of knowledge for knowledge's sake can be called nourishment at all. If all people followed this rule, then the effects on history would be monumental. Greece would never have been enslaved; Caesar would have spared his countrymen their woeful plight; America would have been discovered peacefully, and gradually; and the empires of Mexico and Peru would never have been destroyed.

But I am moralizing in the most interesting part of my tale; and your expression reminds me to proceed.

My father never criticized me in a letter, but only took notice of my silence by inquiring into my occupations more pointedly than before. Winter, spring, and a second summer passed, as I worked in my laboratory night and day. I saw no blossoms or budding leaves in the spring, though such sights had always produced great happiness in me, for my project engrossed me that completely. The leaves of that year had withered before my work drew near its completion; and now every day revealed to me more clearly how well I had succeeded. But my enthusiasm was limited by my anxiety, and I looked more like some one doomed to do slave labour in the mines, or any other wasting trade, than an artist in the midst of doing what he does best. Every evening now I had a slight fever, and I became nervous to an excruciating degree; it was a state I regretted all the more, as I had always enjoyed excellent health, and had often boasted of the firmness of my nerves. But I was persuaded that exercise and well-spent leisure time would drive away such symptoms; and I promised myself both, once my creation was complete.

Chapter IV

It was on a cold and damp November night that I witnessed the realization of my labour. With the greatest rush of anxiety I had ever known, I gathered the instruments of life near myself, so I could finally put the spark of being into the lifeless form at my feet. It seemed as if I had just taken my evening meal, but it was somehow one in the morning. The rain pattered against the windows; my candle had become only a nub, and was growing dim. By the glimmer of this half-extinguished light, I saw the dull yellow eye of the creature open; it breathed hard, and its limbs quivered with convulsions.

How can I describe my emotions in the face of this catastrophe, or how describe the wretch whom I had given so much of myself to form? His limbs were in proportion, and I had chosen his features with beauty in mind. Beauty!—Great God! His yellow skin imperfectly covered the muscles and arteries of his face. His hair was shiny and black, his teeth white like pearls; but these attractive traits only made a more horrid contrast with his watery eyes, nearly the same colour as the gray-white sockets in which they were set, his shriveled complexion, and straight black lips.

The things that seem to happen randomly during a human lifetime are less changeable than the feelings we have about them. I had worked hard for nearly two years, with the sole purpose of infusing life into an inanimate body. For this I had deprived myself of rest and health. I had been pushed forward by a passion far exceeding moderation; but now that I had finished, the beauty of the dream vanished, and breathless horror and disgust filled my heart. Unable to endure the living face of the being I had created, I rushed out of the room, and took to pacing my bed chamber for some time, unable to quiet my mind sufficiently for sleep. Eventually exhaustion overcame the power of the endlessly racing thoughts within me; and I threw myself on the bed in my clothes, with the goal of knowing at least a few moments of forgetfulness. But there were no such moments to be had; I slept indeed, but I was disturbed by the wildest dreams. I thought I saw Elizabeth, in the bloom of health, walking in the streets of Ingolstadt. Delighted and surprised, I embraced her; but as I put the first kiss on her lips, they went the gray-blue colour of death; her features appeared to change, and I thought that I held the corpse of my dead mother in my arms; a shroud enveloped her body, and I saw the grave worms crawling in the folds of the flannel. I started from my sleep with horror; a cold dew covered my forehead, my teeth chattered, and every limb became convulsed. Then, by the dim and yellow light of the moon, as it forced its way through the window shutters, I saw the wretch—the miserable monster whom I had created. He held up the curtain of the bed; and his eyes, if eyes they may be called, were fixed on me. His jaws opened, and he muttered some inarticulate sounds, while a grin wrinkled his cheeks. He might have spoken, but I did not hear; one hand was stretched out, as if to detain me, but I escaped, and rushed downstairs. I chose as a refuge the courtyard belonging to the house where I lived; and there I remained for the rest of the night, walking up and down in the greatest agitation, listening carefully, catching and fearing each sound as if it foretold the arrival of the demoniacal corpse to which I had so miserably given life.

Oh! no mortal could withstand the horror of that face. A mummy brought back to life could not be as hideous as he. I had looked at him closely before he came to life and he was ugly then; but when those muscles and joints were made able to move, it became a thing that no imagination, not even Dante's, could have created.

I passed the night pitifully. Sometimes my pulse beat so quickly and forcefully that I felt the palpitation in every artery; at others, I nearly collapsed from nervous exhaustion. Mingled with this horror, I felt the bitterness of disappointment; dreams that had been my food and rest for so long a time had become a hell to me, and the change was so rapid, the overthrow so complete!

Dawn came, damp and dreary, with the minor brightening of the courtyard and a slate gray sky becoming visible overhead. My weary eyes perceived the white steeple and clock of Ingolstadt's main church, the clock face showing six. The porter opened the courtyard gates, and I set off into the streets at the fastest pace I could maintain. There was much to propel me forward, despite my exhaustion. Above all, there was the memory of the creature, whose face I feared seeing with each turn of the street. I did not dare return to the apartment, and felt my feet hurrying me forward of their own accord, as I made my way through the cold rain pouring from a black and comfortless sky.

I continued walking for some time, trying, through exercise, to ease the load that weighed upon my mind. I made my way down several streets, with little idea where I was, or what I was doing. My heart beat wildly in the sickness of fear, and I rushed forward with irregular steps, not daring to look around me:

Like one who, on a lonely road,
  Doth walk in fear and dread,
And, having once turn'd round, walks on,
  And turns no more his head;
Because he knows a frightful fiend
  Doth close behind him tread.

Continuing along, I eventually arrived across from the inn where various carriages and coaches stopped. I paused here, without knowing why, and remained with my eyes fixed on a coach coming towards me from the other end of the street. As it drew nearer, I saw it was the coach connecting Ingolstadt and Switzerland; it stopped just where I was standing; and when the door opened I observed Henry Clerval, who, on seeing me, instantly darted out.

"My dear Victor!" he exclaimed. "How glad I am to see you! how fortunate for you to be here at the moment of my arrival!"

Seeing Henry was like being ejected from Hell; his miraculous arrival brought my father, Elizabeth, and everyone at home to mind, as well as all of the memories in which each of them figured. I grasped his hand, and in a moment forgot my horror and misfortune. I felt, for the first time in many months, a calm serenity verging on joy; after I welcomed my friend warmly, we walked towards my college. Henry spoke enthusiastically about our mutual friends, and about his good fortune in being allowed to come to Ingolstadt.

"You will have no trouble believing," he said, "how difficult it was persuading my father that it was not absolutely necessary for a merchant not to understand anything except bookkeeping; and, truthfully, I think I left him unconvinced until the very end, for his constant response to my tireless pleading was to quote the Dutch schoolmaster in *The Vicar of Wakefield:* 'I have an income of ten thousand florins a year without Greek; I eat very well without Greek.' But his affection for me eventually overcame his dislike of learning, and he has decided to allow me to undertake a voyage of discovery to the realm of knowledge."

"It makes me truly happy to see you; but tell me about my father, brothers, and Elizabeth."

"They are all very well, and very happy, just a little uneasy that they hear from you so seldom. By the bye, I have intended to lecture you a little on their behalf myself; but, my dear Frankenstein," he continued, stopping short, and gazing full in my face, "I did not notice before how ill you appear; so thin and pale; you look as if you have kept awake for several nights."

"You have guessed right; I have lately been so deeply engaged in one occupation that I have not allowed myself sufficient rest, as you see; but I hope, I sincerely hope, that all these employments are now at an end, and that I am finally free."

I was trembling to an excessive degree; I could not bear to think of, let alone describe, the happenings of the preceding night. I walked with a quick pace, and we soon arrived at my college. It occurred to me, and the thought made me shiver, that the creature whom I had left in my apartment might still be there, alive, and walking about. I had a deep dread of seeing this monster; but I was even more fearful that Henry would see him. Earnestly asking him to stay a few minutes at the bottom of the stairs, I darted up towards my own room. My hand was already on the lock of the door before I remembered the danger of the situation. I paused a moment; and a cold shivering came over me. I threw the door open forcefully, as children will when they expect to see a ghost waiting for them on the other side; but nothing appeared. I stepped fearfully in; the apartment was empty; and my bedroom also had been freed of its hideous guest. I could barely believe that so great a piece of luck could have come my way; but when I was sure that my enemy had indeed fled, I clapped my hands for joy, and ran down to Clerval.

We climbed to my room, and the servant soon brought breakfast; but I was unable to contain myself. It was not joy alone that possessed me; I felt my flesh tingle with excess of sensitiveness, and my pulse beat rapidly. I was unable to remain for a single instant in the same place; I jumped over the chairs, clapped my hands, and laughed aloud. Clerval at first credited my unusual spirits to joy over his arrival; but when he observed me more carefully, he saw a wildness in my eyes for which he could not account; and my loud, unrestrained, heartless laughter, frightened and astonished him.

"My dear Victor," he exclaimed, "What, for God's sake, is the matter? Do not laugh in that way. How ill you are! What is the cause of all this?"

"Do not ask me," I said, putting my hands before my eyes, for I thought I had seen the dreaded fiend slide into the room; "let him tell you! Oh, save me! Save me!" I imagined that the monster took hold of me; I struggled furiously, and fell down in a fit.

Poor Clerval! how must he have felt? A meeting he anticipated with such joy had strangely turned to bitterness. But I was not the witness of his grief; for I was lifeless, and did not recover my senses for a long, long time.

This was the start of a nervous fever that confined me for several months. During all that time Henry was my only nurse. I afterwards learned that, knowing my father's advanced age, his unfitness for such a long journey, and how distressing my sickness would be to Elizabeth, he spared them this grief by concealing the extent of my disorder. He knew that I could not have a more kind and attentive nurse than himself; and, sure in the hope he felt of my recovery, he was confident that, instead of doing harm, he was performing the kindest action that he could towards them.

But I was in reality very ill; and surely nothing but the sustained, selfless attentions of my friend could have restored me to life. The image of the being whom I had brought into existence was always before my eyes, and I raved incessantly regarding him. My words no doubt surprised Henry; he at first believed them to be the wanderings of my disturbed imagination; but the persistence with which I returned to the same subject persuaded him that my disorder originated in some bizarre and terrible event.

At a pitifully slow pace, and with frequent relapses that frightened and worried my friend, I recovered. I remember the first time I became capable of seeing the world with any kind of pleasure, I observed that the fallen leaves had disappeared, and that the young buds were springing forth from the trees that shaded my window. It was an especially beautiful spring that year, which did much to spur my recovery. Soon, forgotten joys and the old ties of affection began to fill my heart again; my gloom disappeared, and in a surprisingly short time I became as cheerful as before I was attacked by the fatal passion.

"Dearest Clerval," I said, "how kind, how very good you are to me. This entire winter, instead of studying as you promised yourself, you have been occupied tending to your old friend. How will I ever repay you? It pains me to have burdened you this way, but I know you will forgive me."

"If you continue getting better," Henry said, "it will be more than adequate repayment; and since you appear in such good spirits, I wonder if I can ask you about one subject?"

I trembled. One subject! what could it be? Could he be referring to an object on whom I dared not even think?

"Collect yourself," said Henry, who observed my change of colour, "I will not ask again, seeing the effect it has on you; but your father and cousin would be very happy if they received a letter from you in your own handwriting. They barely know how sick you have been, and are uneasy over your long silence."

"Is that all? my dear Henry—how could you imagine my first thought would not fly towards those I hold most dear, and who are so deserving of my love?"

"If this is your current frame of mind, my friend, you will be glad to see a letter that has been lying here for some days; it is from your cousin, I believe."

Chapter V

Clerval then put the following letter into my hands.

"To V. Frankenstein.

"My dear Cousin,

"I cannot describe to you the uneasiness we have all felt concerning your health. We cannot help imagining that your friend Clerval is concealing the extent of your disorder; for it is now several months since we have seen your handwriting; and all this time you have been forced to dictate your letters to Henry. Surely, Victor, you must have been exceedingly ill; and this makes us all despondent, almost as much as after the death of your dear mother. My uncle was nearly certain that you were indeed dangerously ill, and could hardly be kept from undertaking a journey to Ingolstadt. Clerval always writes that you are getting better; I eagerly hope that you will make his assurances unnecessary in your own handwriting; for indeed, indeed, Victor, we are all miserable about this. Relieve us of this fear, and we will be the happiest creatures in the world. Your father's health is so much improved, that he looks ten years younger since last winter. Ernest also is so much improved, that you would hardly know him: he is now nearly sixteen, and has lost that sickly appearance which he had some years ago; he has become quite robust and active.

"My uncle and I conversed a long time last night about what profession Ernest should choose. His health when young made it impossible for him to apply himself; and now that he is at full strength, he is constantly in the open air, climbing the hills, or rowing on the lake. I therefore proposed that he become a farmer, which you know, Cousin, is a favourite scheme of mine. A farmer's is a very healthy happy life; and the least hurtful, or rather the most beneficial profession of any. My uncle had an idea of his being educated as an attorney, that through his interest he might become a judge. But, leaving aside that Ernest is not well suited for such an occupation, it is certainly more honourable to feed a man's stomach than it is to feed his vices, and that is what the profession of being a lawyer is. I said that the doings of a prosperous farmer, if they were not inherently more honourable, at least comprised a happier type of occupation than those of a judge, who was doomed always to meddle with the dark side of human nature. My uncle smiled and said that I ought to be a lawyer myself, which put an end to the conversation on that subject.

"I must tell you a story sure to amuse you, and hopefully bring you a moment's happiness. Do you remember Justine Moritz? Probably you do not; I will relate her history, therefore, in a few words. Madame Moritz, Justine's mother, was a widow with four children, of whom Justine was the third. Justine was always the favourite of her father, but, for some unknown reason, her mother could never stand the sight of her and treated her accordingly. Your mother noticed this, and when Justine was twelve, she convinced Justine's mother to allow her at her house. Now, because Switzerland is more enlightened than the monarchies that surround it, there is less oppression of the unfortunate here; one result is that being a servant in Geneva is far less demeaning than in France or England. Justine, received with dignity into our family, learned the duties of a servant, but never at the expense of her humanity.

"After what I have said, I dare say you will remember the lead character of my little tale, for Justine was a great favourite of yours; and I remember you once announced that if you were in a bad mood, one glance from her could make it disappear. You said it was because she was as admirable as any lady described by a poet, being blessed with an honest and happy disposition. As you remember, your mother adored Justine, so much that she not only made sure she received the kind of education given to servants here, but indeed that she received the same sort usually reserved for children in the best families. And the kindness was repaid: Justine was the most grateful girl I have known, not based on what she said, I do not think I ever heard her say that she was thankful for what had been done for her; rather, you could see in her eyes that she almost adored this woman who had chosen to protect her. While she was a lighthearted girl, and in some ways inconsiderate, she paid close attention to everything my aunt said and did, taking her as a model of behaviour and speaking and acting as she did; even today, Justine reminds me of her.

"When my beloved aunt died, everyone was too focussed on their own grief to notice poor Justine, who had cared for her during her illness with the most anxious affection. Poor Justine was very ill; but other difficulties awaited her. One by one, her brothers and sister died. Her mother, with the exception of Justine, was now childless and concluded that the deaths of her children was a judgment from heaven for favouritism she had shown. She was Catholic, and her priest confirmed her belief; thus, a few months after you went to Ingolstadt Justine was sent for by her repentant mother. Poor girl! She was crying when she left. The death of the woman who changed her life had given her a softness and gentleness she had lacked, even though she was good-hearted from the start. When she moved back in with her mother, Madame Moritz was anything but consistent in her repentance. At times, she begged Justine to forgive her past unkindness, but more often she accused her of causing the deaths of her sister and brothers. Long stretches spent in worry threw the woman into ill health, which at first increased her irritability, but she is now at peace. She died on the first approach of cold weather, at the beginning of this last winter. Justine has returned to us; and I find that I love her tenderly. She is very clever and gentle, and extremely pretty; as I mentioned before, her appearance and expressions continually remind me of my dear aunt.

"I must say also a few words to you, my dear cousin, of little darling William. I wish you could see him; he is very tall for his age, with sweet laughing blue eyes, dark eyelashes, and curling hair. When he smiles, two little dimples appear on each cheek, which are rosy with health. He has already had one or two little wives, but Louisa Biron is his favourite, a pretty little girl of five years of age.

"Finally, I dare say you would like to be indulged in a little gossip concerning the good people of Geneva. The pretty Miss Mansfield has been receiving congratulation visits on her engagement to a young Englishman of noble descent, John Melbourne. Meanwhile, her much less pretty sister, Manon, married a rich banker, Monsieur Duvillard, last fall. Your old school friend Louis Manoir has gone through a series of misfortunes after Henry left for Ingolstadt, but he is already back in good spirits and said to be engaged to a very lively and beautiful Frenchwoman, Madame Tavernier. Although a widow, and much older than he, she is much admired and a favourite with everyone.

"I have written myself into good spirits, and yet I cannot end without inquiring once more about your health. Good Victor, if you are not too weak, please write back. You will make your father, and all of us, happy. I cannot bear to think of the other side of the question; my tears already flow.

"Adieu, my dearest cousin.
"*Elizabeth Lavenza.*

"*Geneva, March 18th, 17——.*"

"Dear, dear Elizabeth!" I exclaimed, when I had read her letter. "I will write immediately, and relieve them of the anxiety they must feel." I wrote, and this exertion exhausted me; but my convalescence had begun, and continued its course. In another two weeks I was able to leave my bed chamber.

One of the first duties of my recovery was to introduce Clerval to the various professors of the university. In doing this, I underwent a kind of ordeal, ill suiting the wounds that my mind had sustained. Ever since the fatal night, the end of my labours, and the beginning of my misfortunes, I had conceived a violent loathing even for the name of natural philosophy. When I was otherwise quite restored to health, the sight of a chemical instrument would renew all the agony of my nervous symptoms. Henry saw this, and had the porter remove all the apparatus from my view. He had also arranged for a different apartment; for he observed that I had acquired a dislike for the room which had previously been my laboratory. But these efforts by Clerval were rendered fruitless when I visited the professors. Professor

Waldman tortured me when he praised, with kindness and warmth, the astonishing progress I had made in the sciences. He quickly saw that I disliked the subject, but assumed modesty was to blame. He changed the topic of conversation from my accomplishments to the science itself, with a desire, as I soon saw, of drawing me out. What could I do? He meant to please, and he tormented me. I felt as if he had placed carefully, one by one, within my view those instruments that were to be used afterwards in putting me to a slow and cruel death. I squirmed with his every word, but was careful not to show the true depths of pain I felt. Clerval, whose eyes and feelings were always quick in understanding the reality of others, professed a lack of interest in the subject, blaming his complete lack of training in it. Mercifully, the conversation took a more general turn. Without saying a word, I looked to my friend with gratitude in my eyes. I saw that he was surprised, but he would never attempt to draw my secret out of me; even though I loved him with a mixture of affection and admiration that knew no bounds, I could still never persuade myself to confide to him the event that was so often present to my recollection, but which I feared describing to some one would only impress more deeply.

Professor Krempe was not so easily dissuaded; and in my condition at that time, of barely tolerable sensitivity, his harsh blunt compliments caused me even more pain than the more mild and general praise of Professor Waldman. "Damn your friend and his modesty," he said, speaking to Henry. "I assure you that he has left us behind with his research. Aye, stare at me if you please, but it is nevertheless true. A very young man, indeed, who only a few years ago took Cornelius Agrippa to be a great scientific mind, is now at the head of the university. If he continues on the same course, we will all be made fools of, if we have not been already." As he spoke, he glanced my way from time to time and saw on my face the suffering his flattering words caused me. "Monsieur Frankenstein is modest, an unusual and excellent quality in a young scholar," he said to Henry. "Those who are inexperienced should not think too highly of themselves, it is true. Even I was young once."

Professor Krempe had now started eulogizing himself, turning the conversation from a subject that was so annoying to me.

Clerval was no natural philosopher. His imagination was too vivid for the minutiae of science. Languages were his principal study; and he sought, by acquiring their elements, to open a field for self-instruction on his return to Geneva. Persian, Arabic, and Hebrew claimed his attention, after he had acquired perfect understanding of Greek and Latin. For my own part, idleness had always been unpleasant to me; and now that I was motivated to avoid reflection, and hated my former studies, I felt great relief in being the fellow-pupil with my friend, and found myself fascinated as well as soothed by the work of the orientalists. Their melancholy is consoling, and their joy uplifting to a degree I never experienced in studying the authors of any other country. When you read their writings, life appears to consist in a warm sun and garden of roses—in the smiles and frowns of a fair enemy, and the fire that consumes your own heart. How different from the manly and heroic poetry of Greece and Rome.

Summer passed away in these endeavours, and my return to Geneva was fixed for the latter end of autumn; but being delayed by several accidents, winter and snow arrived, the roads were deemed impassable, and my journey was delayed until the forthcoming spring. I felt the postponement very bitterly; for I longed to see my native town, and my beloved friends. My return had only been delayed so long from an unwillingness to leave Clerval in a strange place, before he had gotten to know anyone. The winter, however, was spent cheerfully; and although the spring was unusually late, when it came, its beauty compensated for its tardy arrival.

The month of May had already begun, and I expected the letter daily which was to fix the date of my departure, when Henry proposed a pedestrian tour in the region surrounding Ingolstadt, so that I could bid a personal farewell to the country where I had so long been living. I agreed to his suggestion with pleasure. I was fond of exercise, and Clerval had always been my favourite companion in the rambles of this nature that I had taken in my native country.

We passed two weeks in these jaunts; my health and spirits had long since been restored, and they gained additional strength from the refreshing air I breathed, the events that occurred along the way, and the conversation of my friend. Study had isolated me from my fellows, and left me antisocial; but Clerval called forth the better feelings of my heart; he again taught me to love the ways of nature, and the cheerful faces of children. Excellent friend! how sincerely did you love me, and seek to elevate my mind, until it was on a level with your own. A selfish pursuit had cramped and narrowed me, until your gentleness and affection warmed and opened my senses; I once again became the happy young man who, loving and beloved by all, had no sorrow or care. When happy, inanimate nature had the power of raising within me the most delightful sensations. A serene sky and green fields filled me with ecstacy. The present season was indeed divine; the flowers of spring bloomed in the hedges, and those of summer were already in bud. I was undisturbed by thoughts which during the preceding year had pressed upon me, despite my strivings to throw them off, diminishing me by the day.

Henry rejoiced in my happiness, revelling in my progress and newfound hope sincerely. His efforts to draw me forth kept on, and he gave voice to the delights of his own soul. The resources of his mind on this occasion were truly astonishing; his conversation was full of imagination; and very often, in imitation of the Persian and Arabic writers, he invented tales of wonderful fancy and passion. At other times he recited my favourite poems, or drew me out into arguments, which he supported with great insight.

We returned to Ingolstadt on a Sunday afternoon; as we made our way through the last miles of countryside before the city walls, the peasants were dancing and rejoicing as they celebrated a local holiday. My own spirits were as high as I could remember them ever having been. I walked along as one without a care in the world, propelled by joy and laughter.

Chapter VI

Upon my return, I found the following letter from my father:

"*To V. Frankenstein.*

"My dear Victor,

"You have no doubt been waiting for a letter fixing the date of your return to us; I was tempted to write just a short note, simply mentioning the day I wanted you to join us. But that would be a cruel kindness, and I dare not do it. What would be your surprise, my son, when you expected a happy and joyful welcome, and found, on the contrary, tears and wretchedness? And how, Victor, can I tell you of our misfortune? Absence cannot have left you immune to our joys and griefs; and how shall I inflict pain on an absent child? I want to prepare you for the sorrowful news, but I know it is impossible; even now your eyes skim over the page, to seek the words that will convey to you the horrible tidings.

"William is dead!—that sweet child, whose smiles delighted and warmed my heart, who was so gentle yet so joyful! Victor, he has been murdered!

"I will not attempt to console you; but will simply relate the circumstances of what has occurred. Last Thursday (May 7), my niece, your two brothers, and I went for a walk in Plainpalais.

The evening was warm and pleasant, and we prolonged our walk farther than usual. It was already dusk before we thought of returning; and then we discovered that William and Ernest, who had been ahead of us, were not to be found. We thus rested on a seat until they should return. Very soon Ernest came, and asked if we had seen his brother, saying that they had been playing together, that William had run away to hide himself, and that he looked for him without success, and afterwards waited for him a long time, but that he did not return.

"This news rather alarmed us, and we continued to search for him until night fell, when Elizabeth had the idea that he might have returned to the house. He was not there. We returned again, with torches; for I could not rest, when I thought that my sweet boy had become lost, and was exposed to all the damps and dews of the night; Elizabeth also suffered extreme anguish. About five in the morning I discovered the lovely boy, whom the night before I had seen blooming and active in health, stretched on the grass blue and motionless; the print of the murderer's finger was on his neck.

"He was carried home, and the sorrow that was visible on my face betrayed the secret to Elizabeth. She was very keen to see the corpse. At first I attempted to prevent her; but she persisted, and entering the room where it lay, hastily examined the neck of the victim, and clasping her hands exclaimed, 'Oh God! I have murdered my darling child!'

"She fainted, and was restored with extreme difficulty. When she was alive again, it was only to weep and sigh. She told me, that that same evening William had teased her to let him wear a very valuable miniature she owned of your mother. This picture is gone, and was doubtless the temptation which urged the murderer to the deed. We have no trace of him at present, although our efforts to find him out are unending; but they will not restore my beloved William.

"Come, dearest Victor; you alone can console Elizabeth. She weeps continually, and accuses herself unjustly as the cause of his death; her words pierce my heart. We are all unhappy; but will that not be an additional motive for you, my son, to return and comfort us? Your dear mother! Alas, Victor! I now say, Thank God she did not live to witness the cruel, miserable death of her youngest darling.

"Come, Victor; not brooding thoughts of vengeance against the assassin, but with feelings of peace and gentleness, that will heal, instead of festering the wounds of our minds. Enter the house of mourning, my friend, but with kindness and affection for those who love you, and not with hatred for your enemies.

"Your affectionate and afflicted father,

"Alphonse Frankenstein.

"Geneva, May 12th, 17—."

Clerval, who had watched my face as I read this letter, was surprised to see despair come so soon after the joy I at first expressed on receiving news from my friends. I threw the letter on the table, and covered my face with my hands.

"My dear Frankenstein," exclaimed Henry, when he observed me weep with bitterness, "are you always to be unhappy? My dear friend, what has happened?"

I motioned for him to pick up the letter, while I walked up and down the room in the most extreme agitation. Tears also streamed from the eyes of Clerval, as he read the account of my misfortune.

"I can offer you no consolation, my friend," said he; "your catastrophe cannot be undone. What do you intend to do?"

"To go this moment to Geneva; come with me, Henry, to order the horses."

During our walk, Clerval strove to raise my spirits. He did not do this with typical topics of consolation, but by showing the truest sympathy.

"Poor William," he said, "the dear child now sleeps with his angel mother in heaven. His friends mourn and weep, but he is at rest. He no longer feels the murderer's grasp; the earth covers his gentle body, and he knows no pain. Pity for him would be a waste; it is the survivors who are suffering, and for them the only thing which will help is time. No one should urge the example of the Stoics; even Cato cried over the dead body of his brother."

Clerval spoke in this fashion as we hurried through the streets; the words fixed themselves to my mind, and I remembered them afterwards in solitude. But now, as soon as the horses arrived, I hurried into a cabriolet, and said goodbye to my friend.

My journey was one of profound sadness. At first, I wanted to arrive in Geneva as quickly as possible, being anxious to console and sympathize with my loved and sorrowing friends. But when I got closer to the city, I slowed the horses, barely able to make sense of the conflicting thoughts rushing through my mind. I passed through areas known to me in my youth, which I had not seen for nearly six years. How much would everything have changed during that time? One sudden and devastating change had taken place; but a thousand small circumstances might have by degrees achieved other alterations which, although done more tranquilly, might not be any less decisive. Fear overcame me; I dared not continue, dreading a thousand nameless evils that made me tremble, although I could not define them.

I stayed at Lausanne for two days in this painful state of mind.

I looked on the lake; the waters were still; all around was calm, and the snowy mountains, the "palaces of nature," were not changed. By degrees the calm and heavenly scene restored me, and I continued my journey towards Geneva.

The road bordered the lake, becoming narrower as I approached my native town. Before arriving, I saw more distinctly the black sides of the Jura mountains and the brilliant white summit of Mont Blanc. Without warning, I was weeping like a child: "Sweet mountains! my beautiful lake! how will you welcome this long lost friend? Your summits are free of storms, and even clouds; the sky and lake are blue and calm. Are these signs of peace, or messages sent only to mock at my unhappiness?"

I fear, my friend, that I will make myself tedious by dwelling on these early circumstances, but they were days of comparative happiness, and I think of them with pleasure. My homeland, my beloved homeland! Who but some one from this part of Switzerland can tell the delight I felt looking at the streams, the mountains, and our perfect lake?

But as I drew nearer home, grief and fear again overwhelmed me. Night also closed around; when I could hardly see the dark mountains, I felt even more gloomily. The picture appeared a vast and dim scene of evil, and I had a shadowy inkling that I was destined to wind up the most miserable of human beings. And while I was correct about it, there was no way for me to know the depth of sorrow that awaited.

It was completely dark when I approached Geneva. The gates of the city were shut, and I was forced to spend the night in Secheron, three miles away. As I was too upset to rest, I made a decision to visit the location where beloved William had been murdered. With the gates shut and the city impassable, my only option was to cross the lake in a rowboat in order to reach Plainpalais. During the short voyage, I saw the lightning playing on the summit of Mont Blanc in beautiful forms. The storm appeared to approach rapidly; and, on landing, I climbed a low hill, to watch its progress. It advanced; the heavens were clouded, and I soon felt the rain coming down in large drops, but its violence quickly increased.

I left the place where I had been sitting, and walked on, although the darkness and storm increased every minute, and the thunder burst with a terrific crash over my head. It echoed from Salève, the Juras, and the Alps of Savoy; vivid flashes of lightning dazzled my eyes, illuminating the lake, making it look like a vast sheet of fire. Then, for an instant, the darkness returned, and my eyes recovered from the flash. The storm, as is often the case in Switzerland, appeared at once in various parts of the sky. The most violent quadrant was directly to the north of Geneva, over the part of the lake lying between Belrive and Copêt. Another piece of it flashed less threateningly over Jura, and a third section was illuminating the Môle, a mountain peak to the east of the lake.

The whole thing was at once beautiful and terrifying. I continued my walk at a fast clip and found that the dramatic war in the sky was actually cheering me up. I clasped my hands together and spoke my thoughts, as lightning erupted overhead.

"William, dear angel!" I said. "This is the funeral the heavens have made for you!"

As I finished speaking, I saw in the gloom a shadowy form emerge from behind a group of trees; I stood fixed, gazing intently: I could not be mistaken. A flash of lightning illuminated the object, and revealed its shape plainly to me; its gigantic stature, its unnatural and ugly shape, more hideous than that of any human being; there was no denying that it was the wretch, the filthy demon to whom I had given life. Why was he here?

Could he—I shook at the thought—be the murderer of my brother? No sooner had the idea crossed my imagination than I realized it was true. My teeth chattered, and I was forced to lean against a tree for support. The figure passed by me, and I lost it in the gloom. Nothing in human shape could have destroyed that fair child. He was the murderer! I could not doubt it. The very presence of the idea was its own proof. I thought of pursuing the hateful creature, but it would have been in vain. Another flash showed he was moving at an almost incredible pace and possessed climbing skills that defied reason. He was already on the cliff face of Mont Salève, a mountain bordering Plainpalais on the south. He quickly reached the summit, and disappeared.

I remained motionless. The thunder ceased; but the rain continued, and the scene was enveloped in an impenetrable darkness. I revolved in my mind the events that I had spent the better part of two years trying to forget. All of it leapt forth from memory— the lengthy process of creating the monster; its visit to my bedside; its departure. Two years had now nearly passed since the night he first received life; and was this his first crime? Alas! I had turned loose into the world a depraved wretch, who delighted in carnage and misery; had he not murdered my brother?

No one can imagine the torment I suffered during the remainder of that night, which I spent cold and wet in the open air. I did not feel the discomfort of the weather; my imagination was busy in scenes of evil and despair. I considered the beast whom I had sent among mankind, and endowed with the will and power to create scenes of horror, such as the deed which he had now done, as if in a vampire form of myself, let loose from the grave, and forced to destroy all that was dear to me.

Day dawned, and I directed my steps towards the town. The gates were open, and I hurried to my father's house. My first thought was to tell everyone what I knew about the murderer, and cause an immediate search to be launched. But I paused when I thought about the story I had to tell. A being whom I myself had formed, and imbued with life, had met me at midnight among the precipices of an inaccessible mountain. I remembered, too, the nervous fever that had overcome me while making the creature, which would give an air of delirium to a tale that was, in all its other respects, utterly improbable. I knew that if anyone else told such a story to me, I would have looked upon it as the ravings of insanity. Besides, the strange nature of the animal would elude all pursuit, even if I were believed sufficiently as to persuade my relatives to start such a hunt. Who could arrest a being capable of scaling the overhanging sides of Mont Salève? These reflections dissuaded me, and I committed myself to remaining silent.

It was nearly five in the morning when I entered my father's house. I told the servants not to disturb my family members, and went into the library to await their usual hour of rising.

Six years had elapsed, passed as a dream except for one indelible trace, and I stood in the same place where I had last embraced my father before my departure for Ingolstadt. Beloved and respectable parent! He still remained to me. I gazed on the picture of my mother, which stood over the mantelpiece. A piece of family history, and painted at my father's desire, it represented Caroline Beaufort in the depths of her anguish, kneeling by the coffin of her dead father. Her clothing was rustic, and her cheek pale, but there was an air of dignity and beauty, that hardly permitted the sentiment of pity. Below this picture was a smaller one of William, and my tears rained down as I looked at my brother's face. In a few moments, Ernest came into the room; he had heard my arrival and rushed to my side, expressing sorrowful delight at seeing me. "Welcome home," he said. "How

I wish you had been here three months ago! You would have found us happy. But now we are miserable, and I am sorry that tears, instead of smiles, are your only gifts. Our father looks so sorrowful: this terrible event has brought back his grief on the death of Mamma. Poor Elizabeth, too, is beyond consoling." He began to cry.

"Do not welcome me in this way," I said. "Do try to be calmer; I cannot stand to be completely miserable at the moment I return. Tell me—how is my father getting through this? And how is my poor Elizabeth?"

"She needs the support of all of us," Ernest replied. "She blamed herself for William's death, and for a time we could not convince her otherwise. But since the murderer has been discovered—"

"The murderer discovered! Good God! how can that be? who could attempt to track him down? It is impossible; you might as well run after the wind, or try to dam a mountain stream with a piece of straw."

"I do not know what you mean; but we were all very unhappy when she was found out. No one would believe it at first; and even now Elizabeth will not see the truth, despite all the evidence. Indeed, who would ever imagine that Justine Moritz, who was so affectionate, and fond of all the family, could all at once become so extremely wicked?"

"Justine Moritz! Poor, poor girl, is she the accused? But it is wrongfully; everyone knows that; no one believes it, surely, Ernest?"

"No one did at first; but several things that have happened have forced us to admit she is the one. It does not help that her behaviour has been so strange since William's death; it only adds to the evidence, and sadly there is now little room for doubt. She will be tried today; you can hear everything in court."

Ernest related that on the morning on which the murder of William had been discovered, Justine had taken ill and been confined to her bed. After several days, one of the servants happened to come across the clothing Justine had worn on the night of the murder and in one of Justine's pockets had found the locket with the picture of my mother, the very thing judged to have been the temptation for the murderer. The servant immediately showed what she found to one of the others, who, without a word to anyone in the family, had gone to a judge. After hearing the woman's story, the judge ordered Justine arrested; upon being charged with the fact, the poor girl confirmed the suspicion by becoming utterly disoriented.

This was a strange tale, but it did not shake my faith; and I replied earnestly, "You are all mistaken; I know the murderer. Justine, poor, good Justine, is innocent."

At that instant my father entered. I saw unhappiness etched on his face, but he made an effort to welcome me cheerfully; and, after we had exchanged our mournful greeting, would have brought forth some other topic than that of our disaster, if Ernest had not exclaimed, "Good God, Papa! Victor says that he knows who was the murderer of poor William."

"We do, too, unfortunately," said my father. "I would rather have remained ignorant than to have learned of so much depravity and ingratitude in one I valued so highly."

"My dear father, you are mistaken," I said. "Justine is innocent."

"If she is, God forbid that she should suffer as guilty," he said. "She is to be tried today, and I hope, I sincerely hope, that she will be acquitted."

This speech calmed me. I was firmly convinced in my own mind that Justine, and every other human being, was innocent of this murder. It seemed impossible, because of this, that sufficiently strong circumstantial evidence could be brought forward to convict her, and I allowed this line of thinking to calm me, and even began looking forward to the trial with eagerness.

We were soon joined by Elizabeth. Time had changed her appearance since I had last beheld her. Six years before, she had been a pretty, good-humoured girl, loved by all, and showered with affection. Now she was a beautiful woman with a high, intelligent forehead, a frank and honest glance, and hazel eyes that showed an inner calm. Still, the recent events had left sadness within her eyes, too. Her reddish-brown hair was lustrous, her complexion fair, and her figure slight and graceful. She gave me her usual warm embrace. "Your arrival, my dear cousin," she said, "fills me with hope. Perhaps you will be able to prove Justine's innocence? For who is safe, if she is convicted? I rely on her innocence as much as I do on my own. Our misfortune is doubly hard; for we have not only lost our darling boy but this poor girl, whom I sincerely love, is to be torn away by an even worse fate. If she is condemned I will never know joy again. But she will not, I am sure she will not; and then I shall be happy again, even after the sad death of my little William."

"She is innocent," I said, "and it will be proven. Do not fear the trial, but let your spirits be lifted by the fact that she will be set free."

"How kind you are!" Elizabeth said. "Everyone else is so sure of her guilt, and that made me miserable; for I have known all along it was outrageous! To see everyone else prejudiced in such a deadly manner left me hopeless and despairing." She wept.

"Sweet niece," said my father, "dry your tears. If Justine is, as you believe, innocent, then rely on the wisdom of our judges and on my own efforts to ensure their fairness."

Chapter VII

We passed a few sad hours, until eleven o'clock, when the trial was to begin. My father and the rest of the family were required to attend as witnesses, and I accompanied them to court. During the whole of this wretched mockery of justice, I suffered living torture. For today would determine if the result of my curiosity would be responsible for the deaths of two of my fellow-beings: one a smiling young boy, full of innocence and joy; the other murdered in an even uglier way, with the instruments of justice brought to bear for the crime. Justine was a good person with a promising life ahead of her; now, her time on earth was at risk of ending in a shameful burial, with myself as the cause. A thousand times over I would have preferred admitting my own guilt for William's death to save Justine, but I had been nowhere near Geneva when his murder was committed, and my confession would have been considered the ravings of a madman, and would not have exonerated the one suffering on account of my actions.

The appearance of Justine was calm. She was dressed in mourning; and her face, always pretty, was made more so by the solemn feelings coursing through her. She was confident, knowing herself to be innocent, and showed no sign of fear, despite having been stared at with the purest contempt by thousands. In any other circumstance, her beauty would have won her at least a few supporters. But such was the condemnation among the public for a crime so gruesome that her attractive appearance probably made things worse for her. While the expression on her face was one of serenity, you could see it might not remain that way. Everyone in Geneva believed her guilty of the crime; her confusion when questioned the morning after the murder appeared to remove all doubt. Still, she put forth the most hopeful face she could in self-defence, knowing herself to be in an impossible situation. When she entered the courtroom, she looked around it and quickly saw our family seated together. Her eyes filled, but she kept the tears from falling. A look of sad affection she directed our way only underscored her guiltlessness.

The trial began; and after the prosecutor had stated the charge, several witnesses were called. Several strange facts combined against her, and these would have been persuasive for anyone lacking the proof of her innocence that I had. She had been out the whole of the night on which the murder had been committed, and towards morning had been observed by a marketwoman not far from the spot where the body of the murdered child had afterwards been found. The woman asked what she was doing there; but she looked agitated, and only returned a confused and unintelligible answer. When she was shown the body, she became hysterical, and was bedridden afterwards for several days. The picture was then produced, which the servant had found in her pocket; and when Elizabeth, in a faltering voice, confirmed it was the same which, an hour before the child had gone missing, she had placed around his neck, a murmur of horror and indignation filled the court.

Justine was called on to speak in her own defence. As the trial had proceeded, her face had changed: surprise, horror, and misery had replaced the serenity of the morning. Sometimes she struggled with her tears, but when she was called to plead she collected her powers and spoke in an audible, if variable voice.

"God knows," she said, "how completely I am innocent. But I do not pretend that saying so will spare me the verdict of the court. Nonetheless, I have a plain explanation of the facts laid out against me and hope that the character I have always maintained will dispose the judges in my favour, in spite of the weight of what has been presented."

She then explained that, with Elizabeth's blessing, she had spent the evening of the murder at an aunt's house in Chêne, about three miles from Geneva. On her way home, at around nine o'clock, she met a man who asked her if she had seen anything that might help locate a missing child. She was upset by the man's story, and spent several hours looking for him, during which the gates of Geneva had been shut. She was forced to spend several hours in a barn, preferring not to wake the farmers whose barn it was, despite the fact that she was well known by them. Unable to sleep, she left her place of refuge early and renewed her search for my brother. If she ever went near the spot where the body was lying, it was without knowing it. The fact that she had been bewildered when the woman on the way to the market spoke to her was not surprising, since she had just spent a sleepless night, and the fate of William was still unknown. As for the locket, she had no idea how it had come to be on her person.

"I know," continued Justine, "how bad it looks, but I have no way of explaining the locket's presence to you. I have wracked my brain as to how it could have been placed in my pocket, but even in my wondering, I am limited; I cannot believe that I have an enemy on this earth, let alone one hateful enough to destroy me for no reason. Did the murderer place it there? I know of no opportunity he had to do so. But if he did, why would he have stolen the jewel only to get rid of it again so soon?

"I beg your mercy, knowing I have no reason to feel the slightest hope. I only ask permission to have a few witnesses testify regarding my character. If their statements cannot remove my seeming guilt, I know that I must be condemned; and yet I swear upon my immortal soul that I am innocent."

Several witnesses were called who had known Justine for many years, and all of them spoke well of her; but fear, and hatred of the crime they imagined her to have committed, made them less forceful than they would otherwise have been. Each of them failed in a different way to back her up to the extent needed. Elizabeth saw that these last hopes of Justine's, her fine character and years of contributing to society without a stain, were not going to save her. Overwhelmed by emotion, my cousin requested and was granted permission to address the court.

"I am," she said, "the cousin of the unhappy child who was murdered, or rather his sister, for I was educated by and have lived with his parents nearly my entire life, and indeed since long before he was born. Some will judge me for coming forward today, but when I see a good person about to die because of the cowardice of her supposed friends, I feel myself compelled to say what I know of her character. I am well acquainted with the accused; I have lived in the same house with her, at one time for five years, and more recently for two years. During all our time together, she was the friendliest and kindest of people. She nursed Madame Frankenstein, my aunt, in her final illness with great affection and care. Afterwards, she did the same for her own mother during a lengthy illness, in a way that earned the admiration of all who knew her. Following her mother's death, she returned to my uncle's home, where she was beloved by the entire household. It is worth noting that she was warmly attached to the child who is now dead. For my own part, I do not hesitate to say that, despite all the evidence to the contrary, I believe in her absolute innocence. She had no temptation to do such a thing. As to the piece of jewelry taken as proof against her, if she had ever wished to have it, I would have given it to her without hesitation, which she would have known. For that is how much I trusted, and loved her, and do still."

A murmur of approval was heard in the courtroom, but this was stirred by Elizabeth's generosity of spirit, rather than by any new compassion or understanding in favour of Justine, whom the public despised, if anything, more than before. For now, the public knew beyond doubt how well-loved Justine had been by all of us and added to her list of imagined sins that of betraying our family. As Elizabeth spoke, tears ran from Justine's eyes, but now she sat stone-faced. My own discomfort and anguish were unbearable. Justine's guiltlessness was not merely a thing that I believed in; rather, I knew her to be innocent, with absolute certainty. Meanwhile, I had begun to wonder whether my creation, who had, no doubt, murdered my brother, had actually framed Justine for the crime. The horror of the situation was beyond anything I could withstand; when it became clear from the judges' faces they would follow the popular opinion within the city and condemn my second victim, I rushed from the courtroom in agony. The tortures of the accused could not equal mine; she was comforted by her own innocence, but the fangs of remorse tore at my heart, and would not give up their hold.

I passed a night of pure torment. In the morning I went to the court; my lips and throat were parched. I could not ask the fatal question; but I was known and the officer on duty guessed the reason for my visit. The three judges' votes had been cast, he told me; they were all black, and Justine was condemned.

I cannot pretend to describe what I then felt. I had already experienced a sense of horror; and I have tried to convey adequately what it was like, but mere words cannot impart the heart-sickening despair that I felt upon hearing the fate of Justine. The officer told me she had, in the end, admitted her guilt. "Her confession," he said, "was hardly needed in so straightforward a case, but I am glad of it; and, indeed, none of our judges like to condemn a criminal upon circumstantial evidence, even when so decisive."

When I returned home, Elizabeth eagerly asked the result.

"My cousin," I said, "it is as you may have expected; all judges would prefer that ten innocent people suffer rather than that one guilty person escape. But she has confessed."

The twin blows of the verdict and her friend's confession were devastating to Elizabeth, whose trust in Justine had never wavered. "It is too much for me," she said. "How can I again believe in human kindness? Justine, whom I loved as a sister, how could she put on her smiles of innocence and then betray us this way? Her bright eyes seemed incapable of harshness of any kind, and yet she has committed murder."

Soon word was brought that the poor victim wished to see my cousin. My father wished her not to go; but said that he left it to her own judgment and feelings to decide. "Yes," said Elizabeth, "I will go, although she is guilty; and you, Victor, shall accompany me: I cannot go alone." The idea of this visit was torture to me, yet I could not refuse.

We entered the gloomy prison-chamber, and saw Justine sitting on some straw at the far end; her wrists were manacled, and her head rested on her knees. She rose on seeing us enter, and when we were left alone with her, she threw herself at the feet of Elizabeth, weeping bitterly. My cousin wept also.

"Oh, Justine!" she said. "Why have you taken my last consolation from me? I counted on your innocence; and while I was full of sorrow before, it is worse now."

"And do you believe, as the others do, that I am the monster they say? Do you join with them to destroy me?" Her voice was cut off by sobs.

"Stand, my poor girl," said Elizabeth. "Why do you kneel, if you are innocent? I am not one of your enemies. I argued for your purity, despite all evidence, until I heard that you had admitted your own guilt. That report, you say, is false; and be assured, dear Justine, that nothing can shake my confidence in you for a moment, short of your own confession."

"I did confess, but I confessed a lie. I confessed to receive absolution; and now that falsehood is the greatest burden I have to bear. God in heaven forgive me! Ever since I was condemned, my priest has besieged me; he threatened and menaced, until I almost began to think that I was the monster that he said I was. He threatened excommunication and hell fire in my last moments, if I did not tell them I was guilty. Dear lady, I had no one to support me; all looked on me as a wretch doomed to dishonour and the loss of my soul. What could I do? In a moment of weakness and darkness I accepted a lie, and now my sorrow is complete."

She paused, weeping, and then continued—"It caused me great pain when I thought you would believe your Justine's confession. For we both know that your aunt honoured and loved me, and I know that you did as well; for you then to believe that I was a creature capable of a crime no one but the devil himself could do made me shudder with horror. Dear William! dearest blessed child! Soon I will see you in heaven, where we shall all be happy; and that consoles me, going as I am to suffer this shameful death."

"Oh, Justine! forgive me for having for one moment distrusted you. Why did you confess? But do not mourn, my dear girl; I will everywhere proclaim your innocence, and persuade all of the truth. Yet you must die; you, my playfellow, my companion, my more than sister. I never can survive so horrible a misfortune."

"Please do not weep," Justine said. "Rather, console me with thoughts of the better world I am on the verge of seeing, and raise my thoughts above this injustice and hardship. Do not, sweet friend, drive me to despair."

"I will try to comfort you," Elizabeth said. "But this, I fear, is an evil too great to be lessened by consolation. There is, perhaps, no hope for you now, not on this earth. Yet, I know heaven will bless you with the peace of the hereafter. How I hate the workings of fate, when one of us is murdered, and another, also innocent, is deprived of life in such a slow and torturous manner. It is awful to contemplate the executioners, their hands reeking with the blood of innocence, believing that they have served the world in some way! Around the city, they are calling it retribution; obscene word! When I hear it said, I know a worse punishment will be delivered than even the cruelest tyrant has imposed. But none of this is any consolation to you, even if you are looking forward to leaving our dark world, which no one could fault you for doing. All of this is enough to make me wish I were joining you in heaven with my aunt and our beloved William. Who would not want to escape from a place so hateful and be freed of people so worthy of judgment themselves?"

"What you offer, good friend, as resignation, is hopelessness in disguise," Justine said. "I must not learn the lesson that you would teach me. Speak of something else, something that will bring real peace, and not further sorrow."

During this conversation, I had retreated to a corner of the prison-room, where I could hide the horrid anguish that possessed me. Despair! Who dared talk of that? The blameless Justine tomorrow would pass through the curtain separating life and death, and yet she did not feel half the pain I did. I gnashed my teeth, and ground them together, uttering a groan that came from my innermost soul. Justine shook with surprise. When she saw who it was, she approached me, and said, "Dear Sir, you are very kind to visit me; you, I hope, do not believe that I am guilty?"

I could not answer. "No, Justine," said Elizabeth. "He is more convinced of your innocence than I was; for even when he heard that you had confessed he never accepted it."

"I truly thank him," said Justine. "In these last moments I feel the deepest gratitude towards any who can still think of me with trust and affection. How sweet is the affection of friends to one as hopeless as I am! You have taken away the larger part of my misfortune, which comes from being alone; I can die in peace now that my innocence is acknowledged by you, dear lady, and by your cousin."

In this way, Justine tried to comfort Elizabeth and me, as well as herself. She was finally attaining the acceptance she desired. But I, the true murderer, felt grief and guilt tear at my heart. There would be no relief in my case. Elizabeth wept and was miserable, but hers, like that of Justine, was the sadness of innocence. Such sorrow is like a cloud passing over the bright moon, briefly hiding it but never diminishing the moon's brightness. In my case, despair had penetrated the very core of my heart; I was carrying a hell within me that nothing could extinguish. We remained for hours with Justine; it was nearly impossible for Elizabeth to tear herself away. "I wish I were going to die with you," Elizabeth said. "I cannot live in this world of misery."

Justine took on an air of cheerfulness, while she fought back her bitter tears. She hugged Elizabeth tightly and spoke, in a voice choked with emotion, words that few could have said in her place. "Farewell, Elizabeth, my beloved and only friend," she said. "May heaven in its wisdom bless and preserve you. May this be the last misfortune you ever know. Live, and be happy, and make others so."

During our return, Elizabeth said, "You cannot know, my dear Victor, how relieved I am that Justine is innocent of William's death. I could never again have known peace if I had been wrong to trust her. During the hours I believed her guilty I felt sorrow that could not have been borne for long. Now, my heart is again my own. An innocent soul is suffering, but the sweet girl I took to be friendly and good never betrayed the trust I put in her, and I am consoled."

Sweet cousin! such were your thoughts, mild and gentle as your own dear eyes and voice. But as for me, my whole being was coursing with shame; and none ever imagined the misery that I then endured.

Volume II

Chapter I

Nothing is more painful to the human mind, than, after a quick succession of difficult events, the dead calmness of inaction and certainty which follows, depriving the soul of both hope and fear. And after the appalling things that had transpired since my return from Ingolstadt, such is what happened within me. Justine was dead; she was resting. I, however, was alive. Blood flowed in my veins, and a weight of hopelessness and regret pressed on my heart. Restful sleep was a distant memory. I wandered around my ancestral town like an unwholesome spirit. I had been a participant in the direst acts of evil, and yet I suspected even worse events were to come. Amazingly, though, my heart was full of kindness, and I appreciated the goodness I saw around me in my family, friends, and the people of Geneva more than ever. I had begun my life with the best of intentions, and had always looked forward to making the world better for my fellow human beings. Now, those hopes were dashed. Instead of the satisfaction that comes from doing good deeds, I was awash in remorse. My conscience had transformed daily life into a torture chamber, one too dark to be described with mere words.

This state of mind preyed upon my health, which had completely recovered from the first shock it withstood. I was once again avoiding human contact. All sound of joy or normalcy was torture to me; solitude was my only consolation—deep, dark, death-like solitude.

My father took note of the changes in my routine, and tried to reason with me about the risk of mourning too deeply. "Remember, Son," he said, "I am suffering as well. No one could love a child more than I loved your brother." Tears came into his eyes. "But it is a responsibility for those of us left behind to avoid going too far into our grief, which only adds to the world's unhappiness. You owe it to yourself and to the rest of us not to descend too far into the tomb of sorrow. Past a certain point, sadness gets in the way of living, and of becoming a better person. I know you know these things in your heart."

My father's advice was wise, given with love. But it did not apply in my case. Always before, I had been the first to hide my grieving, and console my friends, when we had endured losses, including the death of my mother. But now guilt tinged every other feeling I had. I could only respond to my father with a look of sadness, and try to keep myself away from him as politely as possible in the future.

About this time we moved to our house at Belrive, as we did each year. The transition was a blessing to me especially. The shutting of the city gates each night at ten o'clock and the inability to remain on the lake afterwards had been a hardship to me. Now, though, after everyone else was in bed for the night, I would take the boat and pass hours on my beloved body of water. Sometimes, sails raised, I was carried by the wind; at other times, I would row to the middle of the lake, let the boat drift with the sails down, and allow my morbid thoughts to roam. I was often of a mind, when all was peaceful, and I the only unquiet thing on the lake—excepting some bat, or the frogs, whose harsh and interrupted croaking was heard only when I approached the shore—often, I say, I was tempted to plunge into the silent lake and let the waters close over me and my strife forever. But I was restrained when I thought on the heroic and suffering Elizabeth, whom I tenderly loved, and whose life was bound up with mine. I thought also of my father and my surviving brother. On top of the shame of such an act for my family, if I were to choose an ending of this sort, I would be leaving them unprotected from the cruelty of my creation, who was currently roaming only God knew where.

Often I wept during these times on the lake, my world a shroud of sorrow. I wished for peace, in order to be able to console my grieving family members; but it was not to be. Guilt was unavoidable, no matter how many times I tried to drive it away; I had been the accidental author of horrifying violence and suffering, and I lived in the expectation that the monster I had created would act again. Although I cannot explain it now, I knew somehow that the story was not finished. And as long as there were people I loved still living, these fears would stalk me. For this reason, my hatred for the monster took on a life of its own. When I thought of him, my teeth clenched, and I hungered to extinguish the life that I had so naively brought into the world. When I thought about his cunning and cruelty, my desire for revenge became uncontrollable. I would have made a trek to the highest peak of the Andes, if, there, I could have thrown him to their base. I wished to see him again, so that I could wreak the greatest extent of anger on his head and avenge the deaths of William and Justine.

The house at Belrive was the house of mourning. My father's health, until then robust, was deeply shaken by the horror of recent events. Elizabeth was tormented, and incapable of taking comfort in daily life; all joy seemed to her a sacrilege towards the dead. Permanent sorrow was, she thought, the only way to honour the innocent lives we had seen destroyed. She was no longer the same person who in better days had walked with me on the banks of the lake speaking about our shared future. She had become solemn, and on the occasions she did talk it was about the precarious nature of life.

"When I think about the death of Justine, I no longer see the world in the same way I once did," she said. "Before, when I heard or read about evil things done in the world, it seemed imaginary. At a minimum, I knew that the dire events I had been made aware of were far away, and they all seemed to me then not to be completely real. But now sorrow has come home, and the people of Geneva seem like monsters thirsting for one another's blood. I know that I am not being fair, and that everyone sincerely believed Justine guilty. And if she had indeed committed the crime for which she was brought to death, then she would have been a fiend. Who else would have murdered the son of her benefactor and friend, a child whom she had taken care of from the moment of his birth, and seemed to love as if he had been her own, merely for a few jewels? In principle, I am against the taking of a single life, but even I would not have wanted a person capable of such a crime living among us.

"Yet, she was innocent; I know, and feel, she was innocent. And the fact that you have said the same thing confirms my belief. When lies can resemble the truth so well, who is safe? I feel I am walking on the edge of a cliff, with thousands crowding towards it, and all of them pushing me towards my doom. William and Justine were assassinated, and the murderer is out there, free, and perhaps respected. But even if I were to be hanged for Justine's and William's deaths, I would not change places with such a horrible person."

I listened to my cousin's words in agony. For I, not in what I had done, but rather in what I had set in motion, was the true murderer. Elizabeth saw anguish on my face and took my hand.

"You have to become more serene, my dear," she said. "These events have done more damage to my soul than anything I have experienced, but God knows I am not as affected as you. There is a look of hopelessness, alternating with revenge, on your face, that frightens me. Be less spiteful, I ask you. I would give up my own hope of contentment for you to know even a little peace. We will at least be happy in our native country, you and I, keeping to ourselves. What is there to make us unhappy now?"

Unable to fully believe her own gentle words, tears slid down her cheeks. But at the same time she smiled in a brave attempt to lessen the darkness that she could see had taken hold of me.

My father, who knew only part of my situation, was struggling to make sense of the depth of sadness he saw in his eldest son. He thought to restore me with a family excursion to the valley of Chamounix. I had made the trip before, but for Elizabeth and Ernest it would be their first time seeing the great valley. Both had often expressed desire to see the scenery of this place, which had been described to them as among the prettiest anywhere. Accordingly we left from Geneva on this tour around the middle of August, nearly two months after the death of Justine.

The weather was uncommonly fine, and if my grief had been of the sort to be banished by any light circumstance, the trip would have had the effect my father intended. And, in fact, despite my inner struggles, the sights did cheer me, just never completely, and never for more than a few minutes.

During the first day on the road, we travelled by carriage. In the morning before departing, we had seen the mountains from a distance. As we progressed alongside the Arve, whose course we followed, we perceived that the valley formed by the river was closing in on us almost imperceptibly. After the sun set, we perceived great mountains and overhangs rising above us on every side, and heard the river's raging torrent down among the rocks, and the perpetual splashing from waterfalls above.

The following morning, we continued the journey on mules. As we progressed higher on the trail, the valley became lush, a world unto itself. Vibrant pine forests and castles in ruins clung to the sides of the mountains. The rushing river and cottages that peeped out from among the trees made a scene of splendour and peace. And what was beautiful in our immediate vicinity was made more so by the great Alps themselves, rising above in white peaks and domes. It is easy to understand why the Greeks pictured their gods among the mountains.

We soon crossed the bridge at Pelissier. Looking up, we saw the great ravine formed by the river. Soon, we were climbing an even steeper part of the road alongside the rushing water, and then, seemingly all at once, we came into the valley of Chamounix. Compared to the beauty of the valley of Servox, through which we had just passed, the valley of Chamounix was more serene and stately, if less green. High, snowy mountains framed it, and here there were no more castles or fertile fields. Instead, vast glaciers approached the road. We heard the rumbling thunder of an avalanche and saw the smoke left by its passage. Mont Blanc, the supreme and magnificent Mont Blanc, raised itself above the surrounding lesser peaks, and its tremendous dome overlooked the village.

During this journey, I had sometimes stayed beside Elizabeth and appreciated the sights with her. I often slowed my mule to lag behind and spend time alone with my dark thoughts. At other times, I spurred the animal forward, ahead of the others, in order to forget them, the world, and, above all, myself. When I was far enough ahead not to be seen, I dismounted, threw myself on the grass, and writhed in terror and despair.

At eight in the evening, we arrived in the village. My father and Elizabeth were exhausted. Ernest, though, was full of energy and in high spirits. The only complaint he had was that a south wind blowing likely foretold rain for the following day, which neither he nor any of us wanted. We all retired early, though in my case sleep would remain an impossibility for a long time. I remained for several hours at my window, watching lightning flash above Mont Blanc and listening to the rushing water of the Arve.

Chapter II

The weather the next morning, contrary to the guides' predictions, began dry, though cloudy. We made a visit to the source of the Arve and spent the rest of the day riding around the valley. The scenes of natural beauty the trip was allowing me to witness provided the most consolation I had felt since returning to Switzerland. The views did not free me of grief, but they did afford all the detachment I was capable of feeling, and softened the brooding mindset I had developed. When I returned in the evening I was tired, but less morose. My family, with whom I was again happy to converse, took note of the change. My father was pleased, and Elizabeth overjoyed. "My sweet cousin," she said, "do you see how much your happiness affects the rest of us? Do not let the darkness take hold of you again!"

The following morning the rain fell down in torrents, and thick mists hid the summits of the mountains. I was up earlier than usual, and sorry to see that my mood of the evening before had been but a brief interlude between bouts of sorrow. The rain made it much easier for my old thoughts to take hold once more, and I found myself depressed. It was clear how disappointed this would leave my father, and I thought of ways to avoid him until better thoughts might return. I knew the rest of our group would remain at the lodge for the day, and decided on a means of avoiding them and possibly of regaining some of my hope.

As I had long before become impervious to rain and cold, I decided to ascend the summit of Montanvert. The effect the view of the glacier had produced within me the first time I saw it high above the valley had been exceedingly profound. It had given my imagination wings to soar from this dreary world to a realm of light and joy. The most sublime scenes in nature had indeed always made me content, by making it possible for me to forget my petty concerns. I was determined to go alone this day, for two reasons. First, I was acquainted with the path, which was difficult, and preferred to be able to hike without being slowed by another; second, I wished to view the glacier in silent contemplation.

The rocky trail up Montanvert is steep, but it is cut into continual and short windings, which enable you to overcome the perpendicularity of the mountain. It is a scene terrifically desolate. In a thousand spots the traces of the winter avalanche may be perceived, where trees lie broken and strewed on the ground; some entirely destroyed, others bent, leaning upon the jutting rocks of the mountain, or transversely upon other trees. The path, as you ascend higher, is intersected by ravines of snow, down which stones continually roll from above; one of them is particularly dangerous, as the slightest sound, such as even speaking in a loud voice, produces a concussion of air sufficient to draw destruction upon the head of the speaker. The pines are not tall or luxuriant, but they are sombre, and add an air of severity to the scene. Making my way upwards, I struggled to see the valley below through the mist rising from the river. The thick mist also obscured the mountains on the opposite side of the Arve, and the mountain's highest elevations were completely hidden by dark clouds and the rain that came down. How dismal it all was! We human beings are wrong to take pride in our subtler feelings, which lead to misery far too often. Many times I have thought it would be better to possess only the senses of hunger, thirst, and physical desire. Without more than these, we might be nearly free. As it is, we are blown about by the winds of fate and conflict, and can be devastated by chance words and the things that we happen to witness with our eyes.

> *We rest; a dream has power to poison sleep.*
>   *We rise; one wand'ring thought pollutes the day.*
> *We feel, conceive, or reason; laugh, or weep,*
>   *Embrace fond woe, or cast our cares away;*
> *It is the same: for, be it joy or sorrow,*
>   *The path of its departures still is free.*
> *Man's yesterday may ne'er be like his morrow;*
>   *Nought may endure but mutability!*

It was almost noon when I reached the top of the trail. I chose as my seat a rock overlooking the sea of ice, and contemplated the scene. Although the rain had ceased, a layer of mist hovered over the glacier, making the view of the mountains less distinct; soon, though, a breeze arose and dissipated the cloud. With the scene transformed into the crystal vision I remembered from my first visit, I walked onto the glacier. The ice was broken by the pressures exerted within it, its white surface alternately rising and falling like waves on a troubled sea. The glacier is only three miles wide, but I spent more than two hours in crossing it. From the side where I now stood Montanvert was exactly opposite, three miles distant. Above it stood Mont Blanc, in silent majesty. I put myself in a comfortable, protected space between two rocks and looked upon this wonderful and stupendous scene. The sea, or rather the river, of ice I had just traversed wound among the mountains that fed it; glistening white peaks framed the scene above. Suddenly, my heart, which had spent the morning in its familiar sorrow, swelled with something like joy.

Before I knew it, I was shouting, "Wandering spirits, if you visit places like this, do not rest on your beds but bless this moment of happiness of mine. If you cannot, then let the joys of life end for me here and take me away to wherever it is you hide."

The moment I finished saying the words, I observed a man in the distance. He was moving in my direction with incomprehensible speed, bounding across the crevasses that I had needed to traverse slowly and with care. His physical size, I noted as he neared, was larger than that of a human being. I was overwhelmed. Some kind of mist blinded me, and I began to lose consciousness, but the frigid wind from the mountains returned me to my senses. I saw that the tall being drawing nearer was the creature that I had made. Rage and horror set me to trembling; I decided to let him get close enough that I could fight him to the death. He never slowed until he was just a few paces away. I saw that his face showed deep sorrow, combined with an arrogant cruelty, its unearthly ugliness making it almost too horrible for human eyes to behold. Anger and hatred at first left me silent, but then I found that I could speak to the giant standing before me, with words intended to harm.

"Beast! How dare you come near me? Do you not fear what I will do in response to the crimes that you have committed against me and my beloved family? If you were wise, you would have avoided the vengeance of my arm. If only by bringing you and your miserable life to an end I could bring back the victims whom you so hatefully murdered!"

"I expected this reception," the demon said. "For human beings, the urge to hate those beneath them runs strong, and, so, how natural it is to hate me, as I am miserable beyond all living things! Yet you are wrong, my creator, to allow yourself to despise me, for there are ties forever binding a man to any living being he has made. You speak of killing me, and would do so, I see, if I allowed it. Do you have no conscience? You have created life, but you would destroy it so swiftly? If you uphold your duty to me, I will uphold mine to you—and to the rest of the human race. You should know that I have set certain conditions for you to meet. Do you have ears to listen? If you comply with what I ask, I will leave all of humanity, including you and your family, in peace. If you refuse, I will feed the bloody jaws of death with the flesh of your remaining loved ones."

"Hell awaits you, fiend, but even its fires will not pay you back for what you have done," I said. My voice and body both shook. "You complain about having been made by me? Come near, so that I may extinguish the spark that I was foolish enough to ignite."

The fury within me was like nothing I had known. I jumped towards his huge form as though I myself were a devil who could prevail in battle with him, for anger gives courage where nothing else would. My attack was the easiest and most natural thing I had ever done. But he quickly stepped aside, eluded my assault, and then turned towards me calmly. I was still in my white-hot rage, but he was evidently prepared to continue having a rational discussion.

"Be calm," he said, as a parent speaks to a misbehaving child. "You will listen to me. And you will not do what you have imagined to my loyal head. Do you not know anything of my suffering? What else could explain the fact that you would make me suffer more? Know that, as hard and painful as life is, it is dear to me, and I will defend it. And do not forget, you made me stronger than yourself, taller than yourself, and more flexible and cat-like than yourself. No matter how you wish it, I will not allow this to come to a physical contest between us. I am your creation, and I will be generous and decent to my natural lord, if you will do your part, which is something that you owe me. You must not, Frankenstein, be fair and just to everyone else and awful to me. For I am the one, above all, to whom you owe your courtesy, kindness, and justice. While you did make me, you cannot unmake me. I am your creation. You should look upon me in the same way that God looked on Adam, but instead I am an angel cast out of heaven, despite being guilty of no crime. Everywhere I look I see laughter and joy, and know that neither can ever be for me; this despite the fact that I felt warmly towards you and all humanity from the moment I first drew breath. Only misery made me a fiend. If you consent to make me happy, I can again live in the light."

"Be gone! there will be no harmony between us. We are, and ever will be, enemies. Be gone, I say, or you will see that I can force you to fight me, with only one of us surviving."

"What would give you ears to hear my pleas? Is there nothing I can say that would let you see me with the goodness and compassion that I know you possess? You have to believe me: I was warmhearted from the start, my soul glowing with love and humanity. Do you not see how far I have fallen while in the harrowing isolation to which you have abandoned me? If you, the one who made me, can do no better than shun me, then what hope is there for me among the rest of your kind? These others owe me nothing and yet spurn and hate me, out of fear. The empty mountaintops and forlorn glaciers are my only refuge; I have wandered here for many days. The ice caves in the region, which men fear, are my home, the only one that your fellow human beings do not begrudge me. The solemn and bleak skies above are my only friends, gentler to me by far than you and your kind. If the people of this region knew of my existence, they would think as you do, and arm themselves for my destruction. Do you imagine it possible for me not to hate those who would kill me without knowing me? There is no honour required in such situations, no code to follow. I was born into injustice, with you as my original teacher, and it is from your lessons that my hatred springs. In my misery, I am bound to share my wretchedness with others, as the only duty I know. Yet it remains in your power to give me peace, to prevent the unleashing of rage within me that you are on the verge of imposing on the world in your cowardice. For not only you and your family but thousands of others will be swallowed in the whirlwinds of my rage. Let the nobler part of you be moved to act; do not be unkind to me! You have only to listen to my story. When you have heard what has happened during my brief time on earth, you will be in a position to make the decision to abandon me or to show me the compassion that you must have originally hoped to feel towards me. The guilty are allowed, in your society, bloody as they may be, to speak in their own defence before they are condemned. Listen to me, then, Frankenstein. You accuse me of murder, and yet you would, with a clear conscience, destroy your own creation. How filled with irony are the ways of human justice! I will not ask for your favourable decision, merely that you listen. After you have heard what I have to say, if you still wish and are able, then steal back the life you gave."

He dared to reason with me, this fiend that had done violence to a child.

"Reminding me of the circumstances of your creation does nothing to help you," I said. "How often have I cursed the day that you first saw light! Cursed be the hands, though they be my own, that formed you! You have stolen all happiness I ever knew and left me too numb to consider whether I am fair to you, or not. Be gone! you are torture to my eyes."

"I will put an end to your torture," he said, placing his hated hands over my eyes so that I could no longer see. I violently pushed his hands away and stared at him with hatred, but he continued his pleading: "If your eyes do not help you feel compassion, then let it be your ears. In the name of the innocence with which I drew my first breath, I beg this of you, to hear my story. It is long, and strange. But not here—the air over the ice is too cold for you, as a member of your sensitive species. Come to the hut on the mountain to listen in safety. The sun is still high in the sky. Before it descends behind the snowy precipices in the west and lights another world, you will have heard my tale and be able to decide. You alone will judge whether I depart from the neighbourhood of man to lead a peaceful life, or continue with my vengeance against you and your species."

As he said this, he led the way across the ice: I followed. My heart was full, and I did not answer him; but, as I went along, I weighed the various arguments he had used, and committed to at least listening to his tale. I was partly drawn forward by curiosity, although I admit that there was a trace of compassion as well; I realized that I did not truly know whether he was the murderer of my brother, and confirming it one way or the other was vital. And, for the first time, I felt my duties to him as the one who had given him life, and understood that I should strive to make him happy before presuming him evil to the core. We made our way across the ice, therefore, and ascended the opposite rock. The air was cold, and the rain had started coming down again: we entered the hut, the monster with a look of joy, and

I with a heavy heart and depressed spirits. But having agreed to listen to him, I found a place near the fire which my loathsome companion had lighted, and settled in to hear him tell his tale, which he then began.

Chapter III

It is with considerable difficulty that I remember the original era of my being: all the events of that period appear confused and indistinct. Without knowing what a single one of my senses was communicating to me, I was caught in a maelstrom of sights, feelings, sounds, and smells. It took time for me to be able to disentangle each sense from the other, and then to learn the purpose of each. The first to overwhelm me was vision. I remember progressively brighter light bearing down on my nerves, forcing me to shut my eyes tightly to protect myself. When I did, darkness took over, and it was troubling. Then, I now suppose, I opened my eyes, and the light poured in again. I walked, and, I now believe, descended. Soon, all around me had changed again, and the confusing storm of sensations revisited me. Before, dark, shadowy bodies had surrounded me, which I could not interpret with my hands or eyes; but now I found that I could wander on at liberty, with no obstacles which I could neither climb over or avoid. The light became more and more oppressive to me; and, the heat tiring me as I walked, I sought a place where I could receive shade. This was the forest near Ingolstadt; and here I lay down by the side of a brook resting from my fatigue, until I felt tormented by hunger and thirst. This roused me from my nearly dormant state, and I ate berries that I found hanging on trees, or lying on the ground. I satisfied my thirst at the brook; and then lying down, was overcome by sleep.

"It was dark when I awoke; I felt cold also, and half-frightened as it were instinctively, finding myself so solitary. Before I had left your apartment, noting a sensation of cold, I had covered myself with some clothes; but these were not enough to protect me from the dews of night. I was a poor, helpless, miserable wretch; I knew, and could distinguish, nothing; but, feeling pain invade me on all sides, I sat down and wept.

"Soon a gentle light emerged in the heavens, and gave me a sensation of pleasure. I started up, and beheld a radiant form rise from among the trees. I looked upon it with a kind of wonder. It moved slowly, but it provided light to my path; and I again went out in search of berries. I was still cold, when under one of the trees I found a large cloak, with which I covered myself, and sat down upon the ground. I perceived light, hunger, thirst, and darkness; uncountable sounds rang in my ears. Smells from the forest and from the nearby fields confused me even more. The only object I could clearly see was the bright moon, and I stared at it with pleasure.

"Several changes of day and night passed, and the orb of night had greatly lessened, when I began to be able to distinguish my sensations from each other. I gradually saw the clear stream supplying me with water, and the trees that shaded me with their leaves. When I learned that the little winged animals who sometimes passed between myself and the sky were the same ones producing the sweet sounds I heard everywhere in the forest, it made me overjoyed. I was seeing everything around me with increasing clarity, including the bright green canopy high over-head. More than once, I attempted to imitate the sounds that the flying animals made, but I lacked skill. Sometimes, too, I tried to give voice to what I felt, with the same exuberance as my flying friends, in my own mode, but the ugly sounds that broke from me frightened me into silence again.

"The moon had disappeared completely in the night, and then returned in its smallest form again, while I remained in the forest. By this time, my sensations were all distinct, and my mind was increasing in power, as the lessons of each thought multiplied. My eyes became accustomed to the muted light, and to perceiving objects in their true forms. I could distinguish the insect from the herb and, increasingly, one herb from the next. I learned that the sparrow's song was harsh, while those of the blackbird and the thrush were sweet and enticing.

"On one occasion, when I was oppressed by cold, I came upon a fire left by some wandering beggars, and was overcome with delight at the warmth I received from it. In my joy I stuck my hand into the live embers, but quickly drew it out again with a cry of pain. How strange, I thought, that the same cause could generate such opposite effects! I examined the makings of the fire, and saw that it was composed of wood. I ran to collect some branches, but they were wet and would not light. I was pained by this, and sat watching my fire as it burned down. The wet wood I had left near the fire dried, however, and began to burn where it lay. I thought about what I had witnessed for a time. Then I began collecting a huge quantity of wood that I could dry the same way, and thus have a plentiful supply of fire. When night fell and I found myself drifting to sleep, I was in the greatest fear that my fire should be extinguished. I covered it carefully with dry wood and leaves, and placed wet branches upon it; and then, spreading my cloak, I lay on the ground, and sunk into asleep.

"It was morning when I awoke, and my first thought was to visit the fire. I uncovered it, and a gentle breeze quickly fanned it into a flame. I observed this also, and fashioned a fan of branches, which roused the embers when they were nearly extinguished. When night came again, I found, with pleasure, that the fire gave light as well as heat; and that the discovery of this element was useful to me in my food; for I found some of the food the travellers had left had been roasted, and tasted much more savoury than the berries I gathered from the trees. I tried, therefore, to make my food in the same manner, putting it on the live embers. I found that the berries were ruined by this operation, and the nuts and roots much improved.

"Food, however, became scarce. I often spent the whole day looking for a few acorns to lessen the pangs of hunger. I decided, after reflection, to seek a place where my simple existence could continue more comfortably. The most difficult part of the change to a new locale was the loss of my fire, which I had obtained by accident and had no idea how to re-create. I spent hours trying to imagine a way to carry some of the fire with me safely, but I was obliged to give up all attempt to supply it; and, wrapping myself in the cloak, I trudged through the woods towards the setting sun. I spent three days in these rambles, and eventually discovered the open country. A great fall of snow had taken place the night before, and the fields were of one uniform white; the appearance was desolate, and I found my feet chilled by the cold damp substance that covered the ground.

"It was about seven in the morning, and I longed to find food and shelter; after some time, I perceived a small hut, on a rising ground, which had doubtless been built for the convenience of some shepherd. This was a new sight to me; and I examined the structure with great curiosity. Finding the door open, I ducked my head and went in. An old man sat near a fire, over which he was making his breakfast. Hearing me enter, he turned in my direction, saw me, shrieked loudly, and ran from the hut and across the fields faster than seemed possible for some one so debilitated. His appearance, different from any I had ever before seen, coupled with his flight, somewhat surprised me. His hut, on the other hand, was enchanting. Here the snow and rain could not reach; the ground was dry; it was as though suffering and hardship had been banished here. I devoured the remnants of the shepherd's breakfast, which consisted of bread, cheese, milk, and wine; the latter, however, I did not like. Then overcome by exhaustion, I lay down among some straw, and fell asleep.

"It was noon when I awoke. The warmth of the sun, shining brightly on the white ground, called me outdoors, and I prepared to restart my travels. Putting the remnants of the peasant's food in a knapsack I found, I journeyed across the fields for several hours, until at sunset I arrived at a village. How miraculous did this appear! the huts, the neater cottages, and stately houses, called forth my admiration by turns. The vegetables in the gardens, the milk and cheese that I saw placed at the windows of some of the cottages, brought my appetite to life. One of the best of these I entered; but I had hardly placed my foot within the door, before the children shrieked, and one of the women fainted. The whole village was roused; some fled, some attacked me, until, badly bruised by stones and many other kinds of missile weapons, I escaped to the open country, and fearfully took refuge in a low hovel. It was a grim place to sleep, particularly after seeing the beautiful homes back in the village. This hovel, however, was joined to an attractive cottage, which I knew not to enter. My place of refuge was built of wood, but so low, that I could only with difficulty sit upright in it. No wood, however, was placed on the earth, which formed the floor, but it was dry; and although the wind entered by innumerable chinks, I found it an agreeable hideaway from the snow and rain.

"Here then I retreated, and lay down, happy to have found a shelter, however miserable, from the harsh elements of the season, and still more from the cruelty of man.

"When morning dawned, I crept out and inspected the adjacent cottage and looked to see if it would be possible to stay in my kennel for any length of time. It was situated on the back of the cottage and had a pig-stye and a clear pool of water backing onto it. Standing on the outside, I quietly covered every crack and crevice through which I might be seen with stones and wood, in such a way that I could move them on occasion to exit: all the light came from the stye, and that was sufficient for me.

"Having thus arranged my dwelling, and carpeted it with clean straw, I hid myself within it; for I saw the shape of a man at a distance, and I remembered too well my treatment the night before, to risk being in his presence. I had first, however, secured my sustenance for the day, by a loaf of coarse bread, which I pilfered, and a cup with which I could drink, more easily than from my hand, of the pure water which flowed by my retreat. The floor was a little raised, so that it was kept perfectly dry, and by its nearness to the chimney of the cottage it was tolerably warm.

"Being thus provided, I made up my mind to dwell in this hovel, until something should occur which might alter my plan. It was indeed a paradise, compared to the bleak forest, my former residence, the rain-dropping branches, and dank earth. I ate my breakfast with pleasure, and was about to remove a plank in order to obtain for myself a little water, when I heard a heard step, and, looking through a small chink, I witnessed a young creature, with a pail on her head, passing before my shed. The girl was young and of gentle demeanour, unlike what I have since found cottagers and farm-house servants to be. She was crudely dressed, a coarse blue petticoat and a linen jacket being her only garb; her fair hair was braided, but not adorned; she looked patient, yet sad. I lost sight of her; and in about a quarter of an hour she returned, bearing the pail, which was now partly filled with milk. As she walked along, seemingly flustered by the burden, a young man met her, whose face showed a deeper unhappiness. Uttering a few sounds with an air of melancholy, he took the pail from her head, and bore it to the cottage himself. She followed, and they disappeared. A short time later I saw the young man again, with some tools in his hand, cross the field behind the cottage; and the girl was also busied, sometimes in the house, and sometimes in the yard.

"After examining my dwelling, I found that one of the windows of the cottage had once occupied a part of it, but the panes had been filled with wood. In one of these was a small and almost imperceptible chink, through which the eye could just see. Through this crevice, a small room was visible, whitewashed and clean, but very bare of furniture. In one corner, near a small fire, sat an old man, leaning his head on his hands in mournful reflection. The young girl was performing chores around the cottage; but soon she took something out of a drawer, which required use of her hands, and sat down beside the old man, who, taking up an instrument, began to play, and to produce sounds, sweeter than the voice of the thrush or the nightingale. It was a lovely sight, even to me, poor wretch! who had never witnessed real beauty before. The silver hair and sweet face of the aged cottager, won my admiration; while the gentle manners of the girl drew forth my love. He played a sweet mournful tune, which I perceived drew tears from the eyes of his kindly companion, of which the old man took no notice, until she sobbed audibly; he then pronounced a few sounds, and the fair creature, leaving her work, knelt at his feet. He raised her, and smiled with such kindness and affection, that I felt feelings of a peculiar and overpowering nature: they were a mixture of pain and pleasure, such as I had never experienced, either from hunger or cold, warmth or food; and I withdrew from the window, unable to bear these emotions.

"Not long afterwards, the young man returned. He had a load of wood on his shoulders, and the girl met him at the door to help relieve him of his burden. She took a few logs and placed them on the fire. Then the two of them went into a nook, where he showed her a large loaf of bread and a piece of cheese. She seemed pleased; and she went to the garden for some roots and plants, placing them in water and then over the fire. She afterwards continued her work, while the young man went into the garden, and looked busily employed digging and pulling up roots. After he had been employed with this about an hour, the young woman joined him, and then the two of them entered the cottage together.

"The old man had, in the mean time, gone back to somber contemplation; but on the return of his companions, he took on a more cheerful air, and they sat down to eat. The meal was quickly dispatched. The young woman was again occupied in arranging the cottage; the old man walked before the cottage in the sun for a few minutes, leaning on the arm of the youth. There could be nothing more beautiful than the contrast between these two excellent creatures. One was old, with silver hairs and a face beaming with benevolence and love; the younger was slight and graceful in his person, and his features were moulded with the finest symmetry; yet his eyes expressed the greatest sadness and despair. In a short while, the older man went back in the cottage, and the younger, with different tools from the ones he used in the morning, directed his steps across the fields.

"Night quickly shut in; but, to my extreme wonder, I found that the cottagers were able to prolong the light in their living space through the use of candles, and was delighted to find, that the setting of the sun did not put an end to the pleasure I experienced in watching my human neighbours. The girl and the young man were at work on tasks I did not understand; and the old gentleman again picked up his instrument, which produced the divine sounds that had so affected me in the morning. As soon as he had finished, the youth began, not to play, but to utter sounds that were monotonous, and neither resembling the harmony of the old man's instrument or the songs of the birds; I since found that he read aloud, but at that time I knew nothing of the science of words or letters.

"The family, after having been thus occupied for a short time, extinguished their lights, and left the common room, as I imagined, to rest."

Chapter IV

I lay down on my straw, but I could not sleep. I thought of the things that had happened during the day. What chiefly struck me was the kindness that these people showed one another. It made me yearn to present myself to them, but I remembered too well the violent abuse I had received the night before at the hands of the villagers. I decided that, whatever else I might do sometime in the future, for the present I would remain quietly in my kennel, watching, and striving to discover the motives that influenced their actions.

"The cottagers arose the next morning before the sun. The young man was constantly employed out of doors, and the girl in various strenuous chores within. The old man, whom I soon perceived to be blind, employed his leisure hours on his instrument, or in contemplation. Nothing could exceed the love and respect which the younger cottagers showed to their venerable companion. They performed towards him every little form of affection and duty with perfect gentleness; and he rewarded them with his heartwarming smiles.

"They were far from entirely happy, though. The young man and the young woman often separated themselves from the center of the main living area and seemed to weep. I saw no reason for their sadness, but I was deeply affected by it. If such sweet-natured creatures were miserable, it made it less strange that I, imperfect and solitary as I was, should be full of sorrow myself. But, I wondered, why was there any unhappiness? They possessed a wonderful home, or so it appeared to my eyes, and every convenience and luxury in existence. They had a fire to warm them when they were cold, and delicious foods when they were hungry. They were dressed in warm and appealing clothing, as well. But most important, they clearly enjoyed one another's company and speech, interchanging warm looks and kind words every day without exception. So, what did their tears signify? Were they really expressions of sorrow? I was at first unable to solve these questions; but with constant attention, and time, I was eventually able to glean some understanding of their situation.

"A considerable period of time elapsed before I discovered one of the causes of the sorrow within the sweet family; it was poverty, and they suffered that evil in a very distressing degree. Their nourishment consisted entirely of the vegetables of their garden, and the milk of one cow, who gave very little during the winter, when its masters could barely obtain food to support it. They often, I believe, suffered the pangs of hunger very sharply, especially the two younger cottagers; for several times they put food before the old man, when they kept none for themselves.

"This trait of kindness moved me deeply. I had at the beginning of my stay, during the night, stolen for my own consumption food they kept stored; but when I found that in doing this I inflicted pain on the cottagers, I stopped, and satisfied myself with berries, nuts, and roots, which I gathered in a neighbouring forest.

"I discovered also another way through which I was enabled to assist them in their struggles. I observed that the young man spent most of each day gathering wood for the family fire. So, during the night, I borrowed his tools, which I quickly learned to use, and brought home enough firewood to last them several days.

"I remember the first time I left my offering. The young woman, when she opened the door in the morning, appeared greatly astonished at seeing a great pile of wood on the outside. She uttered some few words in a loud voice, and the youth joined her, who also expressed surprise. I observed, with pleasure, that he did not go to the forest that day, but spent it in repairing the cottage, and cultivating the garden.

"Gradually I made an even more significant discovery. I found that these people possessed a method of communicating their experience and feelings to one another by articulate sounds. I perceived that the words they spoke sometimes produced pleasure or pain, smiles or sadness, in the minds and expressions of the hearers. This was truly a godlike science, and I yearned to become acquainted with it. But I was baffled in every attempt I made towards that end. Their pronunciation was quick; and the words they uttered, not having any apparent connexion with visible objects, I was unable to discover any clue by which I could unravel the mystery of their reference. With painstaking effort on my part, however, and after having remained during the span of several cycles of the moon in my hovel, I learned the names that were given to some of the most familiar objects of discourse; I learned and applied the words *fire*, *milk*, *bread*, and *wood*. I learned also the names of the cottagers themselves. The youth and his companion each had several names, but the old man only had one: *father*. The girl was called *sister*, or *Agatha*; and the young man was called *Felix*, *brother*, or *son*. I cannot describe the joy I felt when I learned the ideas connected to each of these sounds, and was able to pronounced them. I distinguished several other words, without being able as yet to understand or apply them; such as *good*, *dearest*, *unhappy*.

"I spent the winter in this manner. The gentle manners and

beauty of the cottagers greatly endeared them to me; when they were unhappy, I felt depressed; when they rejoiced, I felt it in my own heart. I saw few human beings beside them; and if any other happened to enter the cottage, their harsh manners and rude bearing only underscored to me the superior accomplishments of my friends. The old man, I could perceive, often strove to encourage his children, as sometimes I found that he called them, to cast off their sadness. He would speak in such a lighthearted way, with such a kindly expression that it brought joy even to me. Agatha listened with respect, her eyes sometimes filled with tears, which she sought to wipe away unperceived; but I generally found that her expression and tone were more cheerful after having listened to the encouragements of her father. It was not this way with Felix. He was always the most downcast of the group; and, even to my unpractised senses, he appeared to have suffered more deeply than his friends. But if the expressions on his face were more sorrowful, his voice was more cheerful than that of his sister, especially when he addressed the old man.

"I could mention innumerable instances, which, although slight, showed the character of these gracious cottagers. In the midst of poverty and want, Felix carried with pleasure to his sister the first little white flower that peeped out from beneath the snowy ground. Early in the morning before she had risen, he cleared away the snow that obstructed her path to the milk-house, drew water from the well, and brought wood in from their shed, where, to his perpetual astonishment, he found his store replenished by an invisible hand. In the day, I believe, he worked sometimes for a neighbouring farmer, because he went forth, and did not return until dinner, yet brought no wood with him. At other times, he worked in the garden; but, as there was little to do in the frosty season, he frequently read to the old man and Agatha.

"This reading utterly puzzled me at first. But, bit by bit, I discovered that the sounds he uttered when he read aloud were the same ones that he spoke in conversation. I speculated, therefore, that he saw on the paper symbols for speech, and I desperately wished to comprehend these. But how could I do so, when I did not even understand the sounds for which they stood as signs? I was improving in this science, but not enough to follow a conversation in its entirety, even though I applied my whole mind to the task: for I readily understood that, however much I longed to make myself known to the cottagers, I would first need to master their language. Once I was capable of expressing myself well, it would be possible to get them to look past my frightening form, so unlike theirs, as I saw daily watching them go about their chores.

"I had admired the appearance of my hosts—their grace, beauty, and delicate complexion: but how terrified I was, when I viewed myself in a transparent pool! At first, I drew away, unable to believe that it was my own image I saw in the mirror; and when I finally became convinced that I was in reality the monster I am, I was filled with the bitterest despair and shame. Alas! I did not yet entirely know the fatal effects of this miserable deformity.

"As the sun grew warmer, and the light of day longer, the snow vanished, and I observed the bare trees and the black earth. From this time, Felix became more employed; and the heartbreaking signs of impending famine disappeared. The family's food, I later discovered, was not elegant, but it was nutritious, and they managed to obtain enough of it. Several new kinds of plants sprung up in the garden, which they prepared; and these signs of comfort increased daily as the season advanced.

"Every day at noon, when it was not raining, the old man

walked outdoors, leaning on Felix. I had heard the word rain several times and finally understood that it meant water falling from the sky; rain was a regular occurrence, but a high wind quickly dried the earth, and the season became far more pleasant than it had been.

"Life in my hovel was the same each day. During the morning I studied the motions of the cottagers; and when they were elsewhere performing various tasks, I slept: the remainder of the time was spent observing them again. When they had retired to rest, if there was any moon, or the night was starlit, I went into the woods, and collected my own food and firewood for my friends. When I returned, as often as it was necessary, I cleared their path of snow, and did the various tasks I had seen done by Felix. I afterwards found that these labours, performed by an invisible hand, greatly astonished them; and once or twice I heard, on these occasions, utter the words *good spirit ... wonderful;* but I did not then understand the meaning of these terms.

"My thoughts now became more active, and I longed to discover the motives and feelings of these lovely creatures; I was curious why Felix appeared so miserable, and Agatha so sad. I thought (foolish wretch!) that it might be in my power to make these deserving people happy again. When I slept, or daydreamed, the forms of the venerable blind father, the gentle Agatha, and the dependable Felix flitted before me. I looked upon them as superior beings, who would judge and determine my future destiny. I formed in my imagination a thousand pictures of presenting myself to them, and their reception of me. I imagined that they would be disgusted, until, with my gentle actions and mollifying words, I would first gain their favour, and afterwards their love.

"These thoughts exhilarated me, and gave me strength to apply myself even more to the learning of their language. My organs were harsh, but supple, and although my voice was very unlike the soft music of their tones, I nonetheless developed the ability to pronounce the words I understood with some ease. It was like the donkey and the lap-dog; for surely the gentle donkey, whose intentions were affectionate, although his manners were rude, deserved better treatment than beatings and insults.

"The pleasant showers and soft warmth of spring greatly altered the appearance of the earth. Men, who before this change seemed to have been hidden in caves, now fared forth in numbers, and were employed in various ways raising crops. The birds sang in more cheerful notes, and the leaves began to bud forth on the trees. Happy, happy earth! fit habitation for gods, which so short a time before was bleak, damp, and ruinous. My spirits were lifted by the enchanting appearance of nature; the past was blotted from my memory, the present was tranquil, and the future was gilded by bright rays of hope, and anticipations of joy."

Chapter V

I now hurry forth to the more moving parts of my story. I will give an account of events which, from what I was, have made me what I am.

"Spring advanced rapidly; the weather became fine, and the skies cloudless. It surprised me, that what had been lifeless and gloomy should now bloom with the most beautiful flowers and greenery. My senses were gratified and refreshed by a thousand scents of delight, and a thousand sights of beauty.

"It was on one of these days, when my cottagers periodically rested from labour—the old man played on his guitar, and the children listened to him—I observed that the face of Felix was sorrowful beyond expression: he sighed frequently; and once his father paused in his music, and I guessed from his manner that he inquired the cause of his son's sorrow. Felix replied with a cheerful voice, and the old man was starting up his music again, when some one tapped at the door.

"It was a lady on horseback, accompanied by a countryman as a guide. The lady was dressed in a dark suit, and covered with a thick black veil. Agatha asked a question; to which the stranger only replied by pronouncing, in a sweet accent, the name of Felix. Her voice was musical, but unlike that of either of my friends. On hearing this word, Felix sped to the lady; who, when she saw him, threw up her veil, and I observed a face of angelic beauty and expression. Her hair of a shining raven black, and curiously braided; her eyes were dark, but gentle, although animated; her features of a regular proportion, and her complexion wondrously fair, each cheek tinged with a lovely pink.

"Felix seemed overjoyed when he saw her, every trait of sorrow vanished from his face. I could hardly believe the transformation; his eyes sparkled; his cheeks flushed with pleasure; and at that moment I thought him as beautiful as the stranger. She appeared affected by different feelings; wiping a few tears from her lovely eyes, she held out her hand to Felix, who kissed it joyfully and called her, so far as I could hear, his sweet Arabian. She did not seem to understand, but smiled warmly at him. He helped her down from her horse, dismissed her guide, and led her into the cottage. Some conversation took place between him and his father; and the young stranger knelt at the old man's feet, and would have kissed his hand, but he raised her, and embraced her affectionately.

"I soon perceived, that although the stranger made articulate sounds and appeared to have a language of her own, she and the cottagers did not understand each other. They made many signs which I did not comprehend; but I saw that her presence spread happiness through the cottage, dispelling their sorrow as the sun dissipates the morning mists. Felix seemed particularly happy, and with smiles of delight welcomed his Arabian. Agatha, the ever-gentle Agatha, kissed the hands of the lovely stranger; and, pointing to her brother, made signs which appeared to mean that he was sorrowful until she came. Some hours passed in this way, while they, by their faces, expressed joy, the cause of which I did not comprehend. Soon I learned, by the frequent recurrence of one sound which the stranger repeated after them, that she was striving to learn their language; and the idea instantly came to me, that I should make use of the same instructions to achieve the same end. The stranger learned about twenty words during her first lesson, most of them indeed were those I already understood, but I profited from the others.

"As night came on, Agatha and the Arabian retired early. When they were saying their goodnights, Felix kissed the hand of the stranger, and said: 'Good night, sweet Safie.' He sat up much longer, conversing with his father; and, by the frequent repetition of her name, I took the stranger to be the subject of their conversation. I fervently wished to understand them, and bent forward for the purpose, but found it utterly impossible.

"The next morning Felix went out to his work; and, after the usual tasks of Agatha were finished, the Arabian sat at the feet of the old man, and, taking his guitar, played some airs so entrancingly beautiful, that they at the same time drew tears of sorrow and wonder from my eyes. She sang, and her voice carried rich feeling, swelling and hushing, like the song of a nightingale of the woods.

"When she finished, she handed the guitar to Agatha, who at first declined it. She played a simple air, and her voice accompanied it in sweet accents, but unlike the wondrous singing of the stranger. The old man appeared radiant with joy, and said some words, which Agatha attempted to explain to Safie, and by which he appeared to wish to express that she produced in him the greatest joy with her music.

"The days now passed as peaceably as before, with the only alteration, that joy had taken the place of sadness on the faces of my friends. Safie was always animated and happy; she and I improved rapidly in the knowledge of language, so that in two months I began to comprehend most of the words uttered by my protectors.

"In the meanwhile also the black ground was covered with vegetation, and the green banks interspersed with innumerable flowers, sweet to the scent and the eyes, stars of pale radiance in the moonlight woods; the sun became warmer, the nights clear and balmy, and my nighttime rambles were an extreme pleasure to me, although they were considerably shortened by the late setting and early rising of the sun; for I never ventured abroad during daylight, fearful of meeting with the same treatment I had formerly endured in the first village which I entered.

"My days were spent in close attention, that I might more speedily master the language; and I may boast that I improved more rapidly than the Arabian, who understood very little, and spoke in broken accents, whereas I understood and could imitate almost every word that was spoken.

"While I improved in speech, I progressed, too, in the science of letters, as it was taught to the stranger; and this opened before me a wide field for wonder and delight.

"The book from which Felix instructed Safie was Volney's *Ruins of Empires*. I would not have been able to understand the meaning of this book, had not Felix, in reading it, given very precise explanations. He had chosen this work, he said, because the rhetorical style was similar to that of the Eastern authors with whom Safie was already familiar. Through this work I obtained some understanding of history, and a view of the different empires presently existing in the world; it gave me insight into the manners, governments, and religions of the different nations of the earth. I learned of the slothful Asiatics; of the stupendous genius and mental activity of the Grecians; of the wars and wonderful virtue of the early Romans—of their subsequent degeneration—of the decline of that mighty empire; of chivalry Christianity and kings. I heard of the discovery of the American hemisphere, and wept with Safie over the hapless fate of its original inhabitants.

"These wonderful narrations inspired me with strange feelings. Was man, indeed, at once so powerful, so virtuous, and magnificent, yet so vicious and base? Humanity seemed both an agent of pure evil, and of all that was noble and godlike. To be a great and virtuous man appeared to be the highest honour to which a sensitive being could aspire; but to be base and vicious, as many on record have been, appeared the lowest degradation, a condition worse than that of the blind mole or harmless worm. For a long time I could not imagine how one man could go forth to murder another, or even why there were laws and governments; but when I learned the details of rage and bloodshed that make up history, my wonder ceased, and I turned away with disgust and loathing.

"Each conversation of the cottagers now opened new wonders to me. While I listened to the instructions which Felix offered the Arabian, the system of human society was explained to me. I heard of the division of property; of immense wealth and squalid poverty; of rank, descent, and noble blood.

"The words prompted me to turn towards myself. I learned that the possessions most highly regarded by your fellow-creatures were, a patrician lineage united with riches. A man could be respected with one or the other, but with neither he was considered, except in rare instances, a peasant or a slave, cursed to waste his life for the profit of the chosen few. And what was I? Of my creation and creator I was ignorant; but I knew that I possessed no money, no friends, no kind of property. I was, besides, furnished with a hideously deformed and hateful appearance; I was not even of the same nature as man. I was more agile than they, and could subsist on coarser diet; I withstood the extremes of heat and cold with less injury to my person than they; my stature far exceeded theirs. When I looked around, I saw not a single soul resembling me. Was I, as seemed increasingly likely, a monster, a shadow on the earth from which all people would run, and which none would come to know?

"I cannot describe to you the agony that these reflections inflicted on me; I tried to dispel them, but the more I learned of history, and of the complexities of the world, the more sorrow I felt. I found myself yearning for the woods outside Ingolstadt and for the innocent time when I had known nothing beyond hunger, thirst, and exposure to the elements.

"How strange a thing is knowledge! It clings to the mind, when it has seized on it, like lichen on a rock. I wished often to free myself of all thought and feeling; but I learned that there was only one sure way to leave behind the sensation of pain, and that was death. The end of life was something that I feared, instinctively, despite not fully understanding it. I still treasured virtue and kindness, and admired the affectionate and honourable ways of my hosts. Yet I was excluded from all contact with them, except for what I could achieve by stealth. Being so near others without being able to be known by them greatly increased the desire that I felt for human contact. The gentle words of Agatha, and the animated smiles of the Arabian, were not for me. The words of wisdom of the old man, and the lively conversation of the loved Felix, were not for me. Miserable, unhappy wretch!

"Other lessons were impressed on me even more deeply. I heard of the difference of sexes; of the birth and growth of children; how the father doted on the smiles of the young child, and the frolicking of the older child; how all the life and cares of the mother were wrapt up in the precious infant; how the mind of the young expanded and gained knowledge; of brother, and sister, and all the various relationships which bind one human being to another in mutual bonds.

"But where were my own friends and relations? No father had ever doted on me; no mother had blessed me with smiles, or caresses. Or, if they had, my previous life was now a blot, an empty void into which I could not see. From my first memory, I was my current size and shape, and so far I had yet to see a single being resembling me, let alone claiming me as kin. What was I? The question kept arising, to be answered only with groans.

"I will soon tell you what all these feelings were guiding me towards; but allow me to return to the cottagers, whose lives excited in me feelings of righteous anger, delight, and wonder, but which all terminated in ever-deeper love and respect for my protectors (as I, in an innocent, half painful self-deceit, liked to call them)."

Chapter VI

Some time elapsed before I learned the history of my friends. It was a tale which could not fail to impress itself deeply on my mind, revealing as it did a number of circumstances each interesting and wonderful to one so utterly inexperienced as I was.

"The name of the old man was De Lacey. He descended from a good family in France, where he lived for many years in affluence, respected by his superiors and beloved by his equals. His son was raised to be a military officer in the service of his country, and Agatha was given all she needed to be a lady of high distinction. Just a few months before my arrival behind their cottage, they had lived in a large and luxurious city called Paris, surrounded by friends, and blessed with every form of happiness that virtue, intellectual seriousness, refined taste, and considerable wealth could bring.

"Safie's father, I learned, had caused their reversal of fortune. He was a Turkish merchant, and had been living in Paris for many years, when, for some reason I could not learn, he became objectionable to the French government. He was seized and put in prison the very day Safie arrived in Paris from Constantinople to join him. He was tried, and condemned to death. The injustice of his sentence was unimaginable; all Paris was outraged; it was judged that his religion and wealth, rather than the crime alleged against him, had been the cause of his condemnation.

"Felix had been present at the trial; his horror and indignation were uncontrollable, when he heard the decision of the court. He made, at that moment, a solemn vow, to free him, and began looking for the means of doing so. After many fruitless attempts to gain entrance to the prison, he found a strongly grated window in an unguarded part of the building, which gave light to the unlucky Muslim; who, loaded with chains, waited in despair the execution of the barbaric sentence. Felix visited the grate at night, and made known to the prisoner his intentions in his favour. The Turk, amazed and delighted, strove to inspire his rescuer all the more by promising him rewards and wealth. Felix rejected his offers with contempt; yet when he saw the beautiful Safie, who was allowed to visit her father, and who, by her gestures, expressed her lively gratitude, the young man could not help admitting to his own mind, that the captive possessed a treasure which would fully reward his toil and risk.

"The Turk quickly took in the impression that his daughter had made on the heart of Felix, and strove to secure him more entirely in his interests by the promise of her hand in marriage, the moment he had been brought to a place of safety. Felix was too delicate to accept this offer; yet he looked forward to the probability of that event as to the realization of his happiness.

"During the next few days, as preparations for the escape of the merchant were moving forward, Felix was warmed by several letters that he received from this lovely girl, who found the ability to express her thoughts in the language of her lover by the aid of an old man, a servant of her father's, who understood French. She thanked him in the most heartfelt terms for what he was doing for her father; and at the same time she gently lamented her own fate.

"I have copies of these letters; for I obtained the implements of writing, during my residence in the hovel; and the letters were often in the hands of Felix or Agatha. Before I depart, I will give the copies to you, and they will prove the truth of what I am saying; but for now, as the sun is already sinking low in the sky, I will only have time enough to tell you what was in them.

"Safie told Felix that her mother was a Christian Arab who had been kidnapped and enslaved by the Turks; as a woman of extraordinary beauty, she had won the heart of Safie's father, who had married her. Safie spoke in the highest praise of her mother, who, born in freedom, denounced the bondage to which she was now reduced. She instructed her daughter in the principles of her religion, and taught her to aspire to higher powers of intellect, and an independence of spirit, forbidden to female followers of Muhammad. This lady died; but her lessons were indelibly impressed on the mind of Safie, who sickened at the prospect of again returning to Asia, and being confined there within the walls of a haram, with only trivial and suffocating amusements, ill suited to the ways of her soul, now accustomed to grand ideas and the noble pursuit of virtue. The prospect of marrying a Christian, and remaining in a country where women were allowed to hold a rank in society, was enchanting to her.

"The date of the execution of the Turk was set; but, the night before it was to take place, he had escaped, and before morning was many miles southeast of Paris. Felix had obtained passports in the name of his father, sister, and himself. He had previously communicated his plan to the elder De Lacey, who, under the pretence of a journey, had closed up his house and hidden with his daughter in an obscure part of Paris.

"Felix accompanied the fugitives across France to Lyons, and across Mont Cenis to Livorno, where the merchant had decided to await a favourable opportunity of passing into some part of the Turkish realm.

"Safie resolved to remain with her father until the moment of his departure, during which time the Turk renewed his promise that she would be united to his deliverer. Felix remained with them in expectation of that event; and in the mean time he enjoyed the company of the Arabian, who showed towards him the simplest and tenderest affection. They conversed with one another through the means of an interpreter, and sometimes with the interpretation of looks; and Safie sang to him the divine airs of her native country.

"The Turk allowed this intimacy to take place, and encouraged the hopes of the young lovers, while in his heart he had formed far different plans. He despised the idea of his daughter marrying a Christian; but he feared the resentment of Felix if he became lukewarm in their dealings, and thus he maintained the same friendly tone with the Frenchman, reasoning, that if he were to anger him, he could find himself being handed over to the Italian state. He conceived of a thousand ways with which he could extend the deceit until it might no longer be needed, with an eye to take his daughter with him when he departed. News arriving from Paris was a great boost to his schemes.

"The French authorities, inevitably, were furious over the escape of such a prominent prisoner, and spared no effort to track down and punish any who had helped him. Felix's role was quickly discovered, and De Lacey and Agatha were found, arrested, and thrown in prison. When the news reached Felix, his dream of happiness came to an abrupt end. Enjoying the company of his beloved and roaming free, while his blind and aged father and dear sister were confined in a loud and dangerous prison, was not something he would contemplate; even the idea of it was torture to him. He quickly arranged with Safie's father that if the man saw an opportunity to escape before Felix could get back to Italy, then Safie would remain in Livorno as a boarder in a convent. After saying his goodbyes to Safie, Felix hurriedly left for Paris where he intended to surrender to the authorities, the only route available to him to free his family.

"He did not succeed. They remained imprisoned for the five months before Felix's trial; the result of which deprived them of their fortune, and condemned them to a perpetual exile from their native country.

"They found a miserable sanctuary in the form of a cottage in Germany, where I discovered them. Felix was told that as soon as the Turk learned Felix and his loved ones were reduced to poverty and exile, he had left Italy with his daughter, sending Felix a ludicrously small sum of money to assist him, he mockingly said, in his future endeavours.

"These events are what had led Felix to become the most unhappy member of the family at the time I took up residence alongside their cottage. If it had been poverty alone afflicting the family, he might have accepted it, or even made rising above it a means of bettering himself. But the betrayal of a man for whom he had risked much, and the loss of his beloved Safie, were misfortunes of extraordinary weight. The arrival of the Arabian now infused new life into his soul.

"When the news had made its way to Livorno that Felix had been deprived of his wealth and position in society, the Turk commanded his daughter to forget about him and prepare to return with him to their native country. Safie's honest nature responded to her father's ultimatum with outrage. She strove to reason with him, but he left her at the convent angrily, repeating on his way out the door his expectation that she do exactly as he said.

"A few days later, the Turk went back to his daughter's convent lodgings and hurriedly told her that he had learned their residence at Livorno had been identified by people who were on the verge of turning them in to the French government. He had hired a boat to sail him to Constantinople; the vessel was scheduled to depart in a few hours. His plan was to leave his daughter under the care of a trusted servant. Safie was to follow her father with the greater part of his property, which had yet to arrive from Paris.

"Once alone, Safie formed a plan more in keeping with her own heart. Living the rest of her days in Turkey was unthinkable, all the more after developing her ties with Felix. The religion her mother had passed down to her and her feelings for the Frenchman were sufficient reasons not to follow her father. She had learned by reading papers of his that fell into her hands the location of Felix and his family, and had learned, too, of their grim situation. She hesitated some time—forsaking her father, however imperfect he might be, was not something she took lightly—but in the end she made up her mind. Taking with her some jewels that belonged to her, and a small sum of money, she quitted Italy, with an attendant, a native of Livorno who happened to speak the common language of Turkish, and the two of them set out for Germany.

"They had made their way to a town sixty miles from the De Laceys' cottage when the servant became dangerously ill. Safie nursed her with warm devotion, but the poor girl died. Now Safie was left alone, unacquainted with the language of the country she found herself in and knowing few of the customs of the world. In her favour, the mistress of the home where she and her servant had been staying took an interest in protecting her. The servant had mentioned to the woman the name of the village inhabited by the De Laceys, and the kind woman made sure that Safie arrived there, sending her with one of her own servants as a guide."

Chapter VII

Such was the history of my beloved hosts. It impressed me deeply. I came, contemplating the sequence of events, to admire the De Laceys' virtues, and to regard the cruelty of human beings with disgust.

"Still at this time I looked upon crime as a truly distant evil. Goodness and generosity were shown every day by the De Laceys and by Safie now, too; together, they inspired me to imitate them and hope to join them in their daily life. Before continuing, I must not forget to tell you about the development of a part of my intellect that took place in early August of that year. One night, during my usual visit to the nearby forest, where I collected food for myself and firewood for my friends, I saw on the ground a large leather case in which I found several articles of clothing as well as a few books. I eagerly took up the prize and brought it back to my cramped abode. Fortunately, the books were all in the language I had learned by studying the cottagers. The books were *Paradise Lost*, a volume of *Plutarch's Lives*, and *The Sorrows of Young Werther*. Merely having them in my possession made me exceedingly happy. I took to spending every moment I could studying and bettering my mind with the volumes, while my friends focused on their daily tasks.

"As the days and weeks passed, the books generated a vast multitude of new visions and feelings within me, sometimes raising me to ecstacy, but more often sinking me into depression. In *The Sorrows of Young Werther*, there is a sad recitation of a hopeless love triangle and the suicide of the young protagonist. There are also so many perspectives on the events of the book, with so many opinions, that I found the whole of it quite over-whelming. This single book served as a source of continual speculation and astonishment on my part. The gentle and civilized manners it describes, combined with so many lofty sentiments and feelings regarding more than just the plight of Werther himself, were easy to connect to my experience with my protectors. The deep loneliness of Werther could just as easily have been a description of the isolation and sorrow that coursed through my own heart. Werther appeared to me almost godlike, so selfless and unpretentious were his actions. The example that he set forth and the wisdom of his decisions left an indelible imprint on my heart. And the reflections upon death and suicide were of great fascination for me, inevitably. I did not feel capable of assessing who was right in the story, but I did feel a deep affinity for Werther, and wept over his death.

"As I read and compared my situation with those in the pages of the book I saw important similarities but also differences between myself and the people described. In the same way that I was listening, uninvited, to the conversations of my protectors, so, too, was I listening in on these written conversations. I sympathized with the characters, and partly understood them. But I simply was not yet fully formed, neither in my mind nor in my heart, and I had none of the connexions giving the lives of the people in the novel their luster and meaning. I could leave, or die, tomorrow, and no one would cry over my absence. My physical self was gigantic, and my appearance frightful. What did any of this mean? Who was I? What was I? From where did I arise? Where was I destined to live out my life? These questions haunted me.

"The volume of *Plutarch's Lives* contained the history of the founders of the ancient republics. The book's effect on me differed much from that of *The Sorrows of Young Werther*. In that book, Werther's story taught me complicated reasons to feel the weight of existence in my own life, but Plutarch did the opposite. He raised me above my sad circumstances to admire and love the heroes of past ages.

"Most of what I read went well beyond my understanding and experience. I possessed only a confused knowledge of kingdoms and governments, of wide swathes of the globe's terrain, of its mighty rivers and seas, and I had no knowledge of towns, cities, or countries. The cottage of my friends was the only school in which I had studied human nature. Plutarch offered new, compelling scenes of action to contemplate. I learned of men of wide influence sometimes governing and sometimes massacring their species, and felt within me a profound desire to do good in the world, and a great distaste for evil. My thoughts and perceptions were immature, but real.

"Guided by the moral sense developing within me, I came to prefer benevolent leaders such as Numa, Solon, and Lycurgus over the less peaceful Romulus and Theseus. The kindly domestic lives of my hosts caused my ethical development to follow its own gentle course. If my first model of humanity had been a young soldier burning for glory and slaughter, my sense of right and wrong and what was important would have been vastly different.

"But *Paradise Lost* excited different and far deeper emotions. Just as with the others I had found, I read it as though it were a true history. As the omnipotent God in the book warred with his creatures, wonder and awe surged in me, and it was impossible not to compare the situations in the book with my own. Like Adam, I had no forebears; but in every other respect we were not alike at all. Adam had been formed by the hands of God as a perfect creature; he was happy and prosperous, and looked over with care by his Creator; Adam was allowed to speak with and learn from exalted beings. I, on the other hand, was pitiful, helpless, and alone. For the most part, I considered Satan's experience in the book to be the better approximation of the life I was living. Often, as was true for him, witnessing the happiness of those near me meant that the bitter taste of envy was one I knew well.

"Another thing that happened strengthened and confirmed my feelings. Soon after taking up residence in my kennel, I discovered some papers in the pocket of a lab coat I had taken from your apartment. Initially, I ignored this find. But now that I was capable of deciphering the characters covering the pages, I began to study them with great interest. You carefully described in these notes each step that you took in the progress of your work, mingling the scientific account with descriptions of other parts of your life. You, no doubt, remember these papers. Here they are—take them. They are full of references to my unhappy start in this world, and the disgusting circumstances that led to my first breath. There are also very careful descriptions of my revolting and evil appearance, in language making your own horror at what you witnessed only too clear. As for myself, the effect on me of seeing these words was unimaginable. I grew ill as I read. 'Heartless creator,' I cried. 'Why did you form a monster so hideous that even you turned from it in disgust? God, in pity and grace, made man beautiful and sympathetic, after his own image. But my face and body are a wretched corruption of yours, all the more gruesome for bearing faint resemblance to human kind. Satan at least had friends, fellow devils, to admire and encourage him. But I am despised, and forever alone.'

"Such were my reflections as I found myself caught in despondency and solitude; but when I thought upon the virtues of the cottagers, of their loyalty and generosity of spirit, I persuaded myself that they would nonetheless accept me, and overlook my deformity, when they learned just how much I admired them. How could they not be moved by the love I had for them and by the kindness that I intended to show them? I decided to hold onto these hopes, and to prepare myself for the moment when my fate would be decided. I postponed introducing myself to them for a few months. The same impetus pushing me towards succeeding in my bid to win them over caused dread at the prospect of failure. There was also the fact that every day's experience added to my understanding of human speech, and all other things; and I was unwilling to make my approach until the passage of time could make me wiser and more articulate.

"Meanwhile, there were significant events transpiring in the cottage. Safie's presence made all of the De Laceys happier, and I saw that there was less poverty than there had been before. Felix and Agatha were able to spend more time doing things they enjoyed, such as engaging in conversation, and were now assisted in their chores by servants. The changed household was not rich, but its members were visibly happier. Their feelings were clearly serene and peaceful, while mine became more turbulent with the continuation of my education. For as my knowledge of the ways of the world expanded, my position as an outcast was causing me deeper pain. I nursed my hopes, yes, but they vanished whenever I saw myself reflected in water, or when my eye caught my oversized shadow cast by the moon.

"I did everything I could to overcome the fears that sometimes took hold of me, and worked to prepare for the crucial discussion I was committed to initiating in a few months' time. Occasionally, I would disconnect my thoughts from the tight leash of reason and let them run through the fields of Paradise. I pictured friendly, beautiful people sympathizing with my feelings and showing me the kind of warmth and kindness they normally reserved for a new exalted citizen in their midst. But it was all a dream. No Eve soothed my sorrows or shared my thoughts. I was alone. I remembered Adam's cry for a human companion to his Creator, but where was mine? He had abandoned me, and, in the bitterness of my forlorn condition, I cursed him.

"Autumn arrived; I saw, with dismay, the leaves turn yellow and brown and begin to fall from the trees. Soon, nature had once more taken on the barren, bleak appearance it had worn when I had seen the glorious moon for the first time in the forest. The grimness of the approaching season did not contribute greatly to my worries, though. I was better prepared by you for the endurance of cold than heat. Still, among my chief delights was the sight of flowers and birds and all the bright scenes of summer, and indeed when those deserted me, the cottagers took up even more of my attention. Their happiness, unlike mine, was not affected by the changing season; they loved and cared for one another as before. The joy they took in this domestic harmony meant whatever happened outside the walls of the cottage was seldom very concerning. The more I witnessed this steadfastness of theirs, the stronger grew my desire to seek their protection and kindness, and to see their sweet faces turned approvingly towards mine. I lacked the courage to consider for a moment any of them turning away from me in terror. And there were objective reasons for the hope I allowed myself to feel. For instance, whenever the poor stopped at the cottage door, they were never driven away, but were always given a little food, and sometimes even rest. I was asking for a greater gift than those asked for by the destitute, for sympathy of a different magnitude. But my hosts' charity was a fact that I held onto in my innermost heart.

"Autumn grew colder and darker; one cycle of seasons had unfolded since I had awakened into life. My entire focus, at this time, was on introducing myself to my protectors successfully. I considered many options, but in the end I decided to enter the cottage when the elder De Lacey, who was blind, was alone. It was clear enough that my unnatural ugliness was what had frightened those who had seen me previously. My voice, though gruff, was within the range of voices possible for a human being, and I thought that if I could start a friendship with the kindly old man, he might unlock the hearts of my younger hosts, despite my appearance.

"One bright, cold morning just after the last of the red leaves had fallen to the earth was when everything changed. With the day promising plenty of sunshine, though little in the way of warmth, Safie, Agatha, and Felix left on a long walk through the countryside. The elder De Lacey, at his own insistence, remained alone in the cottage. When his children had gone, he picked up his guitar and played a series of mournful and exquisitely beautiful pieces, even more moving than those I had heard him play in the past. At first, his face showed the purest serenity, but as he continued, thoughtfulness, and then sadness, followed. Fatigued from his playing, he put down the instrument, and sat absorbed in reflection.

"My heart pounded in my chest. Now was the time; either my hopes or my fears were on the verge of coming to fruition. The servants had been dismissed, in recognition of the beautiful day, and had gone to a neighbouring fair. All was silent in and around the cottage. It was the perfect opportunity. When I started to act upon my plan, my arms and legs failed me, and I sank to the earth. I rose to my hands and knees, took a breath, and removed the planks I had used to conceal me. Cold air on my face sharpened my thoughts, and I approached the door of the cottage and knocked. 'Who is there?' said the old man. 'Come in.'

"I entered. 'Please pardon my intrusion,' I said. 'I am a traveller in need of rest. You would be doing me a great kindness if you would allow me to stay near the fire for a few minutes.'

"'Please, come in from the cold and rest a while,' the elder De Lacey said. 'I will try as I can to make you comfortable, but unfortunately my children are far from home today, and I am blind. I am afraid I shall find it difficult to get you anything to eat.'

"'Do not worry, kind sir,' I said. 'I have food. It is only warmth and rest I need.'

"I sat with him, and a brief silence followed. I knew every minute was precious, but was uncertain how to begin.

"'From your way of speaking, traveller,' he said, 'I take you for my countryman. Am I correct that you are French?'

"'No, but I received my education in a Parisian family and understand that language only,' I said. 'I am on my way to ask for the protection of friends whom I much love. I am full of hope today.'

"'Are your friends German?' he asked.

"'No, they are French,' I said. 'But let us change the subject. I am an unfortunate and forsaken soul; I have no one on earth with whom to share this life. The kind people I am travelling to see have never laid eyes on me, and know little of me. I am so full of fear. If I fail with them, I will almost certainly be alone forever.'

"'Do not abandon hope,' he said. 'Not having a single friend is indeed unfortunate, but the hearts of men, when not corrupted, are full of brotherly love and kindness. Hold onto your hopes, I say. If your friends are as you describe them, you are not completely alone, even now.'

" 'They are decidedly generous,' I said. 'In my opinion, they are the most excellent people in the world. Unfortunately, they may become prejudiced against me. I have a tender and kindly heart, and have never harmed a soul, but a fatal prejudice clouding their eyes arises from my appearance, and where they should see a sweet and kind friend, they perceive only a horrifying monster.'

" 'That is very difficult,' he said. 'But if you are totally innocent, is it not possible to get them to see you clearly?'

" 'I am near the point of trying to do just that,' I said. 'And that is why I am so frightened. My love for these friends is total. I have for many months been doing whatever I can to help them with their daily living, unbeknownst to them. But they are sure I want to do them harm, and it is this prejudice I must somehow overcome.'

" 'Where do your friends live?' the elder De Lacey asked.

" 'Near this place,' I said.

"He paused, and then continued.

" 'If you trust me with the details of your situation, I might be able to present your case to them in the favourable light it deserves,' he said. 'I am blind, and cannot judge your face, but there is something about the way you speak that convinces me that you are sincere. I am poor, living in exile. But it would give me great pleasure to be of service to so a deserving person.'

" 'Gracious sir,' I said, 'I thank you and humbly accept. You provide hope where there was none. And I trust that, through your kindness, I may not have to be cast out by these people whom I love so well.'

" 'God forbid that you should be,' he said, 'even if you were truly a criminal! For choosing such a path can only drive a man to act desperately and can never direct him towards the light. Like you, I am unfortunate. My family and I have been condemned, even though we are innocent. Know, then, that I feel your misfortunes deeply.'

" 'I can never thank you enough,' I said. "You are the first and only one to have accepted me; my gratitude will be eternal. Your compassion gives me at least a little confidence that the friends I am going to meet soon will understand me as you do.'

" 'May I inquire the names and residence of your friends?' he asked.

"Here it was—a moment that would deprive me of happiness or make it mine forever; I struggled without success for the courage to answer him. The effort deprived me of my remaining strength, and I sank into my chair, and began to cry like a baby. Suddenly, I heard the footsteps of the others; I had not a moment to lose. Taking the elder De Lacey's hand in my own, I yelled to him in desperation.

" 'Now is the time!' I said. 'Save and protect me! You and your family are the ones about whom I spoke. Do not abandon me, now or ever—I beg you!'

" 'Great God!' shouted the old man. 'Who are you?'

"At that instant the cottage door opened, and Felix, Safie, and Agatha entered. Who can describe the horror and confusion they felt upon seeing me with their beloved father and friend? Agatha fainted. Safie, far too afraid to assist her, rushed from the cottage. Felix darted in my direction to pull me away from his father, to whose knees I was clinging like a little boy. Propelled by protective fury, Felix tackled me to the ground and began striking me violently with a stick. It would have been easy to tear him limb from limb, as the lion does the antelope. But my heart sunk within me as with bitter sickness, and I refrained. I saw that Felix was on the verge of using the stick again, and, overwhelmed with pain and sorrow, I fled from the cottage. With the others still shouting and crying, I managed to take refuge in my hiding place once more."

Chapter VIII

Cursed, cursed creator! Why did I live? Why, in that instant, did I not extinguish the spark of existence that you so naively ignited? The will to live is its own mystery; perhaps it is as simple as that. There was also the fact that complete permanent despair had yet to take possession of me; instead, my feelings now were ones of rage and revenge. I could, with pleasure, have destroyed the cottage and its occupants, and would have rejoiced at the sounds of their shrieks and misery.

"When night came, I departed from my hovel, and wandered in the woods; and now, no longer restrained by the fear of discovery, I gave vent to my anguish in fearful howlings. I was like a wild beast broken free of its cage, destroying the objects that got in my way and hurtling through the forest with stag-like speed. Oh! what a miserable night I passed! the cold stars shone in mockery, and the bare trees waved their branches above me: now and then the sweet voice of a bird burst forth amid the universal stillness. All, with the exception of myself, were at rest or in enjoyment: I, like the arch fiend, bore a hell within me; and, finding myself banished to a life without sympathy, I wished to tear up the trees, spread havoc and destruction around me, and then sit down and enjoy the ruin.

"But this was a luxury of sensations that could not last; I became exhausted from so much bodily exertion, and sank on the damp grass in frustration and despair. There was not one among the great numbers of men that existed who would pity or assist me; and why should I feel kindness towards my enemies? No: from that moment I declared everlasting war against the species, and, more than all, against him who had formed me, and sent me forth to this intolerable misery.

"The sun rose; I heard the voices of men, and knew that it was impossible to return to my retreat during that day. Accordingly, I hid myself in thick underbrush, determined to devote the next several hours to reflection on my situation.

"The pleasant sunshine, and the pure air of day, restored me to a degree of calm; and when I thought over what had happened at the cottage, I could not help seeing that I had been hasty in considering the situation hopeless. I realized that I had acted rashly. It was clear that my conversation had interested the father in my behalf, and I was a fool in having exposed my person to the horror of his children. I ought to have allowed the elder De Lacey to know me more thoroughly, and then slowly have introduced myself to the rest of the family in incremental fashion, when they should have been ready for the approach. But I did not believe my errors to be irreparable; and, after much consideration, I resolved to return to the cottage, seek the old man, and by patient explanation win him to my side.

"These thoughts calmed me, and in the afternoon I sank into a deep sleep, but the fever of my blood did not allow me to be visited by peaceful dreams. The horrible scene of the preceding day was for ever replaying in my mind's eye. The females were fleeing, and the enraged Felix tearing me from his father's feet. I awoke exhausted; and, finding that it was already night, I crept forth from my hiding-place, and went in search of food.

"When my hunger was satisfied, I directed my steps towards

the well-known path that had brought me to the cottage. All there was at peace. I climbed into my hovel and remained in silent expectation of the normal hour that the family arose. When that time came and went, and the sun rose high in the heavens without the cottagers appearing, I began trembling, understanding that some horrible misfortune was unfolding. The inside of the cottage was dark, and no sound reached me. All was silent; I cannot describe the agony of this suspense.

"Soon, two countrymen passed by; but, pausing near the cottage, they entered into conversation, using violent gesticulations; but I did not understand what they said, as they spoke the language of the country, which differed from that of my protectors. Soon after, however, Felix approached with another man: I was surprised, as I knew that he had not left the cottage that morning, and waited anxiously to discover, from his speech, the meaning of these strange happenings.

"'You understand that you will be paying three months' rent,' his companion said to him, 'and losing the produce of your garden? I do not wish to take any unfair advantage, and beg therefore that you will take some days to consider your decision.'

"'It is utterly useless,' replied Felix, 'we can never again inhabit your cottage. My father's life is in danger, due to the bizarre events I have described, and my wife and sister will never recover from the shock they have suffered. I beg you not to reason with me any further. Take possession of your property, and let me fly from this place.'

"Felix trembled violently as he said this. He and the landlord entered the cottage, stayed for a few minutes, and then departed. I never saw a member of the De Lacey family again.

"I spent the balance of the day in my hovel in a state of utter and stupid despair. My protectors had left, and had broken the only link connecting me to the world; as the feelings of hatred and revenge filled my heart once more, I now, for the first time, made no effort to control them; but, allowing myself to be carried away by the stream, I focussed my mind on injury and death. Soon, though, when I thought of my friends, of the kindly voice of the elder De Lacey, of the gentle eyes of Agatha, and of the exquisite beauty of Safie, the violence within me vanished, and a gush of tears somewhat soothed me. But again, when I reflected that they had spurned and deserted me, anger returned, a rage of anger, and, unable to injure any thing human, I turned my fury towards inanimate objects. As night advanced, I placed a variety of combustibles around the cottage; and, after having destroyed every vestige of cultivation in the garden, I waited with forced impatience until the moon had sunk to commence my operations.

"As the night advanced, a fierce wind arose from the woods, and swept away the clouds that had been crossing the night sky until then. The wind was like an avalanche hurtling through the trees, and it created an insanity within me that burst all limits of logic and reflection. I lit the dry branch of a tree, and danced with fury around the devoted cottage, my eyes still fixed on the western horizon, the edge of which the moon nearly touched. A part of its orb was slowly hid, and I waved my brand; it sunk, and, with a loud scream, I ignited the straw, and wild grass, and bushes, which I had collected. The wind fanned the fire, and the cottage was quickly enveloped by the flames, which clung to it, and licked it with their forked and destroying tongues.

"As soon as I was sure that no assistance could save any part of the dwelling, I departed, and sought refuge in the woods.

"And now, with the vast world stretched out in all directions around me, where would I direct my steps? I resolved to fly far from the scene of my misfortunes; but to me, hated and despised, every country must be equally horrible. Eventually, the thought of you came into my mind. I learned from your papers that you were my father, of a sort; at a minimum, you were my creator. It was you, above all others, to whom I should appeal.

"Geography had been among the subjects in which Felix had tutored Safie, and I had paid close attention. I had learned the locations of the different countries of the globe, most importantly those of Europe. You had mentioned Geneva as the name of your native town, and I decided that it would be my destination.

"But how would I make my way to this place? I knew that I needed to travel towards the southwest, but with the sun my only guide it would not be easy. I did not know the names of the towns that I would be passing through; nor would I be able to ask for information from a single human being; but I did not despair. From you only could I hope for assistance, although towards you I felt no sentiment but that of hatred. Unfeeling, heartless creator! you had provided me with awareness and desires, and then cast me into a world that would be a hell to me. Unless you are ever scorned and feared on sight as I am everywhere I go, you will never know what you have put me through. But on you only had I any claim for pity and fairness. I decided that I would approach you and request the justice I vainly sought to gain from any other being that wore the human form.

"My travels were long, and the sufferings I endured were many. It was late in autumn when I left the district where I had so long lived. I travelled only at night, fearful of encountering the face of a human being. Nature decayed around me, and the sun became heatless; rain and snow poured around me; mighty rivers were frozen; the surface of the earth was hard, and chill, and bare, and I found no shelter. Oh earth! how often did I hurl curses against the cause of my being! The sweetness of my original nature had fled; and all within me was turned to rage and bitterness. The nearer I approached to your habitation, the more deeply did I feel the spirit of revenge burning in my heart. Snow continued to fall, and the waters remained hardened, but I would not rest. I was able to interpret the scenery in such a way as to direct my feet where they should go, and I also came into possession of a partial map of the country. Nonetheless, I often wandered far from my path. The agony of my feelings offered me no rest: there was nothing that occurred from which my rage and misery could not extract its food; but a circumstance that happened when I arrived on the confines of Switzerland, when the sun had recovered its warmth, and the earth again began to look green, confirmed in a special way the bitterness and horror of my feelings.

"I generally rested during the day, and travelled only when I was protected by night from the view of man. One morning, however, I saw that my path would take me through a dense, dark forest, and I made the decision to continue my journey after the sun had risen; the day, which was one of the first of spring, cheered even me with the loveliness of its sunshine and the balminess of the air. I felt emotions of gentleness and pleasure, that had long appeared dead, revive within me. Surprised by the unexpected presence of new hope, I allowed myself to be carried away by it, and, temporarily forgetting my loneliness and deformed appearance, I allowed myself to be happy again. Soft tears wet my cheeks, and I raised my mist-covered eyes towards the blessed sun giving rise to such joy in me.

"I continued to wind among the paths of the woods. Soon, I came to a deep and rapid river, into which many trees were dipping their branches, now budding with the fresh spring.

Here I paused, not exactly knowing what path to take, when I heard the sound of approaching voices, leading me to conceal myself under the shade of a cypress tree. I was scarcely hid, when a young girl came running past the spot where I was concealed, laughing as though she might be trying to elude some one in sport. She continued her running along the steep sides of the river, when suddenly her foot slipped, and she fell into the rapid stream. I rushed from my hiding place, and, with extreme effort from the force of the current, saved her, and dragged her to shore. She was unconscious; and I strove, by every means in my power, to resuscitate her, when I was suddenly interrupted by the arrival of a peasant, who was probably the person from whom she had playfully fled. On seeing me, he darted towards me, and, tearing the girl from my arms, raced into the deeper parts of the woods. I followed speedily, I hardly knew why; but when the man saw me draw near, he lowered the girl to the ground, aimed a gun, which he carried, at my body, and fired. I sunk to the ground, and the one who had injured me, with increased swiftness, escaped into the woods.

"This was then the reward of my kindness! I had saved a human being from destruction, and, as a payment, I now writhed in pain from a wound that had scattered flesh and bone. The feelings of goodness and gentleness, which I had known but a few moments before, gave place to hellish rage and gnashing of teeth. Inflamed by pain, I vowed eternal hatred and vengeance to all mankind. But the agony of my wound overcame me; my pulses paused, and I fainted.

"For weeks, I led an agonizing life in the woods, striving to clean the wound as I could, but unable to tell if the ball had stayed in my shoulder or passed through it; at any rate, if it was still there, I had no means of extracting it. My sufferings were made worse by the knowledge that they had been caused by injustice and ingratitude. I vowed throughout each day to have a truly deep and deadly revenge, for nothing else would compensate me for what I was experiencing.

"After some weeks my wound healed, and I started again for Geneva. The physical difficulty of the trek was no longer lessened by the bright sun and gentle breezes of spring; all joy was but a mockery, which insulted my forlorn state, and made me feel more painfully that I was not made for the enjoyment of pleasure.

"But my toils now drew near a close; and, two months from this time, I reached the outskirts of Geneva.

"It was evening when I arrived. I located a hiding place in some fields surrounding the city, and there began to reflect on the best way to approach you. I was weighed down by exhaustion and hunger, and was too unhappy to find consolation in the gentle evening breeze and the brilliant red sun setting amid the snow-capped peaks of the Juras.

"My contemplation led to daydreaming, followed by an unintended nap. The sleep provided relief from my unhappy thoughts and the many discomforts of my body. I was awoken by the approach of a beautiful child, who came bounding into my hiding place with all of the joy of the very young members of your species. As I looked in his bright eyes and upon his small frame, I suddenly had a thought, that here was a creature without prejudice, some one who had lived for too brief a time to look upon me with horror. If I could take him with me and educate him as my companion and friend, then I would not be condemned to a life of perpetual loneliness.

"Spurred by this hope, I grabbed the child as he passed, and pulled him towards me. But the moment he saw me, he put his hands in front of his eyes and screamed. I pulled his hands away from his face and said: 'Child, what is the meaning of this? I do not intend to hurt you; listen to me.'

"He struggled with great determination. 'Let me go,' he cried; 'monster! ugly beast! You wish to eat me, and tear me to pieces—you are an ogre—Let me go, or I will tell my papa!'

"'Boy, you will never see your father again. You are going to come with me.'

"'Disgusting monster—let me go! My father is a judge, his name is Frankenstein. He will punish you, if you do not let me go.'

"'Frankenstein? You belong to the man on whom I have sworn eternal vengeance. You will be my first victim.'

"The more I spoke, the more the little one struggled. He cast heated insults at me, and each word pierced me through. My heart filled with the worst despair it had known. I grasped his throat, to quiet him, and in a moment he was lying dead at my feet.

"I looked down upon his lifeless form, and my heart swelled with gladness and hellish triumph. Clapping my hands, I exclaimed, 'I, too, can create desolation. My enemy is not without his weaknesses. This death will bring sorrow to him, and I shall unleash a thousand other miseries to torment and destroy him.'

"I looked down again at the dead child and saw something glittering on his chest, which I removed. Holding it in my hand, I saw that it was a locket with a portrait of a beautiful woman. In spite of my recent violence and rage, the image softened and called to me. For a minute or more, I stared with pleasure at the woman's dark eyes, long lashes, and lovely lips. But soon, all on its own, my rage returned. I remembered that I was permanently deprived of the delights such a beautiful being could offer. And I realized, too, that the one whose features I was contemplating would have changed her expression from one of kindness to one of abject terror and disgust if she were to see my face.

"Is it at all surprising that such thoughts left me gasping with rage? What I find surprising is that instead of screaming in agony I did not rush among the people of the earth and die in the attempt to destroy them all.

"Overcome with such feelings, I left the spot where I had committed the murder and began to look for a more secluded hiding place. After a short while, I observed a woman passing nearby. Even in the gathering dusk, I could see that she was young, less beautiful than the woman whose portrait I held, but attractive, and in the full bloom of youth. Here, I thought, is one of those whose smiles are shown to everyone but myself. Having learned a great deal about the subtleties of evil from what Felix went through and the books that I read, I quickly thought of a way to turn the palace of this woman's happiness into a burning ruin. I approached her without her noticing and placed the portrait securely in a fold of her dress.

"For a few days, I stayed near the place where these events happened, sometimes hoping to see you and sometimes planning my suicide. Eventually, I let my feet carry me towards these mountains, and I have crisscrossed their vast surfaces, consumed by a burning vision that you alone can satisfy. You and I will not part until you have promised to fulfill my request. I am more alone and more miserable than you can appreciate; no human being will associate with me. But a creature who was as deformed and horrible as myself would not deny herself to me, which is why my companion must be of the same species as I, and have the same defects that I have. You will make her for me."

Chapter IX

He finished talking, and looked towards me in expectation of a reply. But I had listened without the slightest anticipation of where he had been going with the story while he was telling it, and found myself shocked, unable to put my ideas together well enough even to understand the full significance of his proposition. He observed my silence and spoke before I could.

"You must create a female for me with whom I can share the compassion necessary for survival. You are the only man on earth who can do this, and I demand that you do right by me!"

While he had described the early parts of his history that involved living behind the villagers, the urge to avenge William's death by destroying this foul beast had subsided. But the latter part of the tale had reawakened my rage, and when he added his rude demand to the account of his violence against sweet William and innocent Justine, I could control the fury rising within me no longer.

"But I do refuse," I said. "There is no torture that could get me to alter my decision. You may choose to make me the most unhappy man on earth, but you will not force me to betray the principles with which I set forth in life and which guide me still. Do you imagine that I would create another like yourself with whom you might that much more easily devastate the world? Get out of my sight! that is your answer; torture me, if you will, but I will never do as you ask."

"You are in the wrong," replied the fiend. "Instead of threatening, I am content to reason with you. Do you not see that I am malicious only because I am miserable? Do you not see that I am shunned and hated by all humanity? You, my own creator, would tear me to pieces if you could. Tell me why I should pity human beings more than they pity me? You would not consider it murder if you sent me plummeting into one of these ice chasms, destroying my frame, the work of your own hands. Am I to respect individuals like yourself, who loathe me upon sight?

"If people only lived with me in the normal exchange of kindness, then instead of violence I would give every benefit in my power, with tears of gratitude in my eyes. But it cannot be. The human senses are too delicate to allow such interactions. But understand this: I will not live as a slave; I will exact revenge for my injuries. If I cannot inspire love, then I will inspire fear, above all within you, my greatest enemy. For as my creator, you have also given life to bottomless hatred. Know that I will work at your destruction and not stop until I have crushed your soul, and have heard you curse the hour of your birth."

A horrifying rage distorted his face as he said this. His features were wrinkled into contortions too awful for human eyes to behold. But presently he calmed down, and began to talk once more.

"I had intended to use my powers of reason only," he said. "These flights of strong feeling are harmful to me, particularly as you do not see that you are the cause of my mental state. If any person felt warmly towards me, I would return their kindness a hundredfold. For that one individual's sake, I would make peace with your whole species! But no such comfort is to be mine. What

I am asking is reasonable, and it is well considered—a creature of the female sex, as hideous as myself. The gratification is likely to be small, but it is all I can receive, and I will accept it. Yes, we will be outcasts, cut off from the world, but that will serve to make us more attached to each other. Our lives will not be happy, as you experience happiness, but they will be harmless. Above all, we will be free of the misery I now feel every hour. Do this for me, my creator! Allow me to feel gratitude towards you for one kindness! Allow me to know what it is to have another living thing feel sympathy towards me—do not deny me this simple request!"

I was moved. I trembled when I considered the possible consequences of my consent, but there was no denying the justice of his argument. His story, and the feelings he had expressed, proved him a being of fine sentiments, and did I not, as his maker, owe him whatever happiness was in my power to give? He read the thoughts on my face, and continued.

"If you agree," he said, "neither you nor any other human being will ever see us again. We will travel to the vast wilds of South America. Your food is not my food; I do not destroy the lamb and the goat to satisfy my appetite. Acorns and berries are all I require. My companion will be made as I am, and will be content with the same forms of nourishment. We will make our bed of dried leaves. The sun will shine upon us as it does on you and all your kind, and it will ripen our food just the same. The picture that I present to you is peaceful and decent, and the only thing that could cause you to deny it is cruelty. Until now, you have shown me not even the slightest pity, but I finally see compassion in your eyes: let me seize the favourable moment, and persuade you to promise what I so deeply desire."

"You suggest that you will fly from human kind and live in

the wild with the beasts of nature as your only other companions," I said. "But how could you—longing as you have told me you do for the sympathy of civilized people—survive in such an exile? You will return, and once more seek human kindness. When you are confronted with horrified reactions again, your evil passions will be reborn, and then you will have a companion to help you in the destruction you wreak. None of it can be allowed to happen. Do not continue asking for my assistance; I will not be made to unleash dangers of this magnitude."

"You are as changeable as the wind," he said. "Only a moment ago, you were moved by my request. Why do you now harden your feelings again? I swear, with all the good still in me, and by the ties binding you and me together, that I will leave the world of human kind with the companion you make for me. We will live in the most remote places we can find, and my evil passions will never be renewed. They will have been extinguished in the cooling waters of your own human decency. I will spend the rest of my days, including my dying moments, peacefully."

His words had an effect on me. I sympathized with him, and wanted to console him; but when I looked at him, and saw once more the filthy mass that moved and talked, my heart sickened, and my feelings of horror returned. I tried to banish these sensations, telling myself that I had no right to withhold the small portion of happiness still within my power to provide.

"You swear you will be harmless," I said. "But can you not see that the degree of malice you have already shown makes it impossible to trust you? You are surely attempting to trick me, as part of your effort to arm yourself more fully for revenge."

"How can you say this? I saw that I stirred your compassion, but now you again refuse to grant me the one thing that will soften my heart and render me harmless. If I continue on this earth with no ties and no affections, then vengeance will be all there is for me! The warm kindness of a mate will destroy the cause of my crimes, and I will become like a benign animal in the forest that no one knows exists. My violence is the child of an enforced solitude, one that brings me little joy. The better parts of me will flourish when I live in harmony with an equal and know the warm sympathy of a fellow sensitive being. I will become part of the flow of life, from which I am now kept painfully separate."

I kept silent and considered everything that my creation had said. He had presented a complex argument. I thought about the positive traits he had shown at the start of his existence, and about their near total destruction induced by the cruelty and coldness of his protectors. His power and threats were part of my calculations. Here was a creature who could dwell in the ice caves on the glaciers, and who could hide himself as long as he needed from pursuers along the ridges of the tallest peaks of these mountains. His intelligence and brute strength meant that he would likely never be brought to justice. Considering all these things, including the fairness due to him for having been born into such a strange life and the fact that doing as he asked might spare the greatest number of lives, I realized that I was obligated to comply with his request. I turned to him, and let him see with my eyes that I had reached a decision.

"I will give you the mate you seek, on your solemn promise that you leave Europe and every other neighbourhood of man forever. You will do so the moment that I deliver to you the female of your kind."

"I swear by the sun, and by the blue skies of heaven, that if you grant my prayer you will never see me again. Return to your home and begin your work. I will observe the process from a distance, and, when you have finished, I will appear."

With these words, he opened the door and exited the cabin, likely fearing that I would change my mind again. I saw him descend the mountain with greater speed than the flight of an eagle, and quickly lost him among the undulations of the sea of ice.

His tale had taken the whole day; and the sun was upon the verge of the horizon when he departed. I knew that I should hurry my descent towards the valley, as I would soon be encompassed in darkness; but my heart was heavy, and my steps slow. The task of winding among the little paths of the mountains, and fixing my feet firmly as I advanced, perplexed me, distracted as I was by the emotions which the events of the day had produced. Night was far advanced, when I came to the half-way resting-place, and seated myself beside the fountain. The stars shone at intervals, as the clouds passed from over them; the dark pines rose before me, and every here and there a broken tree lay on the ground; it was a scene of wonderful solemnity, and stirred strange thoughts within me. I wept bitterly; and, clasping my hands in agony, I exclaimed, "Oh! stars, and clouds, and winds, which mock me; if you truly pity me, crush sensation and memory; reduce me to nothingness; but if not, be gone and leave me in darkness."

These were wild ideas, brimming with despair. But I cannot describe how the twinkling stars weighed on me during these minutes and how every gust of wind over the ridges sounded like a spirit on its way to destroy me.

Morning dawned before I arrived at the village of Chamounix; but my presence, so haggard and strange, did little to calm the fears of my family, who had anxiously stayed awake all night awaiting my return.

The following day we returned to Geneva. Though well-intentioned, my father's method of curing my grief had, in the end, proved almost fatal to the patient. Unable to understand the slide back into darkness that I was obviously experiencing, he said that we should get home as soon as possible. It was his new hope that the quiet monotony of our everyday domestic life would eventually alleviate my suffering.

For my part, I was willing to do whatever he and others asked, but not even the gentle affection of Elizabeth could pull me out of the depths of my despair; the agreement I had come to with the demon weighed upon me that much. Every satisfaction offered by the beautiful scenery on the return trip was beyond my ability to experience. Does it come as a surprise that periods of insanity took hold during this time, or that I perceived a multitude of filthy animals intent upon my torture, drawing screams and cries from deep within me?

Back in Geneva, these perceptions quieted, and the scenes of daily life did finally begin to soothe me, in much the way that my father and the others had hoped.

Volume III

Chapter I

D ay after day, week after week, after our return from Chamounix, I could not find the courage to take up my gruesome work anew, despite fearing the wrath of my disappointed creation. Alas, the memories of the tasks I had performed to make him were vividly horrifying. I also realized that the process of making a female would require me to expend the same kind of effort and investigation that I had in Ingolstadt, a process that had profoundly threatened my own well-being. Word had come from England of discoveries by a certain scientist which would improve the likelihood of my project's success. Several times I came close to requesting my father's consent to travel to England, but instead I manufactured plausible reasons why I could not. Serenity had only recently become part of my life again, and the prospect of seeing it disappear was too much to bear. Also, my health, until recently poor, was much improved. When I allowed myself to believe that I did not owe the fiend anything, a mental trick I was performing more and more often, my spirits rose, too. My father noticed these changes in me with gladness and turned his thoughts towards driving off the last remnants of sorrow that he occasionally still saw within me. And I did have lingering moments of dark depression. When such bleak moods took over, I sought refuge in complete solitude, passing whole days alone on the lake in a little boat. Watching the clouds, listening to the waves slap the hull, breathing the fresh air, and letting the sun warm me, I felt my composure slowly return. When, in the evening, I had put up the boat and returned to the house, I was able to meet the greetings of my friends with a smile and a more cheerful heart.

After one of these outings on the lake, my father took me aside. "It is good to see you returning to your former pleasures and feeling like yourself again," he said. "And yet I can still see the sorrow in your eyes, and you continue to avoid those of us whom you love. I have spent too many hours wondering about the cause of your suffering, but think I may have found the answer. If my conclusion is correct, I only ask that you confirm it. Remaining silent would help no one, and risk much sadness for all."

I was beginning to shake, and did everything I could to hide it. My father continued:

"I confess that I have always looked upon your eventual marriage to your cousin as the key to our family's happiness," he said. "Part of this hope is understandable, given that I am at a time in my own life when the ending of the journey has come into view.

"The two of you were always so attached to each other, and so content around each other, from your earliest days. When it was time, you studied together and then, too, your inclinations and tastes remained well matched. But in my ambition for this continuation of the lifelong harmony that you have known with your cousin, perhaps I have been blind. Without meaning to, I may have put weight on something that could not, and should not, bear pressure. You may, it has occurred to me, think of Elizabeth as your sister, and have no wish for her to become your wife. Or, just as likely, you may have met another whom you love, and, considering yourself bound in honour to your cousin, the strain between the needs of two families and the needs of your own heart may have become immense. This would explain the depths of sorrow that I know you continue to feel."

"My dear father, rest assured that I love Elizabeth above all others. No one has been more tender to me, or a wiser friend, than she has been throughout my life, and to this day. All my future hopes are bound up in the certainty of marrying my beautiful and charming cousin."

"You have made me happier than I have been in a long time. If you truly feel this way, then no matter how dark the present appears, we will all be happy again—I am sure of it! It is my wish to help you banish the gloom that has taken hold of your thoughts, and for all of us to realize our hopes sooner rather than later. What do you say about a wedding in the coming days? We have experienced great misfortune, and it has gotten in the way of the peace that a person of my years and imperfect health would normally expect, and greatly desire. You are younger than most men when they marry. But with your being in possession of a comfortable fortune, I do not see how a wedding now would interfere with your life ambitions. Please know that I do not wish to dictate the form that your happiness must take, and will accept any delay that you may require. It is good we can be candid with each other in this way."

I heard him out in respectful silence. For some time, I was incapable of responding. Competing reasons why I would eventually say no flitted through my mind as I strove to choose the one that would do the least harm. The truth was that an immediate wedding was so far out of the question as to produce horror within me. I was bound by a solemn promise of a very different kind now, one that I had yet to fulfill and dared not fail to honour. If I were to break my vow to the creature, who knew what he might do, and what sorrows my beloved family would have to suffer?

I knew that I was incapable of feigning the joy that a wedding is meant to bring, with a weight such as this hanging around my neck. I had to perform the gruesome task I had promised before I could rejoice in marrying one I truly loved, as I did my sweet Elizabeth.

By this time, I had become convinced that journeying to England was a virtual necessity. The only other possibility that could provide me with the information I needed was to enter into a lengthy correspondence with the scientists whose discoveries were vital to me. And the truth was that even a long series of letters would be less satisfactory than meeting with the men face to face, and that the prospect of passing a year or two far from the tragic landscape that my homeland had become was deeply appealing on its own. More important, there was the possibility that during my trip abroad I would be able to give my creation what he desired and thereby protect my family from him. Finally, I could hope that as I worked to make him his mate some accident would destroy him and put an end to my slavery once and for all.

Guiding all my thoughts was the prospect that my family could one day know me again as the confident and happy person that I had once been. All of this meant telling my father something I knew he did not want to hear, which was that I could not give him what he desired, not at the present time. I expressed my desire to visit England, hiding the true reason for the request. I mentioned wishing to see the world before settling down within the walls of my native town. And there was at least a little truth in what I said. I made my case earnestly, and my father, the most indulgent and least overbearing parent in the world, complied without protest. Plans for the journey were quickly established.

I would travel to Strasbourg, where Henry would join me. We would spend several weeks in the fine towns of Holland, but we would have a much longer stay in England. We would return by way of France; it was agreed that the entire trip would last exactly two years.

For my father, the idea that I was committed to marrying Elizabeth immediately upon my return was reassuring, and proof that the future had become bright once more.

"The time will pass before any of us knows it," he said. "And this journey will build the foundation for a lifetime of contentment. I look forward to the moment we are all reunited and nothing can upset our domestic sphere again."

"May it be so," I said. "Certainly, by that time Elizabeth and I will both be wiser, and happier, than we currently are." I sighed, but my father was kind enough not to ask the reason. He hoped that the new scenes awaiting, and the pleasant distractions of travelling, would again make me the sociable and even-tempered son he remembered.

As I made my travel arrangements, one thing haunted me. During my absence, I would be leaving my family and the other members of our household vulnerable to a violent enemy. Not one of them had any awareness of his existence, or of his rage towards me and those I held dear. My departure itself could induce him to perform some new act of evil, and the thought was too terrible to contemplate.

Still, he had promised to follow me wherever I should go. There was the at once terrifying and hopeful likelihood that he would pursue me to England, with the consolation being that if he stayed by me as I travelled, he could not harm my loved ones in Geneva. But I had to admit to myself the possibility that he would instead stay in Switzerland and punish me in my absence by harming those I loved. During this whole period, when I was the slave of my creation, I let myself be guided by whatever feelings I might be having in the moment. Intuition is not always prescient, of course. But I sensed that the fiend would follow me and leave my family in safety.

The end of August neared, and I prepared to leave for my two years of exile. Elizabeth understood the given reasons for my departure, and gave her approval. Her only regret, she explained, was not being permitted the same freedom to widen her experience and expand her own sense of the world. She cried when we said our goodbyes, and begged me to come home happy.

"We depend on you," she said. "You must understand that when you are in misery all of us are equally so."

As Henry had a few details to attend to before his own departure, it was decided that he would catch up with me in four or five days. With Elizabeth's tears on my cheeks, I leapt into the coach, barely knowing where I was headed or what was going on at all. The one thing that I remembered, and it was with painful awareness, was to have the servants pack the chemical instruments that I would need while in England, for I was committed to fulfilling my promise there. Indeed, it was my intention to return home a free man. Consumed by dark thoughts, I was transported through a series of beautiful and majestic scenes, but I barely noticed them, my eyes fixed straight ahead and capable of producing no delight within me. All I could think of was the land to which I was travelling and the horrifying task that I would be working on once there.

The whole first part of the journey was spent similarly, with brief stops at various villages. At the end of the third day, I was in Strasbourg, many miles from Geneva. Here, I rested and waited for Henry for two days. His exuberant spirits upon arriving underscored the appalling distance between us. He was alive to every new scene, even the subtleties of every sunrise and sunset; sunrises, especially, delighted him. He pointed to the colours of autumn beginning to dapple the landscape, and to the differing appearances of the sky, day to day, and hour to hour.

"To be alive is a gift, even though I fear it does not feel like one to you," he said during a fine sunset one evening. "Why do you continue along your sorrowful course?"

The truth was that I was preoccupied by the gloomiest of thoughts and could appreciate neither the descent of the evening star nor the golden sunrise playing on the waters of the Rhine. A person would benefit infinitely more by reading the journal Henry kept than by listening to my sad reports of this time. Henry took in the world around him with the eyes and ears of a poet, whereas I was by now like a ghost upon the earth, one whose senses had been dulled to the pleasures of being human.

We would be travelling by boat down the Rhine to Rotterdam, and, once there, securing passage on a ship to London. During our journey on this majestic river, we passed by willow-covered islands and saw dozens of quaint towns. We stayed a day at Mannheim, and then, five days after leaving Strasbourg, we arrived at Mainz. Below this small, refined city, the Rhine gains speed and becomes even more picturesque. Here the river presents a truly varied landscape, with beautiful, ruined castles looking down from precipices, and rugged hills reaching up from the dark waters of the river as it rushes past. Then, as you come around a bend and glide past a promontory, hillside vineyards perched behind green, sloping banks appear before your dazzled eyes. Thriving, manicured towns appear amidst the natural scenery from time to time and give a sense of what a fine place the valley must be in which to spend one's life.

It was the season of the harvest, and the early stages of winemaking. The workers' songs made their way to our boat, and even I, in my depressed state of mind and with my spirit oppressed by worry, even I felt the joy of the season. I was lying on a bed of folded sails at the bottom of the boat, staring through the rigging at a cloudless blue sky, with forested hilltops drifting in and out of the edge of my vision. For a brief moment, I was serene. And if the scenes produced such an effect on me, imagine what effect they had on Henry! For him, it was as though he had been carried to a kind of fairyland, as he experienced a purity of happiness that few ever know. "I have seen the most beautiful sights of my own country," he said, "visiting countless times Lake Lucerne and most of all Lake Uri, where snow-capped mountains descend straight down to the water, and leave magnificent, gloomy shadows on its surface, the effect made hopeful by the lush, green islands so nearby. I have seen the same lake roiled by angry tempests, with the wind spinning up waterspouts, and the waves crashing on the shore with fury. In that very place, a priest and his mistress were buried by an avalanche, and the villagers say that their voices can be heard during pauses of the nightly wind. I have also looked upon the mountains of Le Valais and the enchanting Pays de Vaud, but the region through which we are passing is the most beautiful I have seen. The mountains where we are from are more majestic and strange, but there is a loveliness about the banks of this wonderful river that I have never seen equaled. Look at the castle overhanging that cliff! And the one on the island, shrouded by the leaves of the tall, lush trees! Look upon the workers in the vineyards and the village half-hidden in the fold of that mountain! Surely, the spirit that guards this place is more in harmony with human kind than any overseeing our own glaciers and remote mountaintops."

Clerval! beloved friend! even now it delights me, to remember your words, and to dwell on the praise you so eminently deserve! He was a man formed in the "very poetry of nature." Henry's sublime imagination was made just steady enough by the good-natured common sense flowing from his heart. His soul brimmed with affection, and his friendship was so devoted and thoughtful that most worldly minded folk would have considered it impossible. But even loving his fellow man as he did, his excellent mind required the glorious visions of nature to attain its full fruition. For, what others looked at with admiration, he loved with fervor:

> ———*The sounding cataract*
> *Haunted him like a passion: the tall rock,*
> *The mountain, and the deep and gloomy wood,*
> *Their colours and their forms, were then to him*
> *An appetite; a feeling, and a love,*
> *That had no need of a remoter charm,*
> *By thought supplied, or any interest*
> *Unborrowed from the eye.*

And where does he now rest? Has this gentle and loving soul been lost forever? Has this intellect of his—so full of ideas, of images fanciful and magnificent, that had the power to carry a whole world within it—has this mind come to an end? Does it now exist only in my memory? It cannot be. The memory of your features, divinely wrought, brimming with beauty, visits and sustains me even in my unhappiness, though your form has perished.

Please excuse this rush of sorrow. My words are but a weak tribute to the unequalled character of the greatest friend that I will ever have. But even my poor approximation provides my heart with solace, which it aches for after remembering Henry now. I will continue with the story, as I know I must.

Beyond Cologne, we descended to the plains of Holland; with the wind on our bow, and the flow of the river too gentle to help us, we resolved to complete our journey on horseback.

Our journey here lost the interest arising from beautiful scenery; but we arrived in a few days at Rotterdam, and from there continued by sea to England. It was on a clear October morning that I first saw the white cliffs of Dover. The banks of the Thames presented a new scene; they were flat, but fertile, and almost every town was marked by the remembrance of some story. We saw Tilbury Fort, and were reminded of the Spanish Armada. Next came Gravesend, Woolwich, and Greenwich, places which I had heard of even in my country.

At length we saw the numerous steeples of London, St. Paul's towering above all, and the Tower famed in English history.

Chapter II

L ondon was our present point of rest; we decided to spend some months in this wonderful and celebrated city. Henry was pursuing friendships with the men of talent and genius of the town, but for me the delicacies of the mind were a secondary concern. I was focussed, by necessity, on the fulfillment of my promise, and the information that would make it possible. I presented letters of introduction, and became acquainted with the most accomplished scientists in my field of study living in London at the time.

If this journey had taken place during my early days at Ingolstadt, before the tragedies I had known since, it would have brought me much happiness. But there was darkness hovering over everything in my life by this time, and I merely visited these leading lights of science to absorb the helpful information that they could impart. Being around other people, even ones as fascinating as they, was unpleasant to me now. When I was on my own, I could at least fill my mind with the sights of remembered scenes of nature. At such times, words that Henry had spoken to me during our journey to England soothed me, and I managed to create for myself a passing hour of peace.

The few occasions on which I dared to be in the presence of lively and joyous faces at social gatherings left me heartsick with the knowledge of the barrier between me and my fellows.

The invisible wall separating us had been sealed with the blood of William and Justine; and to reflect on the events connected with those names filled my soul with anguish.

But in Henry there was still the image of my former self. He hungered for knowledge, and was happy to do the work to acquire it. Merely observing humanity was endlessly interesting and satisfying to my friend. He was forever busy, and the only thing that limited his enjoyment at all was my sorrowful and dejected appearance. I tried to conceal my thoughts, with the aim of allowing him to make the most of his time in a new and fascinating place. It was certainly not fair that bitterness and care should be concerns of his; thus, as much as I politely could, I refused to accompany him when he ventured forth around the city. I told him that I had other plans, even though my intention was to be alone. In truth, I was beginning to collect the necessary materials for my creation, with even these early steps in the process feeling like the torture of single drops of water continually falling on one's head. Every thought required to bring the enterprise forward was its own ordeal, and every word I spoke in association with it to my unknowing helpers made my lips quiver, and my heart clench.

After we had spent a few months in London, we received a letter from a person in Scotland, who had previously been our visitor in Geneva. He spoke of the beauties of his native country, and argued for our extending our journey and travelling as far north as Perth, where he lived. Henry was immediately in favour of accepting the invitation. Although I was not interested in visiting anyone, even a man as kind as this friend, I was keen to be among the mountains and streams and other wondrous works of nature that remained dear to me.

We had arrived in England in early October, and it was now

February. We planned to start the journey north the following month, when conditions would be more favourable. We did not intend to follow the main road to Edinburgh, preferring to visit the towns of Windsor, Oxford, and Matlock, as well as the Lake District, along the way. The goal was to finish our tour by the end of July. I packed my scientific instruments, and other materials I had collected, with an eye towards completing my work in an obscure locale somewhere in the northern highlands of Scotland.

We left London on a windy and bright Monday morning. The date was March 27th. We spent a few days in Windsor walking in its beautiful forest. This was another new scene to two men of the Alps, for whom the majestic oak trees, the quantity of game, and the herds of stately deer were all novelties.

From there, we continued to Oxford. As we entered this city, our minds were filled with the events of a century and a half before. The first King Charles had collected his forces here, and the city had remained faithful to him, after the rest of the nation abandoned him in favour of parliament and liberty. The memory of the doomed king and his inner circle—the amiable Falkland, the untrustworthy Goring, and Charles's queen and son— lent interest to every part of the city, which they might be understood to have inhabited. The spirit of elder days found a dwelling here, and we delighted to trace its footsteps.

Even if we had not known the local history, Oxford's beauty commanded admiration. The colleges are ancient and picturesque; the streets are almost magnificent; and lovely Isis, flowing between bands of enchanting green meadows, is a quieting force in a place already serene. Stepping across a footbridge to the far side, you can look back and admire the spires, towers, and domes of the city reflected in the river's waters, the whole scene framed by tall, magnificent trees.

I enjoyed this view; and yet my enjoyment was tinged both by memories of the past and anticipation of the future. I was formed for peaceful happiness. During my youthful days, unhappy thoughts never visited my mind. If, from time to time I knew the boredom common among children and young people, then the beauty of nature in all its splendour would consistently bring back my underlying state of contentment. Or, if even that were not enough to restore my hopefulness, then the shining achievements of humanity—architecture, painting, sculpture, music, and theatre—would do so, without exception. But by this time I was like a blasted tree, with the lightning bolt having gone straight through my soul. By living out my days, grim as they had become, I hoped to serve the world as a warning of how not to think and act.

We spent several weeks at Oxford. Most of our waking hours were devoted to walking around the town, striving to learn each nook's relation to the figures of history, including—but not only—Charles I. Our small voyages of discovery were often prolonged when we came upon new subjects of fascination, including Hampden's tomb and the field on which the great patriot had fallen. Standing upon it in contemplation, my soul was liberated from the fears plaguing it, and I could taste the divine ideas of liberty and self-sacrifice like any other man. Indeed, just for a moment, the monuments awakened me so much that I was able to shake off my chains and look around me with a free and lofty spirit, but, alas, the iron had eaten into my flesh, and I sank once more, trembling and hopeless, into my miserable self.

We left Oxford feeling that we would have liked to stay longer and proceeded to the town of Matlock, in Derbyshire, which would be our next stopping place. In certain respects, Derbyshire resembled the scenery of Switzerland on a smaller scale. The green hills are present, but not the distant white Alps above the pine-covered mountains. We visited the nearby cave system with its myriad hollows and saw curiosities assembled and displayed in the same fashion as at Servox and Chamounix. The name of the latter made me quake, when Henry spoke it, and I immediately yearned to leave Matlock, now connected to the awful events that I had gone through above Chamounix.

Heading northward from Derby, we passed two months in Cumberland and Westmoreland, where I could just about imagine myself in the Alps. The small patches of snow clinging to the northern sides of the mountains, the crystal clear lakes, and the cascading rock-strewn streams were wonderfully familiar sights. We made new, warm acquaintances—friends, really—who almost succeeded in tricking me into being happy again. Henry, meanwhile, was under no like obligation to fight off contentment, and enjoyed his stay enormously. Interacting daily with men of talent, as our new friends were, he found aptitudes and resources within himself that he had never imagined himself possessing. He had in the past, to a degree I occasionally lamented, spent more time than was best with people who were his intellectual inferiors. Now, surrounded by vibrant minds, his spirits and thoughts were soaring.

"I could spend the rest of my days here," he said. "Among these great mountains, I would hardly regret Switzerland and the Rhine."

But the reality of a traveller's life includes much pain among its enjoyments. Constant upheaval leaves one's nerves overtaxed, as carefully as one may try to avoid it, and, whenever comfort is found in a new environment, it must be let go of in favour of those at the next destination, which then must be forsaken for other, newer distractions. The effect is one of weariness.

So it was that we bid adieu to the region, and to our new friends, before we would have wished. Our friend in Scotland was expecting us, and it was time to be leaving. For my own part, the departure was not sorrowful. I had largely ignored my work, and I feared the demon's disappointed wrath. He may have remained in Switzerland and be terrorizing my relatives, for all I knew. The idea tortured and pursued me, and stole moments of serenity and rest that I much needed. I waited for the post from home with feverish impatience. If a packet was late in coming, I was inconsolable, and mobbed by fears. When the letters came, and I saw the addresses written on the envelopes in the hand of Elizabeth or my father, I hardly dared to read what they contained and in the process learn my fate.

At times, I thought the fiend was following me and might push me towards fulfilling my promise sooner by murdering Henry. When these thoughts took hold of me, I refused to leave Henry's side for a moment, but shadowed him to protect him from the rage of my creation. I had the sense that I had personally committed truly disturbing crimes, and pangs of conscience hounded me everywhere I went. I was guiltless, objectively, but I had drawn down a curse upon myself, and my sense of shame was equal to that of any murderer.

I visited Edinburgh as though sleepwalking, and yet the fascination of the city was so strong that even the most unfortunate person would, in any other circumstances, respond to it. Henry did not care for Edinburgh as much as he cared for Oxford, probably because he knew the history associated with the English city better. But the beauty and harmonious architecture of the new portion of Edinburgh, together with its romantic castle and stunning grounds, Arthur's Seat, St. Bernard's Well, and the Pentland Hills still induced both cheerfulness and admiration in my cultivated friend. For my own part, I had by this point become impatient to arrive at the final destination of my journey.

For these reasons, we stayed in Edinburgh for only a week, next journeying through Coupar and St. Andrews, and then along the banks of the Tay to Perth, where our friend expected us. Once there, it rapidly became clear that I was in no condition to laugh and talk with strangers, or to enter into discussions of their hopes and plans with the good humour expected from a guest. I told Henry at the earliest juncture that I preferred to finish the tour of Scotland on my own.

"Enjoy yourself," I said. "I will be back in a month or two to rendezvous. Do not look to join me as I move about. I am in need of peace and solitude for a short while. When I return, it will be with a lighter heart, and I will be less of a burden."

Henry protested, but, seeing that I was determined, he stopped arguing after only a short while. His only request was that I write often.

"I would rather be with you, dear friend," he said, "than with these Scotch people, whom I little know; come back sooner rather than later, so that I can feel at least somewhat at home, which I am unable to do in your absence."

After saying goodbye to my dear Henry and leaving Perth, I began to seek out some hidden place where I might perform my work in solitude. I had become more confident that the monster was nearby and would reveal himself when I had finished his companion.

With this resolution I traversed the northern highlands, and chose one of the most remote Orkney islands as the scene of my labours. My chosen sanctuary was well suited to anonymous work, being little more than a rock with high sides continually hammered upon by waves. What soil there was atop the cliffs was mostly bare of vegetation, offering scant pasture for a few miserable cows and oatmeal for the five human inhabitants. These poor souls had gaunt faces and scraggy limbs, proof of the miserable local diet. Vegetables and bread, when there was money for them, and even fresh water all had to be transported from the mainland, a five-mile trip across the sea.

The small island had only three miserable huts, one of which was vacant when I arrived. I rented it for the duration of my project. The structure consisted of but two rooms, and bore evidence of poverty and the squalor that comes with it. In places, the thatched roof had caved in; the walls were unplastered; the door was off its hinges. I ordered the door repaired, bought some furniture, and took possession of the premises. My appearance on the island and decision to become one of its denizens most likely would have shocked my new neighbours, but for the fact that their hunger and poverty had left them numb. I was left to myself, unstared at and unmolested, and barely thanked for the food and clothing which I gave them. Suffering has a way of killing social niceties over the course of time, and the sorrows here were not new.

I spent mornings devoted to the task at hand, but in the evening, when the weather permitted, I walked the stony beach, listening to the crashing waves as they broke. It was a scene at once monotonous and ever changing. My thoughts ran to my homeland, so vastly different from this desolate and chilling landscape. In Switzerland, tidy vineyards adorn the hills, and handsome cottages dot the plains below, with our lakes reflecting the consistently blue and gentle sky. When rare storm winds rise, the roiling water on the lakes is like a gentle whisper compared to the roaring ocean here.

Such was the division of my hours when I began, but as the

assemblage of material upon which I was labouring took form the work became progressively more horrible and overwhelming. More than once, I could not even force myself to enter the laboratory for several days. At other times, I worked day and night, in order to complete the task. What I was involved in was a filthy process. In Ingolstadt, my fascination and ambition—as well as my hope—had blinded me to the horror unfolding in my own apartment. But now I was going about the same process in cold blood, and my heart rebelled at the work that my hands were performing.

Here, on a forlorn rock, working on the most grisly and appalling project that could exist, I felt my nerves start to come undone. Nothing was capable of distracting me from the scene in which I was engaged, and a sense of foreboding that I had been living with for some time was growing by the hour. Every moment, I feared the prospect of meeting my tormentor. Sometimes, I kept my eyes fixed on the ground, believing that if I raised them I would behold the one I dreaded seeing. When not in the hut, I feared to wander out of sight of my neighbours, lest when alone he should come to claim his companion.

Under these circumstances, I laboured on; and my awful project began to near completion. With a dreadful hope, which I avoided letting myself question, I anticipated the moment when the spark of life would arrive. Still, obscure forebodings of evil made their way into my consciousness, unbidden. My heart had never been heavier.

Chapter III

O ne evening, exhausted by the work and very close to the end of it, I took a moment to sit and rest in my laboratory. The sun had just gone down, and the moon was beginning to rise from the sea. I was so tired that just lighting the candles I required to continue would be a challenge. As I tried to talk myself into the expenditure of energy and into bringing the work to its likely conclusion sometime in the next few hours, a new train of thought began to occupy my mind. The reflections led to my considering the effects that the thing I was creating might have in the world. Three years before, I had been engaged in the same process, and I had created a fiend whose violent actions had shattered my heart, and filled me with remorse that would remain with me forever. Now, I was about to form another being, one whose tendencies I could not know before she came to life. She could, quite possibly, be even more violent than her mate, delighting in murder and wretchedness for their own sake. My first creation had sworn to quit the neighbourhood of man, but his mate, still inanimate, had not. She could refuse to comply with an arrangement entered before her first breath was drawn. She and my first creation might also loathe each other. He had admitted to feeling disgust for his own deformed shape. Might he not feel an even greater aversion for it when it came before him in female form? Or it might just as well be she who was repulsed by her counterpart, in favour of the superior beauty of man. She might leave him in their first hour together, worsening his sense of isolation and provoking him to greater violence than ever.

Even if they were to leave Europe and dwell in the most far-flung place somewhere in the New World, there was the inevitable result of the sympathy that the monster desired from his mate: children. If she gave him progeny, then a race of devils would be put on the earth, and the lives of human beings would be made forever precarious and full of terror. Did I have the right, even if it was to benefit my family, to inflict such a curse on future generations? I realized that I did not. I had allowed myself to be moved by the desperate reasoning of a creature overwhelmed by loneliness, and had been struck senseless by his threats. But now, for the first time, the dangers of my promise came home to me. I shivered at the prospect of future ages cursing me as the one who had ruined the earth for habitation.

I was shaking. My heart was so full of fear that I thought it would stop in my chest any moment. My eyes were drawn up by the light of the rising moon coming through the open window, and, where there should have been only moonlight and stars, I saw the face of my creation, an ugly grin wrinkling his lips. He was looking at me with satisfaction in his intelligent eyes over the fact that I was in the midst of fulfilling the task he had begged me to perform. In the end, he had followed me in my travels, haunting forests, hiding in caves, and taking refuge on the wide heaths of England and Scotland; now he had come to measure my progress, and claim the fulfillment of my vow.

As I began to make out the lines of his face more fully in the imperfect light, I saw that his expression bore both ill will and joyfully satisfied treachery. I was suddenly furious at how I had been manipulated into creating another like him. Shaking with rage, I began tearing to pieces the female that I had so nearly brought to life. The demon watched me destroy the one on whom his future happiness depended, and when I had finished, he let out a howl of deep despair, looked at me with truly devilish rage, and disappeared from view.

I left the room I had been using as my laboratory, locked the door, and vowed never to start the project again. Then, with trembling legs, I walked into my living quarters. I was alone; there was no one to disperse the gloom or distract me from the memory of what I had just experienced and the fears of worse things to come.

Hours passed. I stood at the window, gazing at the sea. I saw its surface was the calmest it had been since my arrival. The reliably strong wind had quieted to almost nothing, and all of nature was at rest under the light of the silent moon. A few fishing boats were on the water, and, now and then, the gentle breeze brought the voices of the fishermen through the window, as they called to one another. I sank into the intervening silence deeply, without being aware of it, until I was pulled back by the sound of oars in the water just off shore. Some one was landing a boat close by.

A few minutes slowly passed. Then I heard the barely audible creaking of my front door, as if some one were trying to open it without being heard. I was trembling from head to foot. I had an idea who was making the sound, and I yearned to wake one of the peasants who lived in the cottage nearest mine; but I was too overcome with fear, frozen in the same way as during nightmares, when you command your limbs to escape a threat and are unable to move. As I struggled for breath, I heard the sound of footsteps come from the front hallway and saw the door to my room open. It was the wretch, returned for reasons I was presumably on the verge of learning. Shutting the door behind him, he approached the place where I was standing, and began to speak in a muffled voice.

"You have destroyed what you began. What is it you intend to do next? You dare to go back on your word? You cannot imagine what I have suffered to stay close by. I left Switzerland and crept along the banks of the Rhine, wading along its willow-topped islands and, when forced, scaling the river's nearby hills and struggling to keep you in sight. I spent long periods on the heaths of England and amidst the wilds of Scotland. I have known exhaustion, cold, and hunger. And now you dare destroy my hopes?"

"Be gone!" I said. "I do now, and forever more, break my promise. I will never make another like you."

"Slave, I have reasoned with you until now, but you have proven unworthy of such respect. Do you doubt my power? You perceive that you are in misery now, but it is nothing compared to what I will make you feel. You will be so unhappy that the light of day will be a punishment to you. You are my creator, but I am your master. You will obey me!"

"The time of my weakness has come and gone. And your power on this earth has ended. No threat you can utter will make me perform this act of wickedness. Your words and what I see in your eyes only confirm my decision. Do you really expect that I would, knowing what I have learned, let loose in the world a female demon who delights in death and mayhem? Be gone, I say! Saying anything else will only enrage me more."

The monster saw from my expression that I was serious and clenched his teeth in frustrated anger. "How is it that every man, good or evil, is able to find a wife with whom to share his bed, and yet I am to be alone?" he said. "I brought feelings of warmth and affection into this world, and they were met with hatred and disgust. You loathe me, man, but beware! The rest of your life will be spent in fear. A lightning bolt will strike and separate you from your happiness forever. Why would I leave you content, as I grovel in wretchedness? You may have the power to stand in the way of my other passions, but revenge remains, and, from this moment forward, vengeance will be more important to me than light or food. I may die in the midst of finding the justice that I crave, but before I do you will curse the sun that shines down on your misery. Remember that I am fearless, and that makes me powerful. I will observe you with the treachery of a snake, and I will sting you as it would. You will regret what you have done!"

"Enough! Do not poison the air further with these evil sounds. I have made clear my intentions, and am no coward. Your words are powerless over me. Leave this place, and know that I am resolved."

"As you wish. But know that I will be with you on your wedding-night."

I lunged at him.

"Abortion!" I said. "Before you threaten such harm, be assured that you are safe yourself."

I would have fought him to the death, but he eluded my grasp. Before I could try again, he ducked out the door and ran from the hut. In a few brief moments, I saw him aboard his boat, moving across the water with an arrow's swiftness, before disappearing among gently lumbering swells.

All was silent, but the fiend's words rang in my ears. I was enraged. My first thought was that I needed to follow him and cast him into the ocean. I paced the floor, and my imagination lashed me with a sequence of terrible scenes. How could I have failed to follow him as he left the cottage and then the island? Why had I not managed to fight him to the death when he was within reach? I had let him leave, and he had sped away towards the mainland, and I quivered trying to imagine whom he would choose for his next victim. I thought again of his words: *I will be with you on your wedding-night.* So, my life on earth would come to an end on the same day that Elizabeth and I said our vows, making the monster happy—at last. This knowledge caused me no fear, but when I thought of my beloved Elizabeth the image of her sorrow over having her beloved snatched from her at a time of such tenderness unleashed the first tears I had shed in months. They flowed down my cheeks, and I swore that I would not fall to the demon without a courageous fight.

The night passed with painful slowness, and the sun rose from the ocean. My feelings became calmer, or, rather, the brilliant colours of my rage dissolved into the dark shadows of despair. I stepped out of the cottage, scene of the previous evening's horrific events, and walked on the shore awhile. The sea appeared to me then an uncrossable barrier between my fellow-creatures and myself, and an idea rose within me—that I should spend the rest of my life here. I would do so in a state of deep weariness, but at least my remaining years would be uninterrupted by any sudden shock or misery. If ever I went back to the mainland, it would be to be murdered or, worse, to see those I loved the most sacrificed by the demon I had created.

I walked around the island like a restless ghost, separated from everyone and everything I loved. With the sun near its zenith, I lay down on a patch of grass and tumbled into a deep sleep. I had been awake the whole of the previous night; my nerves were frayed; my eyes burned from the effort of staying awake and from weeping. The brief sleep refreshed me greatly. Upon awakening, I felt connected to the human race again and began to think more about what had happened, with greater composure. But the words of my tormentor rung in my ears like a church bell on a funeral day. The effect was like a dream, but the things he said possessed a reality that made the threats oppressive.

The sun had far descended, but I remained where I was, sitting and staring at the sea. I was satisfying my appetite, which had become ravenous, with an oaten cake, when I saw a fishing boat land not far away. One of its men brought me a packet containing letters from Geneva as well as one from Clerval, reminding me that I was to join him as soon as I was able. He mentioned that we had been away from Switzerland for nearly a year and that France remained unvisited, earnestly asking me to leave my solitary isle, and meet him at Perth, in a week's time. At that point, he said, we could arrange our future journeying. The letter reawakened me to my normal duties and affections, and I determined to quit the island before two days had expired.

Before my departure, there was work to be done, and picturing it made me shudder. I needed to pack up my scientific instruments and clean the room in which I had performed my gruesome work. I knew that even the mere sight of my tools would sicken me. At dawn the following morning, I summoned my courage, unlocked the laboratory door, and saw the remains of the half-finished creature I had lately destroyed scattered on the floor. It appeared as though I had mangled the flesh of a living human being. I hesitated a moment at the door, and then entered the room. It was clear that I needed to clean up the traces of my craft so as not to cause horror and suspicion among the islanders, and I gathered up the different parts of what was to have been my creation's mate and put them in a basket, covering all with a multitude of stones, and laying up the foul container until night. Under the cover of darkness, I planned to throw the basket into the sea. I made good use of the daylight hours until then, sitting on the beach cleaning and organizing my scientific apparatus.

I had undergone a transformation since the night the creature saw me destroy his mate. Previously, I had gloomily considered my promise to him above Chamounix as a commitment that, whatever the consequences, had to be fulfilled. Now, I felt as if a film had been removed from my eyes and that for the first time in a long while I was seeing clearly. The idea of starting the project again crossed my mind. Yes, his threat weighed on my thoughts, but I had no sense that anything I did could keep the monster from his purpose. I had decided that to make another like him would be an act of the most appalling selfishness, and banished from my thoughts anything that could lead me to reconsider.

Between the hours of two and three in the morning, the moon rose. Putting my basket aboard a little skiff, I sailed out a couple of miles from shore. There I saw a few fishing boats returning to port on the mainland, but I sailed away from them. After a few minutes, I was confident that no eyes could see what I intended to do. Strangely, I felt as if, rather than regaining my decency and humanity, I was performing some hideous new crime. At one point, the moon was overspread by a thick cloud, and the sea was cast into complete darkness. I took advantage of the cover this provided me and lowered the heavy basket over the side and into the sea. As it rapidly sank, I listened to some gurgling sounds that it made for a few moments, and then sailed away from the spot. The cloud which had covered the moon was a harbinger of many others. The sky became overcast, and a cold northwest wind began to blow. The breeze was refreshing after this last bit of grim toil. I decided to stay on the water for a while longer, fixing the rudder in a position that would keep me clear of land, and stretching myself out along the bottom of the boat. With the clouds that covered the moon and stars still darkening the sea, I could only just make out the top of the mast from where I lay, my strongest perception being the sound of the boat as its keel cut through the waves. The murmur lulled me, and in a short time I slept soundly.

I do not know how long I remained in this situation, but when I awoke I saw the sun had already risen high above the horizon. The wind was blowing with much more force than when I had drifted to sleep, from the northeast, and waves continually threatened the safety of my little skiff. I realized with a start that I had travelled a considerable distance away from the coast familiar to me. I attempted to change course, but water filled the boat even more rapidly, leaving me with no choice but to run before the wind. There were moments of real terror now. I had no compass, and such minimal knowledge of the geography of the region that even the sun in the sky was of little help. Meanwhile, I was at risk of being driven into the open Atlantic, where I would feel the tortures of starvation, or, far worse, thirst. Or, more likely, I would be swallowed up any moment by the waters that roared and piled up around me. I had by this time been out many hours, and could already feel the pangs of annihilating thirst. I looked on the heavens, which were covered by clouds that flew before the wind only to be replaced by others; I looked upon the sea, it was to be my grave. "Monster," I yelled, "your task is fulfilled!" I thought of Elizabeth, of my father, and of Henry. I sank into the deepest pit of hopelessness I had known. Even here, with my life coming to its sad end, looking back upon that moment makes my heart freeze with grief and terror.

Glancing up once more, I saw that the sails were torn to shreds.

A few hours passed, with gusts pushing the battered skiff up and down the waves. As the sun sank near the horizon, the wind diminished to a soft breeze and the storm-tossed breakers became a heavy swell. I became so seasick I could hardly hold the rudder, when suddenly I saw a line of high land towards the south.

Nearly overcome by fatigue and the doubt I had endured for several hours regarding my own survival, the sudden certainty of life rushed like a flood of warm joy to my heart. Involuntary tears fell from my eyes. How changeable is the soul of man under duress! We cling to life even in the midst of sorrow! I created another sail using some of my clothing, and joyfully steered a course for land. The coast had a wild, rocky appearance, but as I came nearer I saw signs of farming. There were also vessels near the shore, and I came to understand that I was approaching a civilized place. My eyes traced the curves of land until I eventually saw a steeple rise from behind a low hill.

Weakened by my ordeal, I knew my best hope was to sail in the same direction as the returning fishermen, with the hope of finding something to eat and drink. Thankfully, I had money with me. As I came around a promontory, I saw a small, tidy town with a good harbour. I guided my craft into it, my heart swelling with happiness over my unexpected escape.

As I busied myself organizing the sails and securing the boat, several people crowded towards me, seeming both interested in and surprised by my appearance. But instead of offering me assistance, they gestured in my direction and whispered among themselves in a way I would normally have found slightly alarming. It was reassuring to me when I noted that they spoke English, though. And I addressed them in their own language.

"My good friends," I said. "Will you be so kind as to tell me the name of this town?"

"You will know soon enough," replied a man in a gruff voice. "It may be that you have arrived at a place which will not prove to your liking. Your quarters will be chosen for you, and not by you; of that, I can assure you."

I was surprised to receive such a rude answer from a stranger. Just as upsetting were the menacing faces of his companions.

"Why do you speak to me in this way?" I said. "Surely, it is not the English way to receive a stranger with so little hospitality."

"I would not know," said the man, "what the customs of the English might be; but it is the custom of the Irish to hate a villain."

As this bizarre discussion went on, I saw that the crowd was growing. The people's faces expressed a mixture of curiosity and anger, which I could not understand, and which put me further on guard. I asked to be directed to the inn. No one answered. I moved forward and heard a murmuring sound rise from the crowd as they followed and surrounded me; a fisherman with a pockmarked face came near, tapped me on the shoulder, and spoke.

"Come, sir, you must follow me to Mr. Kirwin's. You are to give an account of yourself."

"Why would I give an account of anything?" I said. "Is this not a free country?"

"Aye, sir, free enough for honest folks. You are to explain before Mr. Kirwin the death of a gentleman who was found murdered here last night."

This startled me, but I was able to regain my composure. I was innocent, after all. I followed the man in silence, and was led to one of the finest houses in the town. I was ready to faint from fatigue and hunger, but being surrounded by the ill-willed crowd, I knew it was important to summon what strength I had, so that my weakness could not be construed as proof of guilt. I had no way of knowing the horrifying news on the verge of changing my life forever and making public shame and death look like nothing to me.

I have to pause for a moment, Captain. It is going to take all of my remaining power to speak of the events that I am about to share with you in the detail that they deserve.

Chapter IV

I was soon brought into the presence of the magistrate, an old and kindly gentleman. His manners were dignified and calm, but he looked upon me with a degree of severity; then, turning towards the men who had brought me, he asked who the witnesses were.

About half a dozen men came forward. One was selected by the magistrate to speak first. He said that he had been out fishing the night before with his son and brother-in-law, Daniel Nugent, when, around ten o'clock, they saw a strong northerly blast rising and quickly made for port. It had been a very dark night, with the moon not yet risen. They had not landed at the harbour, as they usually would, but at a creek two miles downwind. The man speaking said that he had walked ahead of the other two on the way back to town, and that he had been carrying some of the fishing tackle. He said that the other two were just a short ways back. As he moved along on the beach in the darkness, his foot struck something, and he fell onto the sand. His companions quickly came to assist him. By the light of their lantern, the three of them saw that the one walking ahead had fallen onto a man who appeared to be dead. They assumed it was some one who had drowned and been tossed on shore by the waves. But upon examination they discovered that the man's clothing was dry, and that his flesh not yet cold. They carried him to the cottage of an old woman who lived close by, and tried without success to revive him. The one whom they had found was a handsome young man, about twenty-five years old. He appeared to have been strangled; black finger marks on his neck were the only sign of violence.

The first part of the fisherman's statement failed to interest me, but when the marks on the neck were mentioned, a chill went down my spine. I was reminded of the murder of my brother, and became deeply upset. My knees shook, my eyes misted over, and I had to lean on a chair; the judge looked at me with his keen eye all the while. There was, I understood even then, evidence of guilt in my response.

Next was the fisherman's son, who confirmed his father's account. He was followed by Daniel Nugent, the fisherman's brother-in-law, who, when asked to speak, included facts that neither of the others had related. He told the judge that just before his companion fell he had seen a boat a little ways from shore with a single man in it. Nugent said that as far as he could judge by the light of the few stars it was the same boat in which I had recently landed.

A woman was next to speak. She lived near the beach, she said, and had been standing at the door of her cottage waiting for the return of the fishermen about an hour before she heard of the discovery of the body. She, too, had seen a boat with only one man in it. She repeated that the boat had pushed off from the same part of the shore where the body of the man was afterwards found.

The woman whose house had been used confirmed the account of the fishermen bringing the body into her home. The body was not cold, she said, and they had put it on a bed, and rubbed it. Nugent had gone to town for the doctor, but he, too, was unsuccessful in reviving the unfortunate victim.

Several other men contributed their observations regarding my arrival, all of them confirming that with the strong north wind the night before it was probable I had sailed against it for a few hours after depositing the body and then returned to the local harbour for refuge. They all added that it appeared I had brought the body from another place. They said it seemed I did not know the coastline and might have entered the harbour without understanding that it was near the place where I had left the corpse.

Mr. Kirwin, on hearing the evidence, said that I should be taken into the room where the body lay in preparation for burial so that they could observe what effect the sight of it had on me. The idea had probably come to the man when he saw how agitated I was upon hearing the cause of death. I was thus accompanied by the judge and several others to the inn. I could not help but notice the series of strange coincidences that had taken place overnight, but knowing I had been on my island back in the Orkneys talking to my neighbours at around the time the body had been found, I felt little worry about the result of the whole affair.

I entered the room where the deceased lay, and was accompanied to the coffin. How can I describe what I felt upon seeing the dead man's face? Even now, my heart freezes; even now, my body begins to shake. All recollection of the recent proceedings and of the judge and witnesses vanished; I was left gasping for breath. The body on the table was that of Henry Clerval. I threw myself on his lifeless form, and said, "Have my murderous doings deprived you also, my dearest Henry, of your time on earth? Two others are already destroyed, and surely other victims await their destiny as well. But you, my protector, my brother—"

The human form has limits to what it can endure, and I presently had to be carried from the room after collapsing in painful convulsions.

Next came a fever. I wavered near the point of death for two months. I was later told that my ravings had been terrifying. I identified myself as the murderer of William, Justine, and Clerval. At various junctures, I begged those who cared for me to assist in destroying the fiend who was tormenting me. At other times, I felt the monster's powerful fingers grasp my neck, and screamed aloud. Thankfully, as I was speaking in my native tongue, none but Mr. Kirwin understood anything I said. Still, my gestures and pained cries were enough to frighten everyone who observed them.

Why could I not have died then? I was more miserable than any individual who had ever lived. The forgetfulness and rest of death would have been the sweetest deliverance. There is no justice in the world! Death snatches away blooming children— the only hopes of their adoring parents. It sends brides and young lovers to the tomb who have good lives awaiting them. What kind of perverse strength did I possess that I could endure so many shocks, which, like the turning of some invisible wheel, kept renewing my torture?

Alas, I was doomed to live. After two months of ranting, I awakened as though from a dream and found myself on a wretched bed in the local prison. I was surrounded by jailers of various ranks and hemmed in by oaken doors, bolts, and all the miserable equipment of a dungeon. I remember that it was morning; it took me some moments to get my bearings. I forgot, initially, the details of what had landed me in this place. I had a vague sense that a terrible misfortune had befallen me. However, when I looked around and saw the barred windows and squalid conditions of the room, the whole awful history flashed across my memory, and I uttered an anguished groan.

The sound disturbed an old woman sleeping in a chair next to my bed. She was a hired nurse, and the wife of one of the jailers. Her face was anything but elegant, its lines hard and rude, as happens when a person witnesses misery day after day. Her tone of voice expressed a complete lack of concern for my well-being. She spoke to me in English, and I realized that I had heard her voice during the course of my sufferings.

"Are you better, sir?" she said.

I replied quietly, my voice badly weakened.

"I believe I am," I said. "But if everything I remember is true, I am sorry I am still alive to feel this misery and horror."

"If you mean about the gentleman that you murdered," she said, "I believe it were better for you if you were dead. I fancy it will go hard with you, for you will be hanged when the next circuit court session is held, not that it is any of my business. I was hired to nurse you, to get you well, and I perform my work with a clear conscience. If only everyone did the same."

I looked away. It was beyond me how some one could make so unfeeling a speech to a man just back from the brink of death. I was feeling dizzy, and lost the ability to reflect on all that had happened. My life presented itself to me as a dream. I could hardly believe that the events were all true, for they never seemed to hold the weight of reality.

As images floated before my mind's eye and slowly grew more distinct, I became feverish. Darkness pressed in on me. There was no one near me to soothe me with a gentle voice, no affectionate hand to support me. The doctor came and prescribed medicines, which, with a sour look on her face, the nurse prepared. No one was interested in the fate of a murderer, with the possible exception of the hangman, who would soon be paid.

These were my thoughts on an uncomfortable, grim morning. But I soon learned that Mr. Kirwin had shown great kindness. This untidy and unpleasant room was by far the best the prison had to offer, and it was the judge who had insisted I be kept in it under the care of a physician and a nurse. While it is true that the judge seldom came to see me himself, it was clear that it was in his nature to relieve the sufferings of every human creature. But that did not mean he wished to witness the agonies and ravings of a murderer. He would therefore visit the prison occasionally to make sure I was not being neglected, but stay only briefly.

One day, as I continued my slow recovery, I was taken over by despair. Seated in a chair with my eyes half open and my cheeks sunken, I became determined to seek my own death. It would be preferable, clearly, to remaining in prison until I was acquitted, only to be returned to a world of endless sorrow. I considered giving a false confession, in order to be hung. Meanwhile, it occurred to me more than once that I was less innocent of Henry's murder than Justine had been of sweet William's. This was my line of thinking, when the door opened and Mr. Kirwin entered. His face reflected sympathy and compassion, and he pulled a chair close to mine and spoke to me in French.

"I fear this place must be quite shocking to you. Can I do anything to make you more comfortable?"

"Thank you, but I have barely noticed the conditions. At any rate, there is no earthly comfort to be had for me."

"I know that the sympathy of a stranger means less than that of some one whom you know. I also know that your misfortune weighs heavily on you. But you will, I hope, soon leave this place. For, certainly, evidence can be brought to free you from the criminal charge."

"That is the least of my concerns. I have become, by a course of strange events, the most miserable soul on earth. Persecuted and tortured as I am and have been, how can death be anything but a gift?"

"There have indeed been strange occurrences surrounding you of late. You were tossed upon this shore by a surprising accident. Though renowned for hospitality, this place became a hell for you from the start. Seized and charged with murder, the first sight you were met with was the body of your friend. He had been murdered in a terrible manner and put in your path by some fiend."

As Mr. Kirwin spoke, despite the fact that hearing about my circumstances made me upset, I also felt considerable surprise at the knowledge he seemed to possess concerning the facts of my situation. My face must have reflected this, for the judge quickly spoke again.

"It was not until a day or two into your illness that I thought to examine your clothing, to learn of any family you might have, and make them aware of your misfortune and illness. I located several letters, including one I saw was from your father. I wrote to Geneva immediately, but I see that you are shaking and that agitation of any kind is too much for you."

"The suspense is a thousand times worse than anything else could be. Tell me what new atrocity has taken place, and whose murder I am now to suffer."

"Your family is unharmed. And some one, a friend of yours, has come to see you."

I know not by what chain of thought the idea presented itself, but it instantly darted into my mind that the murderer had come to mock at my misery, and taunt me with the death of Clerval, as a new means of inducing me to comply with his hellish desires. I waved a hand before my eyes, and cried out in agony.

"Oh! take him away! I cannot see him; for God's sake, do not let him in here!"

Mr. Kirwin looked at me with a pained expression. There was no way for him to interpret my words as anything other than an expression of guilt. For the first time, he spoke to me in a truly severe tone.

"I would have thought, young man, that the presence of your father would be more welcome than this."

"My father?" I said, feeling every feature and every muscle relax from complete suffering to pure joy. "Has my father truly come? It is a miracle. Where is he—why does he not rush to my side?"

The judge noted my change of demeanour and showed pleasant surprise on his face. He likely imagined that my recent shouts were a brief return of the delirium, and he returned to his kindly manner; he stood, motioned to the nurse, and the two of them left the room. In a moment, my father entered.

There was nothing in the world that could have given me greater comfort than the arrival of my father. I stretched out my hand to him and cried, "Are you safe, then—and Elizabeth—and Ernest?"

My father calmed me with assurances that not only he but the others were perfectly safe and well. He did his best to raise my obviously low spirits by staying on these subjects so dear to my heart, but he soon realized that a prison cannot be a home to happiness of any kind.

"What a spot you have found to live in," he said, as he took in the barred windows and disheveled appearance of the room. "You left home in search of happiness, but ill fortune pursues you. And poor Henry!"

"Yes, it is true," I said. "An ugly destiny hangs over me; I am required to fulfill it, or else I would have died on Henry's coffin."

We were not permitted to talk long. My weakened state of mind made it clear every precaution needed to be taken to assist in my recovery; Mr. Kirwin came in and said I should not be allowed to be exhausted. In the end, though, the appearance of my father was like that of a guardian angel, and I slowly regained my health.

As my physical sickness waned, a bleak melancholy took its place. The image of Henry, as he was when I first saw his lifeless body, was always in my mind. More than once, my dark mood gave the judge and my father reason to dread a dangerous relapse of my delirium. Why did these people conspire to preserve so miserable a life? They were but instruments, perhaps, making it possible for me to fulfill my destiny as my life drew to its close. Soon now, though, very soon, death will end my misery, and relieve me of the oppressive weight of anguish that is carrying me towards the dust. After I belatedly deliver justice for all that has taken place, I will finally be granted rest. But during this time of convalescence at the jail, death, although constantly in my thoughts, seemed far away. I would sit motionless and silent for hours, hoping for an epic cataclysm to bury me and my creation under its weight.

The circuit court session was fast approaching. I had by this time spent three months in prison. Although I remained weak and in danger of relapse, I was required to travel nearly a hundred miles to the county seat, where the court was held. Mr. Kirwin had collected witnesses and also prepared my defence. In the end, the case never got past the grand jury. When the members of this panel heard the evidence establishing that I had been on one of the Orkney Islands at the time that the body of my friend was found, they declined to send such a weak case to the court.

A couple of weeks afterwards, I was pronounced innocent and released from prison.

My father was overjoyed that I could breathe fresh air again, that I was free to return to my native country; but I could not share his joy. For me, the walls of a dungeon and those of a palace were equally constraining. The cup of life had been poisoned forever. Yes, the sun again shone down on me as it did on people brimming with life, but I could see nothing around me except an awful darkness, through which two eyes glared at me. Sometimes, these were the expressive eyes of Henry, as they appeared in death, the dark orbs nearly covered by his eyelids and long black lashes. Other times, they were the watery, yellow eyes of the monster, as I had first seen them in my chamber at Ingolstadt.

My father tried to awaken feelings of affection within me. He spoke often of Geneva, which I would soon be visiting, and of Elizabeth and Ernest. But his words only drew deep groans from me. Sometimes, I felt a yearning for happiness, and I thought of my beloved cousin with melancholy delight. At other moments, I felt a consuming homesickness and yearned to see the blue lake and rapid Rhone that had been so precious to me in childhood.

My general state of feeling was numbness, in which a prison was as inviting a residence as the most exquisite scene in nature. The weight of my thoughts was staggering, with the only interruptions being surges of remorse and fear. I had by now begun to make attempts on my own life; it took vigilance on the part of my father and others to prevent me from accomplishing my goal.

When I had left the prison, one of the guards said something to another which I overheard. "He may not have committed this murder," the man said, "but he certainly has a bad conscience."

I felt my heart sink still lower upon hearing the guard's words. He had no doubt observed the awareness I felt of guilt for the horrible deaths of William, Justine, and Henry, who had all died as the result of my actions and decisions. "And whose death will complete the tragedy?" I cried. "Ah! my father, do not remain in this wretched country. Take me where I can forget myself, my existence, and all the world."

My father happily performed the service I requested. After a courtesy visit to Mr. Kirwin, whom we thanked, we travelled as quickly as we could to Dublin. Once there, I felt relieved of a great burden, all the more when our packet ship sailed for England. I was leaving forever a country that had been to me a scene of profound misery.

At midnight, with my father asleep in our cabin, I lay on the deck looking at the stars, and listened to the splashing of the waves. As Ireland passed from view in the darkness, my pulse beat with a barely remembered joy. Soon I would be in Geneva. The past appeared to me to be a kind of nightmare, but the ship bearing me, the wind pushing us, and the surrounding sea told me beyond doubt that I was neither waking from, nor living, a dream. My extraordinary friend had fallen victim to me and the monster of my creation. I turned over in my memory the course of my life, starting with the simple happiness I had known as a child in Geneva. Next came the death of my mother, and my departure for university. I remembered with a shudder the fever that had driven me to create my hideous enemy in Ingolstadt and the terrifying night he had come to life. That was as far as I could go with my thoughts. Waves of feeling pressed in on me, and I wept for some time; when the last stifled sob had passed, I returned to the cabin.

Ever since I had come out of my delirium I had been in the

habit of taking a small quantity of laudanum to get to sleep. Only by means of this drug was I able to rest enough to function at all, or even to stay alive. Sickened by the recollection of my hideous experiences, on this night I took a double dose and soon fell into a deep sleep. But the sleep did not provide any rest from misery. My dreams were their own form of torture; they were incredibly vivid and populated by a thousand horrifying sights. Towards dawn, there was one final nightmare, during which I felt the grasp of the fiend's fingers around my neck and was unable to free myself. My screams were ringing in my ears when my father woke me and gestured towards the porthole. Glancing through it, I saw the harbour at Holyhead, which our ship was now entering.

Chapter V

My father and I had decided to bypass London in favour of Portsmouth and to embark from there for Havre. I preferred this plan mostly because the prospect of revisiting places where I had enjoyed good moments with Henry was unbearable. I also preferred not to encounter the people whom we had spent time with together, for they would inevitably ask about his whereabouts, the mere idea of which made me relive the horror I felt looking upon my friend's body on the night of my arrival in Ireland.

As for my father, his hopes revolved around seeing me restored to health and a better state of mind. His tenderness and attentions were never ending. Even though my gloom and grief were obstinate, he refused to believe my condition was hopeless. It was his theory that answering a charge of murder had made me despise myself. And he strove to establish to me the wasteful nature of pride.

"Alas, my father," I said, "you overestimate me by considering me to be capable of pride—my condition allows me no such indulgences. Justine was as innocent as myself, suffered the same charge, and died for it, but it is I who was her murderer. And I was the murderer of William and Henry, no less."

My father had heard me say such things before the circuit court session had taken place. On some of these occasions he appeared

212

to need an explanation, and on others he took it as a symptom of my delirium. He seemed to presume that at some point during my incapacitation ideas like this had forced themselves into my imagination and that even during my convalescence they persisted as some form of reality to me. I avoided all explanations, and maintained my silence regarding my project at Ingolstadt. I knew with certainty that if I ever described the monster and how I had created him, I would be presumed insane. Fear of that made it easier to keep my awful secret to myself, although I would have given the world to tell some one. But now, on this occasion, my father did question me.

"What are you saying, Victor?" my father said. "Are you suffering from madness? You must not express such things again."

"I am not mad," I forcefully said. "The sun and the heavens, who have watched my whole life, can attest to that. I am the one responsible for the death of these good people. They died because of my actions. I would have shed my own blood to prevent it, but it was not possible, in the same way that it is likely not possible now for me to save the whole human race."

The last statement of mine especially convinced my father that I was less well mentally than he had wished to believe. He quickly changed the subject, and did his best to distract me from my line of thinking, making it his ambition to erase from my memory the scenes that had taken place in Ireland. He never alluded himself to what had happened there and would not allow me to speak of it, either.

As time passed, I became more calm. Misery maintained her dwelling in my heart, but I no longer spoke incoherently of my crimes. Remembering them silently was punishment enough. Through painful self-discipline, I ignored the voice within telling me to speak the grim truth to the whole world. My manners were becoming more composed than they had been at any time since my journey to the sea of ice above Chamounix.

We arrived at Havre on the 8th of May, and from there departed for Paris, where my father had business that would detain us a few weeks. In this city, I received the following letter from Elizabeth:

"To Victor Frankenstein.

"My dearest Friend,

"I was overjoyed to see the letter from my uncle dated at Paris! You are no longer a vast distance away, and it is possible I will see you within a couple of weeks! Dear cousin, how you must have suffered! I expect to see you looking even worse than when you left Geneva. The winter, in the absence of news from you, was spent in anxious suspense. Still, I hope that seeing your face will restore my hopes and let me know that you are as well as you can be.

"And yet I fear that the same reasons you had to leave will still be with you upon your return, or, worse, have grown stronger with time. I dislike bringing you a new worry when you have so much weighing on you, but I believe I owe you some explanation before we meet.

"What could I have to explain? you are no doubt wondering. Well, if this is indeed the case, then I am relieved, and I can probably just sign my letter your affectionate cousin and be done with it. But you are far from me, and it would be selfish not to bring this to you sooner rather than later. I have often wished to express this to you during your absence, but have never found the courage to begin.

"As you know, our marriage has been the favourite plan of

your parents since the two of us were small children. They told us about their idea when we were very young, and they taught us to look forward to it in the same way they did—as an absolute certainty. You and I were easy, affectionate playmates during childhood, and dear and valued friends to each other as we have gotten older. But just as brothers and sisters often feel a strong affection for each other without wishing for a more intimate bond, could not the same be true for us? Answer this one question I must bring to you in the name of our mutual happiness—Do you love another?

"You have travelled, and spent years of your life at Ingolstadt. I confess that when I last saw you, my friend, your grief and all the time you spent alone forced me to wonder if you regretted our connexion. I knew your sense of honour would lead you to do your parents' wishes, even if they ran counter to your own. But this is false reasoning. I confess that I love you and that when I have thought of a bright future it has always been with you by my side.

"Still, it is your happiness as well as my own which makes me say that I would be devastated if our marriage did not reflect the wishes of your heart. I loathe thinking it, but I have to wonder, too, if amid the suffering you have already known you are not using the word honour to stifle all hope of love and happiness for yourself? Please know that your cousin and playmate has too much affection for you not to be made miserable by this idea. Be happy, my friend! Honour your heart, whatever it may be telling you. If you obey me in this one request, nothing on earth will disturb my happiness again!

"Do not be upset by this letter. Do not answer it tomorrow, or the next day, or even before you come to Geneva. Your father will send me news of your health. If I see a smile on your lips when we meet, caused by this letter or anything else I have done, I will need no other happiness.

                                        "*Elizabeth Lavenza.*

"*Geneva, May 18th, 17—.*"

My cousin's letter brought to mind what I had only just managed to forget—the threat of my tormentor: *I will be with you on your wedding-night.* The penalty for my supposed crime against him was thus established. On the night of the greatest joy I was ever to have again, the demon would use his conniving intelligence to murder me, at last. On that night, of all nights, he would fulfill his ugliest passion through the death of his creator. If this was what he required, I was prepared to face it, and there would be a mortal struggle that would have a welcome end, either way. If he was victorious, then my suffering would have come to an end; if I were to survive the battle, then I would be a free man. Yes, it would be the same freedom known by a peasant who has seen his family massacred, his cottage burned to the ground, his lands ruined, and himself left homeless, penniless, and alone. It would be of that precise kind, but with one major exception. In Elizabeth, I had a treasure to see me through the rest of my time on earth, even if our love would be balanced by the remorse and guilt hounding me until death.

Sweet Elizabeth! I reread her letter more than once, and some softer feelings found their way into my heart. I dared to entertain a few dreams of love, of life as others knew it. But the apple of knowledge had already been eaten, and the angel's arm pointed away from what was to have been my heaven, though I would die to make Elizabeth happy. If the creature fulfilled his threat—*I will be with you on your wedding-night*—my death was all but inevitable. But I wondered if my wedding would bring about my demise any sooner than it otherwise would come. Then again, if my nemesis suspected that I was postponing getting married to escape his threat, he would surely find another, possibly even worse, way of exacting his revenge.

He had vowed to be present on my wedding-night, but that did not guarantee that he would maintain peace until that time. Henry's murder, immediately after the monster's threats, proved as much. I decided, therefore, that if getting married as soon as possible would add to my cousin's or my father's happiness then the fiend's threat would not be allowed to push it back by a single hour.

In this state of mind I wrote to Elizabeth. My letter was calm and affectionate. "I fear, my beloved girl," I said, "little happiness remains for us on earth. Yet whatever tiny bit of joy I may still experience is surely to be found in our shared life together. You can inform your pangs of selfless and courteous jealousy that you are the very center of my life, and I will focus from this moment forward on you alone. I do have one secret, Elizabeth, a dreadful one. When I share it with you, you will feel horror such as you have never known. Afterwards, instead of being confused for the reasons behind my sorrow, you will wonder how it is that I have survived this long. I will tell you everything on the day after our wedding, for there must be perfect trust between us. Until then, do not mention anything about it to anyone; I know that you will honour this request."

About a week after the arrival of Elizabeth's letter, my father and I arrived in Geneva. My cousin welcomed me with such great affection that I almost forgot the reality of my circumstances. But upon seeing my emaciated frame and feverish cheeks, tears came to her eyes. In her, there were changes as well. She, too, was thinner, and had lost some of the energy, and even a small portion of the charm, that had drawn me, and all others, to her since she first came to join our family. Still, her gentleness and tender glances made her a fitting companion for a man as broken down as I had become.

There was a period of peace upon my return, but it was not to last. Being in the location where a succession of grim events had occurred stirred my memory, and I could not keep myself from thinking of all that had happened. More than once, true insanity descended upon me. At times, I was furious, and fumed with rage; at other times, I was overcome with lethargy and sadness. I spoke to no one, avoiding all company, and was generally befuddled by the myriad sorrows hemming me in.

The only one with the ability to draw me out was Elizabeth. Her voice soothed me during my bouts of fury, and restored my hopes when I was seized by depression. When she knew that it would be the best thing for me, she wept with me, and for me. When I was clear-minded again, she would plead with me not to sink so deeply into mourning that I ceased to think of others. She said that resignation was no sin, and that I would need to find it within myself. I could not bring myself to tell her that resignation was fine for good people recovering from misfortune but that for those who are guilty it is no option. If indulging in grief to excess is occasionally satisfying for the bulk of humanity, my attacks of conscience were for me the purest poison.

Soon after our return to Geneva, my father spoke to me of the forthcoming wedding. Though in favour of Elizabeth's and my intention to marry as soon as possible, he wished to inquire about any secrets that might be troubling me.

"Is there another person, my son, to whom you have given hopes? Is there some other attachment?"

"Your fears are misplaced. I love Elizabeth, and am looking forward to my life with her. Let us, indeed, set the date! And I will commit myself, whether I live or die, to Elizabeth's lasting happiness."

"My precious son, do not talk this way. We have suffered grave misfortunes, but let us transfer our love for those we have lost to those who are still here. Our circle is smaller, but it is bound more securely than ever by the ties of affection and the experiences we have had. When your grief finally dissipates, new beloved faces will appear to replace those whom we have so painfully lost."

Such were the lessons of a supremely good man. But to me the remembrance of the threat returned; nor can you wonder that, with the fiend having been so effective in his bloody retribution to this point, I considered him to be invincible and his threat—*I will be with you on your wedding-night*—to be an unavoidable fate. Death held no fear for me, especially when I balanced it against the potential loss of Elizabeth. And so, in a more cheerful way than I would have thought possible, I agreed with my father that if Elizabeth would give her consent, the ceremony should take place in ten days. I was, as near as I could tell, signing my own death sentence.

God in heaven! If for a moment I had guessed the fiend's true intention, I would have fled my native country forever and wandered as a friendless outcast across the earth. But, as if he were in possession of magical powers, my creation had blinded me to his real intentions. While I believed myself to be pushing up the date of my own death, I was in fact hastening that of a far more innocent soul.

As the date of the wedding neared, either because of cowardice or some inkling of what was to come, I felt an icy grip upon my heart. I hid my feelings with boisterous displays of hilarity, which brought smiles to my elderly father, but failed to deceive the ever-observant Elizabeth. She appeared to be looking forward to our wedding with calm contentment, mixed with vague fear. She had seen too many hardships up close to count upon even what appeared to be certain happiness, which is what our wedding feast would normally have represented.

Preparations were made for the event; congratulatory visits were received; and all wore a smiling appearance. I shut up, as well as I could, in my own heart the anxiety that feasted there, and entered with seeming earnestness the plans of my father, although they might only serve as the decorations of my tragedy. An attractive home was bought for us in nearby Cologny, so we might enjoy the pleasures of the country, and still see my father every day; who would continue to live within the city walls, for the benefit of Ernest, so that he might follow his studies at the schools.

In the mean time I took every precaution to defend myself, in case the fiend should openly attack me. I carried pistols and a dagger constantly about me, and was ever on the watch for trickery the monster might employ in his attack, and by these means found a greater degree of tranquillity. Indeed, as the wedding day approached, it felt as though my creation's threat had been a nightmare, or perhaps a delusion, not to be regarded as worthy to disturb my peace, while the happiness I hoped for in my marriage was looking more likely by the hour; I heard so many people speaking to me about it so often, that I was coming to believe the future they described was no longer something that could be prevented.

Elizabeth seemed happy; my calm demeanour served greatly to calm her mind. But on the day that was to fulfill my wishes and my destiny, she was heavyhearted, and a sense of evil pervaded her; and perhaps also she thought of the dreadful secret, which I had promised to reveal to her the following day. My father was in the mean time overjoyed, and in the bustle of preparation, only saw in the muted sadness of his niece the agitation of a bride.

After the ceremony was performed, a large party assembled at my father's; but it was agreed that Elizabeth and I would pass the afternoon and night at Evian, and return to Cologny the next morning. As the day was fair, and the wind favourable, we decided to go by water.

Those were the last moments of my life during which I enjoyed the feeling of happiness. Sails filled, we rapidly moved across the surface of the lake; the sun was warm, though we were sheltered by a canopy and could enjoy the beauty of the scene in comfort. As we were spirited forward, we gazed upon Mont Salève, Montalègre, and, in the distance, rising above all, the beautiful Mont Blanc. After a time, we moved to the other side of the lake; there we could see the mighty Jura mountains, which had kept most who contemplated leaving Switzerland from attempting to do so, and had dissuaded any number of armies from attempting to conquer her.

I took the hand of Elizabeth: "You are sorrowful, my love," I said. "Ah! if you knew what I have suffered, and what I may still endure, you would let me taste the quiet, and freedom from despair, that this one day at least permits me to enjoy."

"Be happy, my dear Victor," replied Elizabeth. "I hope that I have done nothing to distress you. If joy is not on my face, know that my heart is at peace in this moment. Yes, there is within me a voice whispering I should not count on the prospect of our happiness, but I choose not to listen. Look how beautifully we are sailing, and at the clouds revealing and then hiding the top of Mont Blanc. Look at the fish swimming below us in the clear waters and the pebbles on the bottom glinting in the sunlight. What a heavenly day! how happy and peaceful all nature appears!"

In this way, Elizabeth sought to distract her thoughts and mine from the sorrows that still seemed close. But her mood was fluctuating; for a few moments, joy shone in her eyes, but soon it gave way to distraction and uncertainty.

The sun sunk lower in the heavens; we passed the river Drance, and observed its path through the higher, and the valleys of the lower hills. The Alps here come closer to the lake, and we approached the ampitheatre of mountains on the eastern shore. The spire at Evian shone under the woods that surrounded it, and the range of mountain above mountain by which it was overhung.

The wind, which had brought us here with amazing speed, sunk at sunset to a light breeze; the soft air just ruffled the water, and caused a pleasant motion among the trees as we approached the shore, from which it carried the delightful scent of flowers and hay. The sun sunk beneath the horizon as we landed; and as I touched the shore, I felt all those cares and fears come back to life, which soon were to grasp me, and cling to me for ever.

Chapter VI

It was eight o'clock when we landed; we walked a short time on the shore, enjoying the twilight, and then retired to the inn, and contemplated the lovely scene of waters, woods, and mountains, obscured in darkness, yet still displaying their black outlines.

From the inn we had watched the last wisps of the evening wind come down from the mountains south of the village and gently sweep the lake, moving away from us. Now, half an hour later, a violent west wind rose. The moon was at her zenith in the sky and was starting to descend. Clouds flew through the heavens with disorienting speed, now dimming the moon, now letting it shine bright, and the rough waters of the lake reflected the busy scene above; within minutes, the lake's waves were crowned in white, as the wind continued to rise. Suddenly, a heavy storm of rain descended.

I had been calm during the day; but the moment night obscured the shapes of objects, a thousand fears rose in my mind. I was anxious and watchful, while my right hand grasped a pistol which was hidden in my vest; every sound terrified me; but I was determined not to sell my life other than dearly, and not to be distracted from the impending conflict until my own life, or that of my adversary, were extinguished.

Elizabeth observed my agitation for some time in timid and

fearful silence; at length, she said, "What is it you are worried about, my dear Victor? What is it you fear?"

"We are safe here, my love," I said. "The night is merely dreadful, that is all."

I passed an hour in this state of wariness; then I thought of how horrifying the combat, expected any moment, would be for Elizabeth. I politely but firmly asked that she make herself comfortable in the room, knowing I could never join her until I had at least determined something about the whereabouts and intention of my enemy.

She left me, leaving me to walk up and down the passages of the inn and inspect every corner my adversary might use as a hiding place from which to launch an attack. But I found no trace of him. I was beginning to imagine that my luck had changed for the better and that something had prevented him from fulfilling his awful threats when I heard a piercing and terrible scream. It had come from the room where Elizabeth had just gone for the night. The moment I heard the sound, the whole truth rushed into my mind. My arms dropped to my sides, and I found that I was rooted to the floor. I could feel the blood moving through my veins and tingling in my hands and feet. The paralysis lasted only an instant, and then the scream was repeated. I rushed into the room.

God in heaven! Why could I not have died then? I have been left to describe the destruction of the finest soul on earth. My pure and beautiful wife was there, lifeless and inanimate, tossed across the bed, her head hanging down, her pale, distorted features halfway covered by her long hair. Everywhere I turn, to this day, I see the same thing: her bloodless arms and splayed form, flung by the murderer onto our bridal bed. Could I see this and live? Sadly, the life force is stubborn, and holds on the most tightly where it is the most loathed. Without warning, I fainted.

When I awoke, I was surrounded by people from the inn. On the faces of the staff and guests was the horror appropriate to the situation, but it was a faint shadow of the feelings inside me. I stole myself away from their murmuring midst and escaped to the room where Elizabeth's body still lay, closing the door behind me. She was no longer in the same position as when I found her. She had been composed, with her head upon her arm and a handkerchief placed across her face and neck. I could almost imagine that she was sleeping, and I rushed to the bed and held her close in my arms, but her body was cold and lifeless. My love, my wife, my Elizabeth, was gone. The murderous marks of my creation's fingers were on her neck; no breath came from her lips.

As I bent over her in an agony of despair, I happened to look towards the window. The shutters had been closed hours before, leaving the windows darkened, but now I saw pale yellow moonlight streaming into the room, and felt a shiver of panic. The shutters had been pulled back from the outside, and I realized, with horror that words could never describe, that I was seeing the frightful beast himself. His grinning face was framed by the window, and he pointed with a long, mocking finger at the body of my wife. I rushed towards the window, drew my pistol, and fired; but he ducked to elude the bullet, leapt from his perch, and, running with the speed of lightning across the grounds, plunged into the lake.

The sound of the pistol shot brought a crowd to the room. I pointed towards the spot where he had disappeared, and we followed the murderer's track to the water's edge, where we climbed into boats. We cast nets for him, but pulled up nothing. After several hours, we returned to the inn, demoralized. Most members of the search party believed that I had seen not the murderer, but only a figment of my imagination. With all again on dry land, new search parties headed off in various directions to hunt in the woods, but I did not go out with them. I was weary, and blinded by tears, my skin hot with fever. I lay on a bed, barely aware of the night's proceedings, with my eyes wandering around the room, as if seeking something I had lost.

After some time, I realized that my father would expect the return of both Elizabeth and myself the next day, and that I would have to return alone. This understanding brought more tears to my eyes, and I wept for a time. While I did, my mind touched on a series of subjects. I reflected on my various misfortunes, and their causes, making sense of very little of it. Indeed, my ideas were cloudier than ever. Wonder and horror vied for my attention, with neither gaining a clear advantage. After the murder of William, the execution of Justine, the hunting down and killing of Henry, and the vicious strangling of my wife, I had no way of knowing whether my remaining friends and family were safe. My father's throat might even now be in the creature's grasp, and Ernest could be lying dead at his feet. These thoughts made me shudder, and snapped me back to action. I stood, collected myself, and resolved to return to Geneva as fast as I could.

I would have preferred to travel by horse, but there were none to be had. I would need to return by water. The wind was not advantageous, and the rain was coming down in torrents. In my favour, it was just past midnight, and I could hope to arrive before dawn. I hired men to row and took an oar for myself, for it had always given me peace to perform physical exercise; but, in the end, my abundance of misery and nervous strain left me incapable of rowing. I threw down the oar, and, leaning my head upon my hands, allowed each gloomy thought arising to carry me where it would. Whenever I looked up, I saw scenes familiar to me from happier times and which I had experienced just the day before with Elizabeth by my side. Now she was but a shadow and a memory. Tears streamed from my eyes. The rain had stopped, and I saw fish shimmering in the waters as they had only hours before; but then they had been seen by Elizabeth. Perhaps nothing is so painful to the human spirit as sudden and profound change. The sun could shine or dark clouds build, but never would anything look the same as it had on the way to Evian with my new bride by my side. A fiend had snatched every hope of happiness from me at the moment that I most hoped to taste it. No man had ever been so wretched as I was then, for no other events as frightening had ever been experienced.

There is no reason to spend much time describing the incidents that followed this last tragedy in my life. My story, I know, has been a tale of horror which has now reached its peak. What I have left to tell will inevitably be tedious for you. But I must at least admit that, one by one, my remaining loved ones were murdered by the fiend. I was left like a castaway, desolate and alone. My strength is now nearly gone, and yet I must somehow give breath to what remains of my sorrowful tale.

I arrived in Geneva. My father and Ernest still lived, but my father collapsed beneath the weight of the tidings that I brought him. I see him still in my mind's eye—excellent and venerable man! His eyes moved from object to object without seeing; the last animating spark for his vision, his more than daughter, had been lost. Here was a creature whom my gray-haired father doted on with all the affection a man can feel in his declining years, when fewer ties bind him to the world, and those that remain take on greater meaning. How I still curse the fiend that brought misery on my father, dooming him to spend his remaining time on earth in wretchedness! He could not live amidst the horrors that had accumulated around him. A stroke was brought on by the nervous strain, and a few days later he died in my arms.

As to what then became of me, I know next to nothing. I lost sensation, and eventually felt chains and darkness pressing in on me. Sometimes, I dreamt that I was wandering across a meadow or traversing a valley with the friends of my youth, but I inevitably awoke and found myself in a dungeon. The deepest mourning of my life followed, and very slowly I gained a picture of what I had gone through and of my current situation. I was, in the end, released from my prison. How had I found my way there? The people of Geneva had, fairly enough, considered me insane and confined me in a solitary cell.

Having my liberty returned to me would have been a useless gift had I not, awakening to reason, also awakened to revenge. As the clearer memory of past misfortunes pressed in on me, I began to think about their cause—the monster I had created, a miserable demon whom I had foolishly sent into the world, and who was still roaming free. I became possessed by sickening rage when I pictured him, yearning, indeed fervently praying, that I would successfully hunt and kill him.

My hate soon evolved beyond this purely imaginative phase. I began to plot ways of deceiving, trapping, and killing the monster. About a month after my release, I sought out a criminal judge in the town, and told him that I had an accusation to make; I told him that I knew the identity of the one who had destroyed my family; and that I required him to do everything in his power to arrest the murderer.

The magistrate listened to me with attentiveness and kindness: "I assure you," he said, "that we will go to all lengths to find and apprehend the villain."

"I thank you," I replied. "Listen, therefore, to the account that I have to make. It is indeed a tale so strange, that I would fear you would not believe it, were there not something in truth which, however astonishing, compels belief. The story is too connected to be mistaken for a dream, and I have no motive for falsehood." My manner, as I spoke, was serious and calm. I had by now committed myself to pursuing my enemy to death, and this knowledge quieted my sorrowful rage sufficiently for me to attend to the details of my life. I provided the judge my history with both firmness and precision, noting the dates with accuracy, and never allowing myself to speak with an excess of emotion.

The magistrate appeared completely skeptical, for a time; but as I continued he became more attentive and interested; more than once I saw him shudder with horror; other times I saw on his face great surprise, unmingled with disbelief.

When I had finished my narration, I said, "This is the being whom I accuse, and for whose detection and punishment I call upon you to exert your whole power. It is your duty as a magistrate, and I believe and hope that your feelings as a man will not lead you to hesitate on this occasion."

Although my listener had shown signs of believing much of what I told him, now that he was being called upon to act officially, the full force of his doubt took hold of him. "I would happily help you," he said mildly, "but the creature you describe appears to have powers which would render my exertions futile. Who can track down an animal which can traverse a glacier, and hide in caves and dens, where no human being would dare enter? Besides, months have passed since he committed his most recent crime; and it is impossible to know where he may be hiding today."

"I do not doubt that he still stalks me; and if he has taken refuge in the Alps, he may be hunted like a mountain goat, and killed like any other beast of prey. Unfortunately, I see in your glance that you do not intend to pursue my enemy, nor to punish him as he deserves."

As I spoke, rage sparkled in my eyes; the magistrate was intimidated. "You are mistaken," said he, "I will exert myself, and if it is in my power to seize the monster, then he will suffer the punishment proportionate to his crimes. But I fear from what you have described in terms of his traits and abilities that no effort of mine will be sufficient to bring him to justice, and that, therefore, you should strive to prepare yourself for disappointment."

"I can never accept his going free; you indicate that you will pursue him, and I thank you for that. While my revenge is of little concern to you, it is the only passion left to me, and I acknowledge I am devoured by it, even though I know it to be a sin. My rage is unspeakable, when I consider that the murderer, whom I set loose in society, still lives. You refuse my just demand: I have but one resource; and I devote myself, whether I live or die, to his destruction."

I was shaking with excess of emotion as I said this. My demeanour had become a frenzied, haughty fierceness, of the kind the martyrs of old are said to have had. But to a Genevan magistrate, whose mind revolved around things other than devotion to cause and heroism, the way I spoke and held myself looked very much like madness. He strove to pacify me, as a nurse does a young child, telling me that the delirium I had recently suffered was responsible for what I thought I had experienced.

"Man," I cried, "you have no idea how ignorant you are, puffed up by your pride in your own wisdom. You do not even understand what you are saying."

I fled the house angry and disturbed, and returned home to meditate on some other mode of action.

Chapter VII

My present situation was one in which all voluntary thought was swallowed up and lost. I was hurried away by fury; revenge alone provided me with strength and composure; it dictated my feelings, and allowed me to be calculating and calm, when otherwise madness or death would have been my fate.

My first resolution was to leave Geneva forever; my country, which, when I was happy and beloved, was dear to me, now, in my adversity, became hateful. I provided myself with a sum of money, together with a few jewels which had belonged to my mother, and departed.

And now my wanderings began, which are to end only when my life ends. I have made my way across the earth, and have experienced every hardship which travellers, in unpopulated wastelands and barbaric countries, typically meet. How I have survived I hardly know; many times I have stretched my failing limbs on the ground and prayed for death, but revenge kept me alive. I instinctively feared dying, while my foe still breathed.

When I set forth from Geneva, my first priority was to find a trace of my enemy, but I had no real plan. I wandered for hours around the edge of town, unable to decide which path to follow. As night approached, I found myself at the entrance of the cemetery where William, Elizabeth, and my father reposed. I went in and approached the tomb enclosing their graves.

Everything was silent, except for the gently rustling leaves on the trees, which the evening breeze now and then stirred. The sky had gone violet, and the scene around me was pitch dark; even a stranger with no dead buried in this place would have felt it to be solemn and touching. Spirits of the departed seemed to flit through the air, and to cast shadows over my head.

What started as grief and hopelessness for me in this sorrowful place quickly gave way to rage. Those I loved were dead; I, meanwhile, was alive. My loved ones' murderer lived as well, and to destroy him I had to continue my woeful existence. I knelt on the grass, kissed the ground, and exclaimed, "By the sacred earth on which I kneel, by the souls that wander near me, by the deep and everlasting grief I feel, I swear; and by you, O Night, and by the spirits that preside over you, I swear to pursue the demon who caused this misery until one of us dies in mortal combat. For this purpose I will spare my own life; solely to exact this precious revenge I will again behold the sun rise, and tread the green grass of the earth, which otherwise should disappear from my eyes for ever. I call on you, spirits of the dead, and on you, wandering ministers of vengeance, to assist and guide me in this work. Let the hellish and cursed monster drink deep of agony; let him feel the despair that torments me.

I had begun my petition solemnly, awestruck, certain that my murdered friends' souls heard and approved of my devotion, but towards the end of my dark prayer, rage choked the words in my throat.

I was answered through the soft night air by a loud, fiendish laugh. It rung among the headstones after it was made; the mountains re-echoed it, and it seemed as though hell itself mocked me with laughter from all directions. Surely I would have taken my own life then, had my vows not been heard; I was being kept alive for vengeance. The laughter died away. Familiar and vile, a voice by my ear spoke in a whisper—"I am satisfied, miserable wretch! you have elected to live, and I am satisfied."

I leapt in the direction of these sounds, but the one making them eluded me. At that moment, the disk of the moon lifted above the horizon and shone upon his monstrously distorted shape, as he fled with more than mortal speed.

I pursued him; and for many months this has been my task. Guided by a slight clue, I followed the Rhone into France, crossing the country's southern half, but in vain. The blue Mediterranean appeared, and by a strange chance I saw the creature hide himself in a vessel bound for the Black Sea. I took passage on the same ship; but he escaped, I know not how.

I followed his trail through the wilds of Tartary and Russia, but he eluded me at every turn. Sometimes the peasants, scared by this horrifying apparition, informed me of his path; sometimes he himself, who feared that if I lost all trace I would despair and die, left some mark to guide me. The snows descended on my head, and I saw the print of his huge step on the white plain. To you first entering on life, how can you understand what I have felt, and still feel? Cold, hunger, and fatigue were the least pains that I was destined to endure. I had been cursed by some devil, and carried around with me my own everlasting hell; yet still some competing spirit of good followed and directed my steps, and when I found myself babbling in exhaustion, this spirit would extricate me from insurmountable difficulties. Hunger could have brought the end of my life, but at such times a humble meal was left for me in the wilderness. The rustic food was akin to what the local peasants ate, but I have no doubt that it was put in my path by the spirits whose names I invoked. It also happened when I was parched by terrible thirst and the sky was an unbroken blue, that a single cloud would darken the heavens, shed the few drops I needed to survive, and vanish.

When I could, I followed the courses of the rivers. Conversely, the demon avoided these, as it was near rivers that the population was the most concentrated. At times, I went long periods without seeing another human being; and I generally subsisted on wild animals that crossed my path. I had money with me, and made friends with the villagers by giving small amounts to them. I also made a point of offering them the game I had killed, once I had taken a small portion for myself. I always gave the best parts to those who had provided me with fire and utensils for cooking.

As the trek unfolded in this way, each day was hateful. Only during sleep could I taste joy. Dear God—the sanctuary that sleep can provide! Sometimes, when I was at my most miserable, I would lie down and let my dreams transport me to a state of rapture. My guardian spirits created these hours for me, so that brief tastes of happiness would give me the strength to continue my pilgrimage. Without these moments, I would not have survived. Through the course of a day, the promise of my dreams later that night gave me the strength to put one foot in front of the other; I knew that in sleep I would see my friends, my wife, and my beloved country; again, I would see the kindly face of my father, hear the gentle tones of Elizabeth's voice, and observe Henry enjoying health and youth. In the midst of my most exhausting marches, I convinced myself that it was the suffering that was a dream, and eagerly awaited the night to be restored to the reality of being in the warm embrace of my loved ones. The longing I felt for those who were gone caused me no end of torment. I hung on to my memory of them so tightly that at times during my waking hours I perceived them around me, as you are with me now. When this happened, the vengeance burning within me was quieted. On such occasions, I continued my quest to destroy the creature, but more to satisfy heaven than to quench my need for revenge. It seemed to me that my feet were carrying me forward of their own accord, spurred by forces that I did not fully understand.

I had no way of knowing the feelings of the demon that I pursued; but sometimes, indeed, he left marks in writing on the barks of the trees, or cut in stone, that guided me, and renewed my fury. "My reign is not yet over," (these words were legible in one of these inscriptions); "you live, and my power is complete. Follow me. I am going to the frozen wilds of the north. There, you will feel the misery of cold and frost, and I will feel no pain. I have left a dead hare for you nearby. If you are not too far behind me, you will find it. Eat, and be refreshed. Come on, my enemy; we have yet to wrestle for our lives, but you will first have to endure many hard and miserable days, until the hour shall arrive."

Scoffing devil! Again, I vow vengeance. I will torture and kill you! I will not stop my pursuit until either you or I breathe no more. And then what ecstasy it will be when I join Elizabeth! I know as well that some others are preparing the reward for my hideous pilgrimage.

As I tracked him northward, the snows deepened and the cold grew unbearable, forcing even the hardy peasants to shut themselves up in their crude huts. Only a few of them fared forth to hunt animals whom starvation had forced from their hiding places in search of prey. The rivers were covered with ice so thick that fishing was impossible. I had, until then, relied on fish as my chief source of sustenance, and I now grew weak and hungry.

The glee and triumph of my enemy increased as the hardships

I went through worsened. One inscription that he left was in these words: "Prepare! your work is only beginning! Wrap yourself in furs and gather what food you can, for we are soon going on a journey where your sufferings will satisfy my everlasting hatred."

My courage and perseverance were invigorated by these scoffing words; I resolved not to fail in my purpose; and, calling on heaven to support me, I continued with utmost passion to traverse immense reaches of uninhabited land, until the ocean appeared at a distance, and formed the utmost boundary of the horizon. Oh! how unlike it was to the blue seas of the south! Covered with ice, it could only be distinguished from land by its greater wildness and ruggedness. The Greeks wept for joy when they beheld the Mediterranean from the hills of Asia, and shouted with rapture upon the end of their exile and hardship. I did not weep; but I knelt down, and, with a full heart, thanked my guiding spirit for getting me to the place where, despite the taunt left by my adversary, I hoped to meet and grapple with him at last.

Some weeks before this period, I had obtained a sled and dogs. My progress over the snows had been achieved with utmost speed. Whether the creature had travelled in like fashion I did not know; but where previously I had slowly lost ground to him, now I was gaining on him, so much so that, when I first saw the ice-jumbled sea, he was only one day's journey ahead of me. I hoped to overtake him before he reached the beach. With all the more passion, therefore, I pressed on, and in two days I arrived at a woeful village of some dozen huts along the seashore. I asked the inhabitants about the fiend, and they gave me important information. A gigantic monster, they said, had arrived after midnight the night before, armed with a rifle and several pistols. He scared away the inhabitants of a solitary cottage with his horrifying appearance. He had helped himself to their supply of winter food, and, placing it on a sled, seized a number of trained dogs, harnessed them, and, the same night, to the joy of the horror-struck villagers, pursued his journey across the sea in a direction that led to no land; and they estimated that he must speedily be destroyed by the breaking of the ice, or frozen by the eternal frosts.

My first response to the news was a rush of discouragement. He had escaped me; and I faced a destructive and almost endless journey across the mountainous ices of the ocean—amidst cold that few inhabitants could long endure, and which I, the native of a forgiving and sunny climate, could not hope to survive. Yet the notion that the creature would live, and triumph, caused my rage and desire for vengeance to come roaring back. All other thoughts were cast aside. After a few hours of rest, during which the spirits of the dead hovered round, and urged me to finish what I had begun, I began preparing for my final journey.

I exchanged my land sled for one made to withstand the unevenness of the frozen ocean, and, having bought a supply of provisions, I departed from land.

I cannot guess how many days have passed since then; but I have endured misery, which nothing but the hope of delivering just vengeance burning within my heart could have allowed me to endure. Immense and rugged mountains of ice often greatly slowed my passage, and I often heard the thunder of the ground sea, which threatened my destruction. But then the frost returned, and made the paths of the sea secure.

Judging by the quantity of provision which I had consumed, I should guess that I had spent three weeks in this journey; and the continual postponement of hope, returning back upon the heart, often wrung bitter drops of grief and despondency from my eyes. Despair had almost claimed her prey when my poor dogs carried me with extreme effort up a steep ice mountain, with one of the courageous animals dying from the effort at the top. I nearly died with him, from heartbreak, viewing the empty expanse below, but just then my eye caught a dark speck among the gathering shadows. I strained my eyesight to discover what I was seeing, and then screamed in ecstasy when I distinguished a sled, and the distorted proportions of a well-known form within. Oh! with what a burning gush did hope revisit my heart! warm tears filled my eyes, which I hastily wiped away so they would not intercept the view I had of the demon; but still my sight was dimmed by the burning drops, until, giving way to the emotions that oppressed me, I wept aloud.

But this was not the time for delay; I untethered the remaining dogs from their dead companion, gave them a good portion of food, and, after an hour's rest, which I hated every minute of but which could not be avoided, I continued my route. The sled was still visible; nor did I again lose sight of it, except at the moments when for a short time some ice rock concealed it with its inter-vening crags. Indeed I imperceptibly gained on it; and when, after nearly two days' journey, I saw my enemy at no more than a mile distant, my heart leapt.

But now, when I appeared almost within grasp of my enemy, my hopes were suddenly extinguished, and I lost all trace of him more completely than I ever had before. There was a deep moaning and then a loud crashing within the ice, as a ground sea developed, causing great movements beneath the ice and a terrifying thunder to sound. The wind rose; the sea roared; and with the violence of a mighty earthquake the ice split and cracked all around us. A tumultuous sea rolled between the monster and me, and I was left drifting, on an iceberg that continually grew smaller, with the knowledge that a hideous death would be mine soon.

I passed many hours in this condition; several of the dogs died, and I was about to sink under the weight of accumulated distress, when to my amazement I spied your ship riding at anchor. Until then, I had no idea that ships came so far north, and I was stunned by the sight of your mast. I quickly destroyed part of my sled to make oars and with them was able, as I fought the most profound exhaustion, to move my ice raft in the direction of your ship. I had decided that if you were travelling towards the south I would trust myself to the mercy of the seas, although it was my hope to persuade you to provide me with a boat with which to chase the monster. But you and your crew were travelling northward! I was soon pulled on board, just as I had expended the last of my energy. I was surely within minutes of death, which I still dread, as my life remains unfulfilled.

Oh! when will my guiding spirit, which has brought me so near the demon, give me the rest that my soul craves? Or will I die, after all, while he lives? If I do, you must swear that you will not let him escape! You must swear to chase him, Captain Walton, and to bring justice on his head. Am I so selfish as to ask you to take on my somber pilgrimage and endure the kinds of cruel hardships I have known? In the end, I am not. But after I am dead, if he should appear before you, if the spirits of divine vengeance should bring him straight to you, you must promise me you will kill him! You must swear by all that is good that he will not taste victory after watching me endure this sequence of hardships, and live to make another pitiful shell of a person as I have become. He is eloquent and persuasive, and at one time his words had power over my own heart, but do not trust him. His soul, in the end, is no less hellish than his outward form, full of treachery and malice. Do not listen to his pleas! Instead, call upon the spirits of William, Justine, Henry, Elizabeth, my father, and my tortured self—and thrust your sword into his heart. I will hover near and direct the steel where it must go.

Walton continues, in his own words.
August 26th, 17—.

You have read this fascinating and bizarre tale, my sister. Did it make your blood run cold, as it does mine even now? At times, in sudden agony, Frankenstein could not continue his story; at others, his voice broken, yet piercing, he dislodged the painful words from his throat by force of will. His intelligent eyes fluctuated between the light of righteous indignation and a chilling darkness, the likes of which I had never seen. On certain occasions, regaining his strength for a short period, he described the most horrifying events as though he were reading from the description of a country garden. On others, the words came forth like a volcano in full eruption, his face taking on the wildest rage, as he screamed out insults against the monster.

His tale possessed a strong logic, as well as the ring of truth, but it was the letters of Felix and Safie, which he showed me, and the sight of the distant giant from on board our ship that convinced me, more than anything he said, of what he had gone through. The beast is no figment of his imagination. I sometimes asked him to tell me more about how he had made the monster, but he would not hear of it.

"Are you mentally unwell, my friend?" he said. "Have you not heard where curiosity leads in a case such as this? Would you create for yourself, and for the world, a monstrous enemy? Why else would you ask me such a thing? Hush—I am begging you, learn from my suffering, and make no effort to increase your own."

When Frankenstein learned that I had been keeping notes regarding the things he told me, he asked to look at them, and corrected them and added to them in many places. He focussed most on giving life to the conversations he had held with his enemy.

"As you have taken the trouble to preserve my narration," he said, "I prefer that a mutilated form of it not be left for posterity."

In such manner a week has passed, as this brilliant man spoke the most astonishing story that ever imagination formed. While his tale unfolded, his gentleness and intelligence, as well as the nature of the events that he recounted, have made me care greatly about his well-being. I would soothe him, if it were within my power, but who am I to give counsel to a man who has gone through what he has, and who has lost every reason to live? No, the only joy left for him will be when he composes his shattered feelings for peace and death. For the moment, his sole source of comfort is the belief that his friends communicate to him when he is dreaming. These perceptions raise his spirits in a way that is unmistakable, although at times seeing their faces and feeling that they are holding his hands again inflames his desire for revenge. Perhaps those of us who have never experienced his degree of solitude and terror are not capable of knowing how he can interpret the visions he has while dreaming as real experiences. To him, his visitors are not the products of delusion but beings who come from the regions of a remote world. So powerful are they to him, that I sometimes share his sense of his dreams' truth.

We sometimes speak of other things than his own history and misfortunes. When our discussions run to literature, he shows vast knowledge and a wonderfully nimble mind. His words, without apparent effort, are pure poetry. When he describes a sad detail from his life with such eloquence, I am very often moved to tears. It is hard to imagine what a glorious individual he must have been before his fortunes turned. Even in ruined form he is noble, and almost godlike. He remains aware of his own human value, and of the immensity of his fall.

"When I was younger," he said, "I somehow knew it was my destiny to be a man of greatness. My feelings are profound, and at the same time I possessed a coolness of judgment that prepared me for illustrious achievements. Knowing what I was capable of gave me enormous energy, where others might have perceived such talents as heavy burdens. It was a question of morality. I considered the failure to use one's gifts to benefit humanity to be criminal. Once I had embraced my potential—by bringing back to life a small animal in my laboratory—I could no longer see myself as one of the lesser, childlike scientists our age knows. My desire to change human history and the ability to do so gave me an abundance of hope at the beginning of my career, but now these same gifts serve only as grindstones that crush their owner into dust. I am like the archangel who wished to have the power of God and is now chained to an eternal hell. My imagination was keen, and my powers of observation and analysis no less so. Above all, I had the ability to apply myself. Through the union of these qualities, I was able to conceive the idea of my life's work, and finally to accomplish the creation of a man. Even now, as I remember the burning intensity of my thoughts while I performed the work, I feel the passion stir within me again. For the briefest of moments, I walked within heaven itself, and had power and visions that other scientists would have done anything to share. From my very youngest childhood, I was brimming with the desire to do good. How I have fallen! If you had known me as I was, you would not recognize me in this state of degradation. Sorrow was all but unknown to me. The pull of destiny carried me forward—until I fell, never again to rise."

Must I then lose this admirable being? I have longed for a friend; I have sought one who would sympathize with and love me. And then, somehow, on these distant, half-frozen seas, I have found one, but it seems I have come to know the man and his value only to lose him. Often, I have tried to convince him to embrace life again, but he will not hear of it.

"Thank you, Walton," he said, "for the good intentions that you show towards one as ruined as myself. But when you talk of new friendships and fresh affection, do you imagine anyone could replace those who are lost to me forever, that another man can mean as much to me as Henry, or another woman fill my heart as Elizabeth did? A man's childhood companions, even if not particularly brilliant and gifted, forever hold sway over his mind. For later acquaintances, even the closest ones, can never come to know us in the way of our childhood friends, who intuitively understand our deepest character and can judge our actions with ease. The truth of our motives is always apparent to them.

"Unless there is good reason for it, established early, a brother or sister will never suspect the other of bad faith. But a friend made later in life, no matter how much affection is present, may find himself the subject of sharp suspicion. My loved ones, though, were not loved by me simply because they were those I knew when young. They were each rich in sensitivity and appreciation for all that is best, and I adored them for these and myriad other reasons. Wherever I am, the voice of Elizabeth and the stirring conversation of Henry will be whispered in my ear. In the loneliness that their deaths have caused me, only one thing could engage me in living fully again. This would be some vast new undertaking or ambition, solely to help my fellow human beings. But such is not my destiny. For me all that is left is to pursue and destroy the being to whom I gave life. When this last goal is accomplished, my purpose on earth will be fulfilled, and I may die."

September 2nd

My beloved Sister,

I write to you hemmed in by danger, and unsure whether I will ever see England and my dear friends there again. I am surrounded by mountains of ice, from which there can be no escape, and that threaten to crush the ship at any moment. The brave members of the crew, whom I persuaded to accompany me on this journey, look to me for ideas about how to save us, but I have none to offer. While the situation is bleak, my hope and courage have not abandoned me. We may yet live, and, if we do not, I will draw upon the wisdom of the stoics through the ages, and die with a full heart.

Still, my friend and sister, I am left to wonder what effect these events will have on you? You will likely not hear of my destruction, but be left never knowing the fate of one you love. Years will pass during which despair may visit often, and then you will be tortured by something worse: hope. What you are facing is more terrible to me than the prospect of my own death. I thank heaven you have a husband and wonderful children. You can be happy, yet! May God bless you, and keep you from worry!

My unfortunate guest looks my way with the tenderest compassion. He strives to renew my optimism, and talks as if life were something he truly valued. He tells me of similar, dire situations survived by other explorers. Even knowing I should not allow them to be, my spirits are lifted by his words. The men are affected by his eloquence as well. When he speaks, their despair leaves them, and they perform their shipboard chores with enthusiasm once more. So long as they can hear his voice, they believe that these great mountains of ice are less substantial than they appear, and that they will yield to the power of focussed effort. The effect is fleeting, though. As each day goes by without expectations for deliverance being met, the men's fear blossoms even more than before. The possibility of mutiny, the inevitable result of a crew in despair, has come to my mind several times, and among the men it has surely come to mind more often than that.

September 5

Something so astonishing has just happened that, although it is unlikely that these papers will make their way to you, I cannot keep myself from writing down what I have witnessed.

Mountains of ice continue to hem us in and threaten us, and the cold has become severe. Several members of the crew have died in the last week, and our desolation has only grown greater. Frankenstein's health is weakening. There is, yet, a feverish fire in his eyes, but it seems on the verge of being extinguished. When something inspires him to full awareness for a brief time, the exertion leaves him exhausted.

In my last letter, I mentioned my fear of mutiny. This morning, as I was looking at the face of my friend—his eyes half open, and his limbs hanging listlessly—six of the men knocked at the door of the cabin seeking entry. I consented, and, when they had entered, their leader spoke. He said that he and the other five had been chosen by the rest to make a demand that no just man could refuse. He said that, while the ice around us was unlikely to release us before the following spring, the crew was concerned about my plans if it were to break up briefly and allow us to set sail again. Specifically, they were concerned that I might dare to continue my pursuit of the northern passage, and asked me to make a solemn promise that if the ship were freed I would set a course towards the south.

The leader's speech upset me. I had not neared the point of despair, and had not once thought of abandoning the expedition. But could I, in good conscience, refuse their demand? I hesitated, and at this very moment Frankenstein stirred. Until now, he had appeared to lack the strength even to listen, but he sat up a little in his bunk and forced himself awake. His eyes sparkled and his cheeks took on a ruddy hue. He looked more alive than I had thought he ever would again. Turning towards the men, he began to speak—

"What are you asking of your captain? Is it this easy to turn you away from your sworn purpose? Was it not yourselves who so recently called this a 'glorious expedition'? You were right to think it so. But it was not glorious because the way was smooth, crossing well-known seas. It was so, precisely because it was full of dangers and terror! It was so, because every day there was the possibility of some new unforeseeable incident that might call forth your courage and strength! It was so, because the danger and risk of death you would have to overcome would summon what was great in you, and reveal your deepest stores of courage! For these reasons, it was a glorious undertaking. You would have the possibility afterwards of being called the saviours of your species, your names spoken with reverence. Few are they who brave as much for the benefit of mankind. And now you show that you are anything but heroic, despite the fact that you are still mostly facing your own imagination of danger! You have barely begun to be tested! You are suddenly content to be known as men who lacked the courage to endure cold and peril. 'They were chilly, and returned to their warm home-fires' will be the judgment of history. Have you then wasted so much effort, and put your captain in so precarious a situation? Do you not take seriously what it means to drag him into a defeat that you cause yourselves? Be men, or be more than men! This ice is less strong than the human heart. If you decide you will outlast it, then you will. It has no courage of its own. Do not return as cowards to your families. They will see it upon your faces from across the square, and you will never again be who you were to them before. No, return as heroes who have fought and conquered, who do not know what it is to turn their backs on an enemy and flee."

He spoke with such a beautifully controlled voice, and with so much personal courage burning in his eyes, that it is little wonder how moved the men were by his example. They looked at one another soberly, in recognition of the greatness of the man before them, and found themselves unable to reply.

"Return to your quarters and stations," I said. "Think about what our visitor has told you. If you still prefer not to continue the voyage, you will not be forced to do so. I hope, however, that with reflection you will find your resolve once more."

The representatives left, and I turned towards my friend, but he was deeply asleep.

It is far from clear how the situation will resolve. I would prefer to die than return home shamefully, my purpose unfulfilled, but it appears likely that the latter will be my fate. The men of the crew, less affected than their captain by visions of glory and honour, can never willingly continue to endure their present suffering.

September 7th

The die is cast; I have agreed to return, if we are not destroyed. Thus are my hopes dashed by others' cowardice and hesitancy. I shall return with no way of knowing whether, or how, I might have completed my voyage, and utterly disappointed. It requires more grace than I possess to bear such injustice with patience.

September 12th

It has happened, and I am returning to England. My hopes of benefitting mankind, and of being celebrated for it, are but memories now. Far more painful, though, my friend has died. I am committed to writing down the heartbreaking circumstances in which it all came to pass. As fair winds are pushing us towards England, and towards you, I will not yield to despair.

September 9th, the ice began to move, and roarings like thunder were heard at a distance, as the islands split and cracked in every direction. We were in grave danger; but as we could not affect the outcome one way or the other, my chief attention was occupied by my unfortunate guest, whose illness had increased to such a degree that he was entirely confined to his bed. The ice cracked behind us, and was driven with force towards the north; a breeze sprung from the west, and on the 11th the passage towards the south became perfectly free. When the sailors saw this, and that their return to their native country was apparently assured, a shout of tumultuous joy broke from them, loud and long continued. Frankenstein, who was dozing, awoke, and asked the cause of the excitement. "They shout," I said, "because they will soon return to England."

"Do you then really return?" he said.

"Sadly, yes. I cannot deny their demands. I cannot lead them unwillingly to danger, and I must return."

"Do so, if you will. I will not. You are able to give up your purpose, but mine was given to me by heaven and I dare not refuse it. Though I am much weakened, surely the spirits who have assisted my vengeance up to this point will give me the strength required to fulfill it." With this, he made an effort to rise from his bed, but the exertion was too much for him; he fell back and fainted.

It was a long time before he was restored, and I often thought that the spark of life was gone. When he finally opened his eyes, he breathed with difficulty, and was unable to speak. The doctor gave him brandy, and ordered us to leave him undisturbed. In the mean time, he took me aside and told me that my friend had not many hours to live.

His sentence was pronounced; and I could only grieve, and be patient. I sat by his bed watching him; his eyes were closed, and I thought that he slept, but he called to me in a feeble voice and motioned me closer.

"Alas, the strength I was counting on is gone," he said. "I feel as though I will die very soon, even as my enemy likely lives. But do not imagine, Walton, that in these last moments of my existence I feel the same intense hatred and desire for revenge that burdened me for so long, and yet I feel justified in desiring the creature's death. Over the course of the last few days, I have been examining my history and past conduct, and do not see myself as a villain in what has happened. In a fit of enthusiastic madness I created a rational creature, whom I was morally obligated to make as happy and healthy as was in my power to achieve. That was my duty; but there was a heavier responsibility to protect human kind. The well-being of my fellow creatures around the earth had to come before the wants and needs of the creature. With this simple fact guiding me, I was correct in refusing to make a companion for him. He had, meanwhile, showed both ambition and skill in the realm of violence and evil, murdering my friends and family, and in the process ending the lives of people brimming with sensitivity, happiness, and wisdom. Nor do I know where his thirst for vengeance may end. Miserable himself, he must die, so that no other lives are ruined by his terrible actions. The task of his destruction was mine, and I have failed. Propelled by selfish motives, I once begged you to finish what I had left incomplete. Now, I renew my request, moved solely by virtue and reason.

"Yet I cannot ask you to renounce your country and friends to fulfill the task. Now that you are returning to England, you will have little chance of running across him. The consideration of these points, and the balancing of what you know to be your duties, I leave to you. My judgment and faculties are being eroded now by the approach of death. I dare not ask you to do what I think right, for I still may be misled by passion.

"The idea that he should live and continue in his ways of evil sickens me. At the same time, the fact that I can see the end of my sufferings approaching is giving me the only contented hour I have known in years. The faces of my beloved dead friends and family pass before my eyes, and I will soon be in their arms. Goodbye, Walton! Be happy in the stillness of a happy home. Avoid ambition, even the innocent one of becoming a great man of science. Why do I tell you this? I have seen myself destroyed by the same hope, although it is possible another will succeed where I have failed."

His voice became fainter as he spoke; and at length exhausted by his effort, he sunk into silence. Half an hour later, he tried again to speak, but was unable. He weakly pressed my hand, and his eyes closed forever, while a gentle smile faded from his lips.

Margaret, what comment can I give about the premature passing of so glorious a spirit? There is nothing I can say to communicate the depth of my sorrow; everything that comes to mind is inadequate and feeble. My tears flow; my mind is dulled by sorrow. Still, I journey towards England, and hope to find consolation there.

I am being interrupted. What do these sounds mean? It is midnight; the breeze blows fairly, and the watch on deck scarcely stir. Again—there is a sound as of a human voice, but hoarser; it comes from the cabin where the remains of Frankenstein lie. I must arise, and examine. Good night, my sister.

Dear God! what a scene has just taken place! I am still dizzy with the memory of it. I hardly know whether I will have the power to detail it, but the tale I have recorded would be incomplete without this final and fantastic catastrophe.

I entered the cabin where lay the remains of my ill-fated and admirable friend. Perched above him was a form that words could never adequately describe—giant in stature, and rough and distorted in his proportions. As he hung over the coffin, his face was concealed by long locks of ragged hair; but one vast hand was extended, its colour and apparent texture like that of a mummy. When he heard the sound of my approach, he paused in his utterances of grief and horror, and sprang towards the window. Never had I beheld a sight so horrible as his face, which was of a hateful and appalling hideousness. I shut my eyes involuntarily, and strove to remember the duties that had fallen to me with the death of the creature's maker. I called on him to stay.

He paused, looking on me with wonder, and, again turning

towards the lifeless form of his creator, he seemed to forget my presence, and every feature and gesture seemed to flow from the wildest rage of some uncontrollable passion.

"This is also my victim!" he said. "In his murder my crimes are perfected; the miserable events of my life are wound to their close. Oh, Frankenstein! generous and caring man! What good does it do now for me to beg you for forgiveness? I, who utterly destroyed you by destroying all you loved. Alas, he is cold, and cannot answer."

His voice seemed suffocated; and my first impulses, which involved obeying the dying request of my friend, in destroying his enemy, were now held in check by a mixture of curiosity and compassion. I approached this tremendous being. I dared not raise my eyes again to his face, for that was how frightening and unearthly his ugliness was. I attempted to speak, but the words died on my lips. The monster kept uttering wild and incoherent attacks upon himself. After some time I gathered my courage to address him, in a pause of the tempest of his passion. "Your repentance lacks all meaning," I said. "For if you had heeded these pangs of conscience and stings of remorse, before you had driven your vengeance to this sad extreme, then Frankenstein would still live."

"And are you dreaming?" the monster said. "Do you think that agony and remorse did not torture me, even then? He—" and here he pointed to the corpse—"he, in these last days, suffered not the smallest portion of the sorrow that I experienced as I led him towards the death of his body, and of his hopes. A terrifying selfishness spurred me on, even as my heart was poisoned with remorse. Do you think the groans of Clerval were music to my ears? My heart was made to feel sweet love and sympathy. When I was forced to violence by spite and hatred, I felt the change as a form of torture, such as you cannot imagine.

"After Clerval's murder, I went back to Switzerland, heart-broken and overwhelmed. I felt pity for Frankenstein, and my sympathy took the form of horror. Above all, I feared and despised myself. But when I learned that the author of my existence and of all my terrible suffering dared to hope for the same matrimonial happiness that he had denied me, a great thirst for vengeance came upon me again. It was simply too much to bear that he would heap hardship upon me, and claim a normal life for himself.

"I remembered my threat to him, and decided that it would be fulfilled. I knew as I planned my revenge that I would be inflicting a new deadly torture on myself, but I was the slave, not the master, of an impulse that I detested even as I responded to it. Incredibly, when Frankenstein's bride died, I felt not the slightest sorrow, such as you would recognize. I had finally cast off all feelings of compassion and was at last free to know the true depths of despair. Evil became my good. Pushed to this point, I had no choice left but to adapt to a way of being that I had willfully chosen. The completion of my hateful plan became an insatiable passion. And now it is ended; there is my last victim!"

I was at first moved by the expressions of his misery, but when I remembered what Frankenstein had said about the monster's powers of eloquence and persuasion, and then looked upon the lifeless form of my friend, my indignation was rekindled. "You are an abomination," I said. "It is bold that you come here to whine over the desolation that you have made. Having thrown a torch into a group of buildings and seen them burn, you sit among the ruins and say a few sorrowful words. Hypo-critical fiend! if somehow the one whom you say you mourn returned to life, you would again seek revenge. It is not true pity you feel but sorrow over the end of your reign of vengeance."

"It is not that way," said the being, "although I understand why you misinterpret what you see, based on the limited knowledge in your possession; but I have no need for compassion, yours, or that of anyone else. I have understood for some time that I would never taste the sympathy that you and other people know. At first I did want it, being full of happiness and virtue myself, and wishing to exchange affection with those I met. At that time, I was overflowing with love, but now that virtue has become but a memory for me, and that happiness and kindness have turned to bitter and hateful despair, to whom will I turn for sympathy? I am content to suffer alone, as long as my suffering lasts. It is satisfying for the hatred that others have for me to fill my memory until the end. At one time, yes, my imagination fixed on dreams of shared kindness and enjoyment; I certainly hoped to be known by people who, forgiving my frightening appearance, would love me for the dignity that I possessed. I took my thoughts of honour and devotion as a food for my soul, but now evil has brought me lower than the jackal at his feast. No crime, no hatred, no sorrow, no misery can be compared to mine. When I consider the catalogue of my deeds, I cannot believe that I am the same one whose thoughts were once full of transcendent beauty and sublime kindness. And yet it is so; the fallen angel becomes a terrifying devil, but even that enemy of God had friends and associates in his desolation. I am quite alone.

"You, who call Frankenstein your friend, seem to have some knowledge of my crimes and misfortunes. But, in the details that he gave you of them, he could not sum up the hours and months of misery I have endured, wasting in frustrated passions. For while I destroyed my maker's hopes, never once did I satisfy my own desires. My yearning for love and companionship never weakened, and still I was spurned. Was there no injustice in this? Am I to be thought the only criminal, when all human kind sinned against me? Why do you not hate Felix, who drove his friend from his door with malice? Why do you not loathe the peasant who tried to kill the one who had saved his child? No, these are good and perfect beings! I, meanwhile, am miserable and abandoned, an abortion, to be rejected, kicked, and trampled on. Even now my blood boils at the memory of this injustice.

"But it is no doubt true that I am wretched. I have murdered the lovely and the helpless. I have strangled the innocent as they slept, and choked the life from a man who never injured me or any other living thing. I have enveloped my creator, a man worthy of love and admiration, in pure misery. I have pursued him in vengeance, until his own soul stood around him in ruins. There he lies, white and cold. You hate me, but your loathing cannot equal the ill will I feel towards myself. I look upon the hands that committed this deed; I think on the heart in which the imagination of it was conceived. And I long for the moment when the memory of my victims will be visible to me no longer.

"You need not fear I will do any more harm. My work is nearly done. Neither yours nor any man's death is required to complete this sequence of events; but it does require my own. And do not think that I will be slow to perform this sacrifice. I will take the ice raft that brought me to you and seek the farthest northern extremity of the globe. I will collect my own funeral pyre and burn to ashes this miserable frame. Only in this way can I be sure no curious and disturbed soul will form another sad wretch like myself. I will no longer feel the agonies afflicting me my every waking hour, or suffer the loneliness that has characterized my life. He is dead who called me into being; and when I am no longer, the memory of us both will quickly fade. I will no longer see the sun or stars, or feel the wind caressing my cheeks. The gifts of vision, feeling, and all sensation, which once rose within me, will pass away, and only in this condition will I find happiness. Years ago, when the images that this world offers first opened to me and I first felt the cheering warmth of summer, and heard the rustling of the leaves and the chirping of the birds, and these were all to me, I would have wept at the prospect of death; now it is my only consolation. Polluted by crimes and torn by the bitterest remorse, where can I find rest but in death?

"Farewell! I leave you, and in you the last of human kind these eyes will ever behold. Farewell, Frankenstein! If you were still living, and still desired revenge against me, it would be better satisfied in my living on, than in my destruction. But that was not to be; you did seek my death, but only so I could not cause greater sorrow. If, in some way I cannot know, you continue to think and feel, I know that you wished to see me perish not for vengeance but to protect your fellow creatures. As tortured as you were, my agony was keener than yours, for the bitter sting of remorse will be in my wounds, until death closes them forever.

"But soon," he cried, with sad and solemn enthusiasm, "I will die, and what I now feel will no longer be felt. Soon, these burning miseries will be quieted. I will climb my funeral pyre triumphantly and relish the agony of the scorching flames. The light of the fire will fade away; my ashes will be swept into the sea by the winds. My spirit will sleep in peace; or, if it thinks, it will have better thoughts than these. Farewell!"

He sprung from the cabin window, as he said this, upon the ice raft which lay close to the vessel. He was soon borne away by the waves, and lost in darkness and distance.

Acknowledgments

This book would not have been possible without careful reading and analysis by dozens of students and teachers at Rocky Hill School. I would like to especially thank Kathy Priest, Holly Cotta, and Whitney Barker for believing in the project and making use of it during its earlier phases. Special thanks also to the members of the English Department: Sean Tinsley, Jessica Russell, Belinda Snyman, and Diane Rich.

The manuscript was read and improved by John Walsh and Kimberly Edge-Ambler. It was heroically edited by Martin Edmunds, who became a good friend along the way.

Great thanks are due to the many members of my family for their encouragement throughout the project; I thank them all with a full heart.

I dedicate the hope that this adaptation represents to my two daughters, Rell and Annalee. And to my beautiful wife, Kim, who not only read but designed the book you hold in your hands, I offer my greatest thanks of all.

—H.B.A.